RETURN OF THE

Cowgirl

MARSHA MOYER

RETURN OF THE

Stardust

Cowgirl

A Lucy Hatch Novel

THREE RIVERS PRESS
NEW YORK

Copyright © 2008 by Marsha Moyer

All rights reserved.
Published in the United States by Three Rivers Press, an imprint of the Crown Publishing Group, a division of Random House, Inc., New York.
www.crownpublishing.com

Three Rivers Press and the Tugboat design are registered trademarks of Random House, Inc.

Library of Congress Cataloging-in-Publication Data
Moyer, Marsha.
    Return of the Stardust Cowgirl : a novel / Marsha Moyer.—1st ed.
      p. cm.
    (alk. paper)
    1. Country musicians—Fiction.   2. Pregnant women—Fiction.   3. Texas—
Fiction.   4. Domestic fiction.   I. Title.
    PS3613.O93R48 2008
    813'.6—dc22   2007036722

ISBN 978-0-307-35155-5

Printed in the United States of America

Design by Chris Welch

10 9 8 7 6 5 4 3 2 1

First Edition

In memory of Sylva Billue

Acknowledgments

Thanks to Allison McCabe, Lindsey Moore, Heather Proulx, Annsley Rosner, Paige Alexander, and Donna Passannante at Three Rivers Press; Barbara Braun and John Baker; Greg, Zoe, and Mya Phelps; Mary Teague; and my family.

RETURN OF THE

Stardust

Cowgirl

Prologue

DENNY

I MARRIED MY daddy. Everybody said so, but I wouldn't listen. I thought Will Culpepper hung the moon, with his skinny gangster hips and his half-cocked smile, the strand of black hair like a comma separating the clauses of his steel-blue eyes. I was hell-bent on having him and nothing would have kept me back, not even a big Day-Glo skull and crossbones in the middle of his forehead, which, come to find out, he did have, one that everybody in the world could see but me. But by the time the smoke from the fireworks had cleared, it was too late, I was Mrs. Will Culpepper, and I guess I'm Mrs. Will Culpepper still, although I'm doing my best to put as much distance between him and me as I can, as fast as I can. Even now, I can feel him out there in the dark like an unseen hand, his nimble, guitar-picking fingers poised to reach down and pluck my speeding pickup off the blacktop, lift it straight up out of the East Texas piney woods and set it down five hundred miles behind me, back in Tennessee.

The rain that's been chasing my tail all the way from Little Rock finally catches up with me, and I flip on the wipers and hit a button to send the windows whirring down, and the cab fills up with old familiar smells, wet pine and wood smoke, everything green and sopping with early spring. The road spools out ahead of my headlights like a loop of black satin ribbon, glistening and treacherous, which is how I'm feeling myself pretty much exactly, and I've got Lucinda Williams in the tape player, a cassette Daddy gave me last year after he was finished going through his latest and, according to him, final broken heart. I'll be as good as Lucinda someday, once I get a few more years under my belt, a little more gravel in my voice. Pretty soon I'll be writing my own heartbreak songs. For now, it's enough to hear her sing *Did you only want me for those three days?* like her voice is coming out of a jagged tear in the middle of her chest and know that somebody, somewhere once hurt as bad as this and lived to tell about it. It's funny, in a way, her singing about getting screwed over by some guy, when anybody with two ears can hear what a warrior she is, how righteous and strong. My guess is the guy couldn't handle it, couldn't keep up. But maybe I'm projecting, and who can blame me? Someday, I'll be able to hear this song without it making me think about Will Culpepper. He'll just be a song request shouted out from the back row, a track on a CD I hardly ever listen to anymore.

Daddy's going to kill me. He's going to stand there laughing his ass off and saying, *I told you so, Denise,* and then he's going to kill me.

To which I'll say, *If you're so damn smart, how come you didn't stop me?*

But I know the answer to that one. There was no stopping me. There never is. In fact, I think the reason I've done as well as I have in the music business and Daddy a little, shall we say, less so, is that I come at things head-on, with all my guns blazing, and I don't quit until I've either gotten what I want or decided I don't want it anymore.

"He's a hoodlum," Daddy said shortly after I married Will, and I laughed because I thought he meant petty crime and Will wasn't a criminal, at least not the regular kind. It might've been easier if he had been; he might be in jail somewhere instead of sitting up in our condo in Nashville, dialing and dialing my cell phone like he did for five whole hours until I finally threw it out the window, watching it bust apart in a thousand plastic pieces on Interstate 40. He might be locked up, and I could at least hope for a clean getaway and some peace. But they don't put folks in jail for stealing hearts. Imagine if they did—Will Culpepper would have plenty of company, my own daddy included, before he stopped drinking and came back to Texas and Lucy and settled down, on lifetime parole.

Taillights appear up ahead like red animal eyes in the dark, and I swing out to pass an 18-wheeler with Illinois plates, switching my wipers on high to catch the dirty spray kicked up by his wake. He toots his horn as I slide back in front of him, flashes his lights, and I flash back and lift my hand, a good old southern-style *adios*-see-you-around. Ever since I passed Texarkana, there's hardly anybody on the road, it being too late and too nasty for ordinary folks to be out and about, only a few semis headed down to Beaumont or Houston and girls in pickups on the run, heading home, getting ready to face the music.

A scattering of lights is coming up on the horizon, the twenty-four-hour fluorescent blaze of Orson's Texaco, and I tap the brakes and move into the right-hand lane and put on my blinker for the exit. Mooney, Texas, population 990, two of whom, at least, I'm counting on to rescue me tonight.

This is only the second time I've been to the new house, but it's easy to find since it's right across the highway from the old one, on a two-hundred-acre parcel of land that used to belong to a farmer, Mr. Bates, who got sick of trying to hack a living out of sorghum and corn and put the whole spread up for sale and moved to Florida. There are three houses on it now: the old Bates place standing empty out near the road, a tumbledown handyman's cottage, and the new house Daddy built back in the trees, a big, beautiful timber-frame cabin with a wraparound porch and the master bedroom full of floor-to-ceiling windows, so that Daddy and Lucy can sit up in bed in the mornings and see nothing but water and sky. There's a lake—an overgrown pond, really—out front, with a pier and an old rowboat that my little brother, Jude, likes to fish from and, for a few days every spring and a few more in the fall, a pair of cranes who stop off on their way to and from their winter home down at the coast, or so the story goes. Cranes, in case you don't know, mate for life, and Daddy claims that just hearing about them from Mr. Bates was enough to make him decide, right there on the spot, to buy the land and build this house. It felt like a blessing to him, and who knows? Maybe it was. He and Lucy seem happy—different from how they were before, more low-key, more careful with each other. But one thing I learned early on, in my family, happiness is not a place where any of us feels at home for very long. It's probably some kind of miracle that I got to hang on to what I had for as long as I did. By Farrell standards, I'm way past due.

I turn in off the blacktop at the county marker and follow the snaky, red-clay road through a dripping canopy of tall pines. I'd forgotten how dark it gets out in the country, true dark, no streetlights or city glow, nothing but my high beams tunneling through the trees. So dark, in fact, that I overshoot the drive and have to back up, my tires spinning for a second before they gain traction and send me rocketing forward again, splattering my truck as high as the hood with thick, red East Texas mud.

As the house takes shape in my headlights, black on black, I ease up on the gas and switch to my running lights. Of course everybody's in bed, like decent people everywhere. A hundred times I thought about calling to say I was on my way, to wait up for me. I just never could make myself do it, couldn't seem to come up with the words. And there's the matter of my cell phone, smashed to bits back on I-40.

But there's a light on in the little house, the old handy-man's place, and all of a sudden I recall Daddy telling me that he'd been working all winter to turn it into a studio. It's been a couple of years since he made a record, and to tell the truth, he hasn't got the greatest reputation anymore back in Nashville. He burned a lot of bridges. That was in his drinking days, though, before he and Lucy got back together, and I remember him telling me when he first moved back down here that he didn't care if he ever wrote another song.

I reach down and eject Lucinda, and then it's just the throaty rumble of the pickup's engine and, down under that but almost like it's keeping time, the hammering of my heart. You think of your family as a bunker, a place to hole up and lick your wounds. But it's not like a business deal; there's no contract promising their support, no money-back guarantee. For the first time since I jumped in the truck back in Nashville, I feel really sorry for what I've done, that I couldn't just have a quiet little breakdown but have managed somehow to turn it into a free-for-all, dragging folks behind me every which way. I don't know what I've got to say for myself, to Daddy or to anybody. No idea at all.

Then the door of the little house swings inward and there he is, silhouetted by the light behind. I know I better identify myself—he's got a shotgun in the closet, and no reason to recognize the truck—but my mouth is so dry I can't even swallow. Wouldn't that make a great headline in the *Nashville Scene*? "Country singer shoots daughter in case of mistaken identity." On the other hand, it might solve a few of my more pressing problems.

I cut the engine, finally, and push open the door. Lord knows, I must look like hell, nine hours on the road with no real break, just five-minute pit stops to buy Cokes and Mars bars, to gas up and pee. The light pours out from the little house like melted butter, and I hope to God it's the light of forgiveness, but I can't tell, it's been the longest twenty-four hours of my life, and I'm not sure anymore what's real and what's not.

I walk around in front of the truck, into the light, and let him get a look at me: *Here I am, your baby girl, the apple that fell so far from the tree, that rolled five hundred miles and back again.* I haven't cried since I left Nashville, but at the look on his face, a sob fills my throat, and just as I'm wondering if it's too late to change my mind, to turn around and get back on the road and just keep driving to someplace nobody knows me, where there's nobody whose life I've turned to crap, he takes four long strides off the porch and into the yard and I fall forward into his arms, breathing him in in big, greedy gulps, sawdust and varnish and soap and something else, one shadowy bottom note I've spent my whole life chasing, and the tears come then, enough for the whole past fifteen months as he holds me against his chest, his hard brown arms a refuge, a throttlehold, and the light shines all around us and the rain just keeps coming down, as soft and noiseless as a baptism.

LUCY

"The subject of our program today is 'Love and Fear.'"

Dr. Phil turns to the camera with his patented look, a half smile and a little hitch of the eyebrows meant to convey that, for all his smarts and his success, he's still just a regular Joe like you and me.

"Please welcome my guests, a clinical psychologist from Boston, Massachusetts, Dr. Norman Stiller, and from Mooney, Texas, Mrs. Lucy Hatch." The studio audience applauds. I lean over and whisper into Dr. Phil's ear, and he nods and adds, to the camera and the audience, "Lucy Hatch *Farrell.*

"Now, Dr. Stiller, you've written a book on this topic, out this week, am I right?" Dr. Phil just happens to have a copy here, and he holds it up. "Why don't you tell us a little bit about your premise?"

The psychologist clears his throat. He's small and rotund, with a pale bald head, gold-rimmed eyeglasses, and a suit that probably cost more than most people who aren't doctors or TV personalities earn in a month.

"After extensive research," he says in a sonorous voice, "my conclusion is that every feeling we human beings experience, therefore every action we take, is motivated by one of two things: love or fear. What's more, the two are mutually exclusive. What that means is that if you love something, you cannot fear it, and vice versa."

"Bullshit."

The camera swings toward me. Nobody looks especially shocked that I've just used a cussword on national TV, but then nobody seems to care that I'm sitting in front of a camera and a live studio audience in my nightgown, either.

I look out at the audience. It's mostly women, mostly middle-aged, with haircuts and outfits two or three years out of style. They're looking at me, waiting to hear what I have to say. I'm one of them—me, a wife and mother from a little town on the edge of nowhere, not these men with their college degrees and their book deals, their hand-tailored suits.

"Are you married, Dr. Stiller?" I ask.

He peers over the top of his glasses at me. "I am."

"Any kids?"

"No."

I know exactly what I'm going to say. If this guy had kids, he'd understand that love and fear go hand in hand. Having kids means giving up the chance to live your life unencumbered, to sleep soundly, sealed off from the world, at night. Even when they're grown and gone, they tug at you; you feel their disappointments and their agitations churning around you like the air before a storm.

That's when I see her, right there in the front row, with her blazing red hair and jeans with the knees ripped out, her worn-out cowboy boots.

A door slams, and I bolt upright in bed, my magazine falling to the floor.

"Denny?" I say.

CHAPTER 1

Denny

OVER AT THE big house the porch light snapped on, and I lifted my face out of Daddy's shirtfront to see Lucy silhouetted against the yellow rectangle of the open door, barefoot in a white cotton nightgown with her hair hanging loose around her shoulders. I couldn't help but think of the first time I'd landed in Mooney, when I was just fourteen, left by my mama on the doorstep of a man who hadn't claimed me since I was six. It was Lucy who answered the door that day, buck naked except for a bedsheet, her face swollen with sleep and, it turned out, about three months' worth of my little brother, Jude, though nobody, not even Lucy, knew that at the time. Her hair had been just like this, wild and uncombed, a dark reddish-brown shot through with strands of copper and gold, and in spite of having every reason in the world to hate her on sight, something inside seemed to pull me to her, to crave getting lost in her musky scent and soft curves.

"Oh, my Lord," she said, rushing down off the steps and into the yard. She took my face between her cool hands and looked into my eyes so hard I had to look away. "For heaven's sake, you're soaking wet," she said. "Get inside, both of you. I'll put on some tea." That's Lucy for you, in a nutshell. The whole world could be coming down like Judgment Day and she'd be filling the kettle, getting out the Celestial Seasonings.

I followed her through the door and down the hall, Daddy bringing up the rear. He pulled out a chair for me at the table, and I sank onto it and looked around the kitchen, still strange to me with its stainless-steel appliances and tile floors covered with scatter rugs, acres of granite countertop. Only the table was familiar, carried over from the old house. Daddy'd made it himself, years before, out of fine blond wood. I would've put my head down on it right then and there if I could have. I don't think I'd ever felt so tired in my life, the kind of tired where you've kept going and going, like the Energizer Bunny, till all of a sudden you sputter to a stop and realize you're out of juice.

"How about I scramble up some eggs," Lucy said. "Or would you rather have pancakes?" Already her head was in the pantry, getting out the tin canister of flour, the Crisco.

"I hope you realize what an honor this is," Daddy said. "I'm lucky if I can get her to make pancakes once a year."

"You're lucky all right, mister." Lucy's voice was matter-of-fact, but Daddy grinned and leaned over and kissed her behind the ear, and she smiled a small, secret smile. It took me straight back to the first summer I'd spent with them, when I'd felt like an alien stranded on the Planet of Love. But there was something comforting about it, too, an ease between them that was missing the year before, when I'd come home dragging Will Culpepper by the shirt collar like a prize I'd won at the craps table in Vegas. I didn't resent Lucy and Daddy's happiness anymore, not like I had when I was too young to know how rare such a thing was, that when you found it you had to fight for it, hang on till your fingernails bled. He nipped teasingly at the back of her neck, and she swatted him with a dish towel. "Go find your daughter something dry to wear. Honey, is your bag in the car?"

"I didn't have time to pack."

"Well, run upstairs, Ash, and fetch her something of mine. And a couple of towels. The good ones, not those old things you dry the dogs with."

For a while the only sounds were the drumming of rain on the metal roof and Lucy's wooden spoon clacking against the side of the yellowware bowl as she stirred baking powder into flour. I sat back and let the truth of the moment sink into me: I was home. Not that Will couldn't touch me here, but he'd have to go through Daddy to do it. And through Lucy, who could be just as tough in her way, though you'd never guess it to see her in her white nightgown with her hair down her back. I watched her cut Crisco into flour with the tines of a fork, really putting her shoulders and back into it. She looked different from the last time I'd seen her—softer around the edges, the sharp planes gone out of her face. It occurred to me that this was what life, and love, did to you, tossed you around like a piece of driftwood, and depending on where you landed, you could end up hard and twisted and pitted, or buffed to a silky, sand-smoothed sheen.

"I was just thinking about you," she said. "And here you turned up. What do you think about that?" She glanced back at me over her shoulder. I tried but couldn't quite get my smile muscles to work.

"Where's Jude?" I asked. My little brother—half brother, if you want to get technical about it—was famous for sleeping like the dead, but the smell of Lucy's pancakes would usually bring him running.

"Sleeping over at his cousin's. Lily orders him around like a slave, and he moons around after her like a sad-eyed puppy. I'm not sure it's healthy." She shook her head and smiled. "But I guess you always worry about your babies. No matter how big they get."

Without warning, tears filled my eyes, and I ducked my head, hiding my face with my hair. Not quick enough, though. Lucy set down her spatula and pulled up a chair right next to mine and put her arms around my shoulders. "Oh, honey," she said as I leaned into the sweet-smelling warmth of her. You had to hand it to Lucy; she'd bring you out of the rain, mix up pancakes and fetch dry towels for your hair, let you cry into the front of her nightgown, but she'd never tell you everything was going to be all right or any of that horseshit.

"Ssh," Lucy murmured, running a hand over my hair as the kettle started to whistle. "You just sit and get warm, drink your tea." She poured me a cup and set it in front of me, and

I lifted it to my face and breathed in the earthy, minty aroma, another smell that reminded me of home.

Daddy came thumping back down the stairs, dumping a mess of towels and clothes in the middle of the table, and started pawing through it all, bringing out a blue satin negligee, one of Jude's Little League jerseys, finally a flannel shirt so old and worn it held only the merest suggestion of plaid. "That," I said, recognizing it as one of his, a thing he'd owned since time immemorial, and he slid the sleeves obligingly over my arms, tugging the collar tight around my neck, then grabbed a towel and began to rub my head with it. "Ow!" I cried, causing Lucy to look back over her shoulder.

"Ash, for goodness' sake. Try to be a little gentler."

I closed my eyes, listening to the batter sizzle in the skillet as she put it over the flame, inhaling the sweet aroma as it began to cook. Under his breath Daddy started to sing: *Across the Red River where the sweet water flows . . .*

Maybe this was the main trouble between Will and me, that our ideas of human comfort were so different. For me, it didn't get any better than a warm kitchen when it's raining outside, somebody rubbing your head with a towel and crooning old cowboy songs in your ear. Whereas Will needed—well, whatever it was, I didn't know, and I doubt I could have given it to him if I had. Of course, I couldn't see that when I met him. He was a master of disguise, Will Culpepper. He was that fancy fly at the end of a fishing line, twisting and twirling under the bright water, calling out, *Here, little fishy, fishy.* He could fool even the wiliest old carp,

I swear. Though, come to think of it, he hadn't fooled my daddy for a second.

Then Lucy was slapping down a plate of pancakes in front of me, setting out the Blackburn's syrup and a little pitcher of melted butter. She shook a gingham-checked cloth napkin over my lap, stuck a fork in my hand. I blinked, turning it this way and that in the light, like a cave person who's never seen such a thing and can't quite get the hang of what it's meant for. I felt a flush of shame at the sight of their faces, all full of concern. For the past three years I'd spent most of my nights looking out over smoky, crowded rooms, and I thought I'd seen every kind of want there was. Folks came to hear me sing about the things they couldn't say, about hurt and anger and love gone wrong. I was proud to do it. I was, as my real mama, Marlene, was fond of reminding me, beholden. But I hadn't known till now how bad I needed somebody to look at me without wanting a thing. I sawed off a bite of pancake and put it in my mouth, letting the sweet dough and syrup mingle on my tongue.

"I'll have some of those, while you're at it," Daddy said to Lucy.

"You would." But she was already setting a plate in front of him. She poured herself a cup of tea and sat down at the table, and for a few minutes the only sounds were the clicking of forks against stoneware and the soft drip of rain off the eaves outside. Daddy cleaned his plate in about half a minute and held it out for a refill. Lucy made a little face, but she got up and poured more batter into the skillet.

"Eat," she said, nudging me with her foot under the table. "You look like a strong breeze could carry you off." I guess I'd lost some weight over the past few months. It seemed like every minute I wasn't onstage I was talking into some radio or newspaper guy's microphone, or signing autographs at some county fair or the parking lot of some small-town Wal-Mart, or on the bus heading from one of those places to another. I went to bed without supper plenty of times.

I started cutting my pancakes into squares and pushing them around on my plate. I was thinking about something Ty, my manager, had said to me a couple weeks earlier, about how relationships were supposed to be about balance and compromise, two words Will Culpepper wouldn't know the meaning of if you hit him over the head with a dictionary. I would have been happy cooking pancakes for Will—not that I knew how to make pancakes, but still—in exchange for his rubbing my head with a towel or singing in my ear. But none of those things was going to happen—not now, not ever. We were both too selfish, according to Ty. We both wanted to be the person up there on that golden chair, riding above the crowd on the shoulders of the adoring minions while they hoisted their spears and waved palm fronds in our wake. Neither one of us was cut out to be a spear carrier or a frond waver. Doomed from the start.

Finally I gave up and set down my fork. Lucy reached over and covered my hand with hers, and we sat like that for a minute or so, then she squeezed my fingers and stood up and ran the sink full of soapy water and set the batter bowl to soak.

She wiped her hands on a dish towel, then turned and cupped a hand under my chin. "You want to sit up awhile and talk?" I shook my head. I was so tired the words were just running around in circles in my head. "Okay, then. There's clean sheets on the bed in your room. Towels in the hall cupboard. Come by and see me at the shop tomorrow, all right?" I nodded, and she bent and kissed my forehead. "You," she said, laying a hand on Daddy's shoulder. "Don't keep her up all night."

"I thought I'd show her the studio."

"That studio will be there in the morning." Daddy smiled and winked at me, and Lucy sighed in a loud, dramatic way. It was a losing battle—the day birds versus the night owls—and she knew it. "I mean it, Ash. One hour, tops. Mrs. Humphries is expecting you first thing tomorrow, don't forget."

"Night, babe," he said, and squeezed her hip.

"I'm serious. If you're not upstairs in an hour, I'm coming out there and dragging you to bed."

"Is that a threat or a promise?"

He raised his face so she could brush her lips against his, then she stood there a second looking down at him, her eyes holding his. I used to think I could read the looks between the two of them, but it wasn't so easy anymore. Maybe the looks had gotten more complicated. Or maybe it was that I understood now firsthand how nobody really knows what's going on inside a relationship besides the two people in it. "One hour," she said again, and slipped off up the stairs.

Once Lucy was gone, quiet seemed to gather like fog, drifting down from the ceiling and settling thick and heavy around our shoulders. The rain had let up, and all I could hear was the steady tick of Daddy's fork against the edge of his plate, the hum of the big stainless-steel icebox. He mopped up a puddle of syrup with the last bite of pancake and popped it into his mouth.

"Well, Denise," he said, dabbing his lips with a corner of his napkin. There was no place to hide from the look in his eyes, and I thought he was going to pin me to the mat right there about me and Will, but, "You gonna eat those?" he asked finally, gesturing at my plate. I shook my head, and he got up and scraped the leftover pancakes into the trash and put our plates in the dishwasher. "So, how about it?" he asked. "You ready to hit the hay, or you want the grand tour first?"

"The tour," I said, getting to my feet and spreading the damp towel over the back of the chair.

I followed him across the yard through a soft mist and in through the door of what used to be the hired man's cottage, back when the Bates family owned the place. It was an impressive setup he had out there, professional. The soundboard was first-rate, and his Martin and Gibson guitars sat in racks alongside a seafoam-green Fender Telecaster and a beautiful maple mandolin. There was an ugly plaid couch with sagging springs I recognized from the old house, along with a beat-up coffee table that held stacks of notebooks and CDs and a jelly jar full of the wildflowers that grew along the edge of the pond in springtime.

I wandered through the room, my pulse pounding, and touched the tip of one finger to the glossy surface of the Martin. I thought back to a few nights before I'd left Nashville, when Ty had taken me to see a movie about the songwriter

Townes Van Zandt. Somebody—one of his musician friends or ex-wives, I couldn't remember who—had talked about how tough Townes had been on the people who loved him; and sitting in the darkened theater, I'd felt like I understood, not what it was like to love someone like him, but to *be* him, torn between wanting a regular life, a home and family, and at the same time driven by music to the point where it canceled out everything else. It was no wonder he'd drunk himself stupid, sniffed glue, shot smack; it was a miracle he'd made it to fifty. It scared me to death, but at the same time I knew how it beckoned, that life, calling you into a dark place where nothing mattered but the words and the notes in your head. I wanted to sink down on that couch and pick up a guitar and fall headlong into the darkness, into the place the music came from. The place I could forget about Will, and Ty, everything I'd left behind.

I looked over at Daddy, fooling with the flowers in the jelly jar, stirring up a little cloud of yellow pollen. "So, have you started writing again?" I asked.

"Not really. Just messing around."

"I want to hear it."

"I'm not sure I've got anything worth hearing."

"Got to start somewhere," I said.

"Tomorrow, maybe," he said. "After I get back from Mrs. Humphries's."

"Sure." I didn't say what I wanted, which was to ask him why was he wasting himself on the likes of Mrs. Humphries. Talent to burn, this beautiful little studio, and here he was, just like before he'd gone to Nashville, remodeling kitchens for small-town biddies. But I kept my mouth shut; I wasn't exactly in a position right then to call a spade a spade.

I started sifting through the CDs on the coffee table. He had Willie Nelson's tribute to the songs of Cindy Walker, a Rodney Crowell I hadn't heard. I picked up *Sweet Old World* and held it up for him to see. "I listened to Lucinda all the way down here," I said. "The one you sent me."

"I had a feeling that would come in handy sooner or later."

Next thing I knew, my face was wet with tears, and Daddy was crossing the room double-time to scoop me up in his arms. "Oh, baby girl," he said. "It's all right. It's all right."

"No, it's not," I sobbed. That was just a lie people told you, to keep you from jumping off a bridge or shooting up the post office, to keep you buying their brand of liquor and popping their pills.

"I know it seems that way now. But this is the bottom of the pit, okay? Just keep telling yourself that. This is the worst night, but every one from here on out will be just a little bit better." I laughed, hiccuping into his shirtfront. "What?" he said.

"Did you learn that in AA? Because, no offense, but it sounds like pure grade-A bullshit to me."

"I guess it does. But you're young, and you've got the whole world on your side. There's no way you're getting side-tracked for more than a day or two, tops, by the likes of Will Culpepper."

I lifted my face and looked at him. He'd walked through the fire a time or two himself, my daddy, and that journey was laid out plain in the lines on his face, deeper than the last time I saw him, his salt-and-pepper hair now mostly gray.

"You want to hang out here awhile?" he asked. "There's stuff to munch on in that cupboard, and a hot plate if you feel like another cup of tea."

"I'll stay, if it's okay."

"Hey, *mi casa, su casa*," he said. I rolled my eyes, and he smiled. He could be so corny sometimes. "I can keep you company if you want," he said. "But maybe you'd rather have the place to yourself."

I thought about it. There was so much I wanted to say, so much I needed to hear. But I felt stupid with exhaustion and the weight of what I'd done, and the words I needed bobbed around in my head like little balloons, drifting just out of reach.

"You go back in," I said. "Lucy's waiting on you."

He stood looking down at me, his eyes so black they seemed to be all pupil. For a panicky second I wondered, not for the first time, if he could see more of me than what was on the surface. What sweet relief it would be to hand over all my secrets, let somebody else clean up after me. But I needed some time first to take it all in, to figure out how I felt about things. I went up on my toes and kissed him on the cheek, and he gave my shoulders a quick squeeze and stepped away.

"Don't stay up too late, okay? You need your beauty sleep."

After he was gone I put *Sweet Old World* in the CD player and turned it on low, then switched off the lights and stretched out on the couch. I could still feel the highway moving under me. My insides felt jangly from the road and the caffeine, and the minute I closed my eyes the old movie started up, in surround sound and Technicolor. The frames were all jumbled, though, the faces blurring from one scene to the next, Will's into Ty's and then back again as I wrapped Daddy's soft old shirt around me and let myself fall into the cradle of Lucinda's voice, let it lift me up and bear me gently, like a leaf upon water, into sleep.

CHAPTER 2

Lucy

I CLIMBED BACK into bed, pulling the sheet up to my
chin, watching the rain track down the window glass, listening to its steady *ping* against the metal roof. I used to
love the rain, loved any kind of wild weather. But I was a different person then, a person without a thing in the world to lose.

For nearly six months now, Ash and Jude and I had been
quietly rebuilding what we'd started eight years back, before
we went to Nashville and things turned sour, before Ash and
I separated and then, after many slow, hard months, reconciled. We'd talked about having another baby, had spent the
first several weeks after he was home from rehab making fer-
vent, unprotected love before I came to my senses. A baby
was not the right thing for us. I couldn't have said why, only
that I'd recognized it in some instinctive, female part of me.
Now finally, tonight, I knew.

Before long I heard the front door open and close, the soft tread of feet on the stairs. I sat up as Ash came into the bedroom, his boots in his hand.

"Hey," I whispered.

"You still awake?" He set his boots beside the rocker in the corner and pulled his T-shirt over his head.

"Waiting on you."

He dropped his shirt on the chair and I held out my arms and he moved into them, stretching his body, still in socks and Levi's, the length of mine. Through the layers I felt the heat of his skin as he kissed my hair, my temples, my eyelids, finally my mouth. I'd been planning to talk to him about Denny, but as I brought his hand inside the unbuttoned neck of my nightgown, I decided that what had seemed so important a few minutes before could wait. He lifted his hips and I reached between us to undo the buttons on his Levi's, and he stood and skinned them off as I threw back the covers and pulled my nightgown over my head. There had been nights, once the baby-making frenzy ended, when we'd lain together in this bed and touched and kissed each other for hours, learning our way back to each other after nearly a year apart; but this would not be one of them. Without overture I took him in my hand and guided him into me, and we both gasped at our readiness, at the first hard thrust of connection. For a blessed few minutes my mind was a blank, my body answering Ash's in that age-old call-and-response.

After, we lay side by side, the ceiling fan cooling the sweat that had gathered on our bellies and thighs. He reached down and pulled the sheet over us, and I rolled onto my side away from him and he wrapped his arm around me and tucked his knees into the backs of mine.

"Lucy?"

"Hm?"

He fitted his chin into the notch between my neck and shoulder. "Are you wearing your diaphragm?"

The rain had started up again, a light patter against the metal roof. I sighed and muttered something wordless, pulling his arm tighter around me, and turned my face into my pillow. It was easier feigning sleep than to tell Ash the truth—that there would be a baby in this house, but not the way he thought, and sooner than he knew.

IN THE MORNING I was dressed and out of the house before dawn, Ash still in bed with the covers over his head. Denny's bed hadn't been slept in. I crossed the yard past her truck and eased open the door of the studio. Lucinda Williams sang softly from the speakers, the one about walking the line to prove her love. In the darkness I could just make out Denny asleep on the broken-down old couch, her face mashed into the pillow. *Oh, child,* I thought, *what you know about walking the line is nothing; it hasn't even begun.*

I drove up the farm-to-market road through stands of pine, past far-off farmers on tractors in fields hazy and golden in the early light. Downtown Mooney was still locked up tight, the courthouse square empty but for the usual handful of pickups and work trucks around the café. The case could be made that this was pretty much as lively as downtown Mooney got anymore. There were a few holdouts—the True Value, the machine shop, Orson's Texaco, the café.

No such thing could be said of Faye's Flowers. Though my boss, Peggy Thaney, had finally taken full retirement, she still owned the place her mama had started from scratch, and Peggy'd always claimed that as long as there was a breath in her body or one person left in town who could remember ordering their Easter wreaths and anniversary bouquets from her mama, Faye's would carry on. I got nervous, though, every time I thought about the bypass that had taken the highway a dozen miles west of town, along with the new superstore chains that were springing up along it like toadstools after a rain. Every Friday when I sat down to do the books, my hands shook on the computer keyboard, and I had to go straight home afterward to take a BC powder and lie with a wet washcloth over my eyes.

I found myself turning into my sister-in-law Geneva's driveway, knowing she'd be up with their new baby, Emmalee. My brother, Bailey, had been working on a housing development up near Naples, and his truck was already gone.

I let myself in without knocking. As I made my way toward the kitchen I could hear the radio playing quietly, smell coffee brewing. "Gen? It's me."

I crossed the threshold and found her sitting at the breakfast table in a ratty chenille robe, spooning oatmeal into Emmy's open mouth. I smiled at the sight of them, my big, blond sister-in-law with her hair going in a dozen different directions and Emmy grabbing for the spoon and crowing,

her black-almond eyes disappearing into a fat-cheeked grin. I
leaned over to kiss the baby and hug Geneva's neck.

"Don't look at me," she said. "I'm a mess."

"But a good mess."

"The coffee's made. Pour me some while you're at it,
would you?"

"I wish I knew your secret," I said, reaching into the cabinet for mugs. "Is that child ever not in a good mood?"

"Ha! You haven't seen her when she's hungry at two in the
morning. I'm surprised you haven't been able to hear her
screaming out at your place."

"Daw!" Emmy declared as Geneva grabbed a facecloth
and wiped oatmeal off the baby's chin.

I set a cup of coffee in front of her and pulled out a chair.
"Everything set for the party?" They'd been back from China
with Emmy for three weeks, and it was time to introduce her
to her new hometown.

"I guess. I thought I'd run up to Wal-Mart later on and
pick up a few more things for the goody-bags. Want to
come?"

"Can't. Work. Anyway . . ."

She looked up at me, the spoon poised in midair. "Ork!"
Emmy complained.

"What?" Geneva said, narrowing her eyes at me suspi-
ciously. "What's going on?"

Geneva was my best friend, but I couldn't tell her what
was really on my mind that morning. First, it was only a
hunch, not a fact. Second, I hadn't decided how I felt about
it. Third, the subject of fertility was a subject we only danced

around, even now that Jude was seven and Geneva was herself the proud adoptive mother of two. My unintended pregnancy just after her sixth miscarriage had thrown our relationship into a tailspin I wasn't sure at the time we'd recover from; I couldn't stand to think about how she might take the news of Denny's.

"Denny showed up last night around midnight, looking like ten miles of hard road." I got up to top off our coffee. "That damn Will Culpepper! I saw this coming the minute I first laid eyes on the man. I just knew he'd wind up leaving footprints all over her heart. But I've got a feeling this isn't just—"

A noise like stampeding elephants had started at the far end of the house, and seconds later Jude and Lily burst into the room, Jude wearing his SpongeBob SquarePants pajamas, Lily in a nightshirt patterned with red number 8's and the squinty eyes and cocky grin of Dale Earnhardt Junior.

"Mama!" Jude cried, and climbed into my lap. I pulled him close and buried my nose in the top of his head. His red hair was darkening by the day, and his bare legs dangled, his feet almost touching the floor. He sat back heavily against me, still sleepy enough to endure my arms around him, my little kisses and words of endearment. He was a piece of work, this son of mine, prone to fits of wild euphoria and deep blue melancholy. Babies are nothing but blank screens; you can't imagine them growing up with flaws and complications. It's a wonder to watch them come into their own, their true selves taking shape beneath the smooth skins and soft bones, to admit that there are some things that, no matter

how hard you work or how much you pray, are just plain out
of your control.

Lily marched over to the pantry for a box of Frosted Mini-
Wheats, and Geneva rose to get out the milk and juice.

"I don't want to go to school," Jude whined into the front
of my blouse.

"How come, baby?"

"I want to stay here with you."

"I'm not staying here. I'm going to work, and Aunt
Geneva's got stuff to do. But guess what? Later on I've got a
surprise for you."

He lifted his face and looked at me, his brown eyes liquid
and trusting.

"When you get home from school today, somebody special's going to be there," I said.

"Santa Claus?"

Lily shot her cousin a dark look across the breakfast table.
"This is April," she said. "Santa Claus is *December*."

"Dale Earnhardt?" Jude glanced shyly at Lily, who scowled
and dug her spoon into her cereal. With her crisp black bob
and stern demeanor, she was as serious as her new little sister
was sunny. Bailey's nickname for her was the General.

"Dale Earnhardt is dead," she said scornfully.

Jude's voice quavered. "No, he's not. He's on your shirt."

"That's Dale *Junior,* dummy," Lily said. "And he's not at
your house. No how, no way. He's at Talladega, for the quali-
fying."

Geneva and I exchanged a look, amused and long-suffering.
I wondered, not for the first time, if God hand-chose our

offspring for us or if he just reached into some big washtub and plucked them out and flung them at us randomly, for his own amusement.

"Don't say 'dummy,' Lil," Geneva said.

"I'll give you a hint," I told Jude. "It's somebody who's related to you. Somebody you haven't seen in a long time, who sings on a stage in front of big, big . . ."

"Denny!" he shouted, sliding off my lap, jostling the table so hard the cereal box fell over. He started to dance, waving his arms and legs, chanting, "Denny, Denny, Denny!" He darted around the table; I reached for him as he shot past, but I wasn't quick enough.

"Jude! Where are you going?"

"To get ready for school, so everything can hurry up and be over with and I can go home and see Denny!" He ran off down the hallway.

"What do you say, Lil?" I asked. "You want to come out and see Denny after school? Maybe sleep over tonight? Or have you got a hot date with Junior?"

She cocked her head and considered this like a CEO mulling over whether or not to buy out some multimillion-dollar corporation. "Sleep over," she said.

I polished off my coffee and stood. "That okay with you?" I asked Geneva.

"Are you kidding?"

"I'll pick up you and your cousin at Aunt Dove's after work, okay?" I said, leaning over to kiss the top of Lily's head. "Maybe we can get your uncle Ash to fix us some burgers on the grill."

"You are coming early tomorrow, right?" Geneva asked as she carried Emmy to the front door to see us off.

"What time does it start, again?"

"The invitations said six, but I could use you around four, if you can swing it."

I reached out and cupped Emmy's ivory cheek with my hand. Happy and fed and grinning her toothless grin, she looked like a little Buddha.

"For you, baby?" I said. "Anything."

I UNLOCKED THE shop as the sun crested the treetops, figuring I had two hours of peace and quiet, tops, before Audrey came in. Not that I didn't love her like a daughter—which is to say with equal measures of tenderness and vexation. But in less than three weeks she'd be graduating from Mooney High and, the very next afternoon, marrying her boyfriend of two years, Joe Grissom, at the VFW Hall, and I feared not just for Audrey's sanity but that of everybody whose lives she touched in the meantime.

I'd put on the coffee and was checking the cooler when I heard a key in the back door lock and Audrey came bursting in. Her hair, four inches of dark roots tipped by two inches of platinum, was spiked out in three or four different directions, her eyes rimmed with thick purple liner. Her T-shirt bore the faded image of a poster for a concert by Big Brother and the Holding Company, whose singer, Janis Joplin, had been dead and buried nearly two decades before Audrey was born. The silver stud she'd worn in her navel for the past couple of years was gone, replaced by a tiny winking diamond—her and Joe's version of an engagement ring.

"Take a look at this," she said breathlessly, dumping an armload of magazines on the counter.

"Why aren't you at school?"

"Please. Do you really think they'll be taking attendance this close to graduation?"

"Well, yes, I think they might. Aren't you already in enough—"

"Here," she said, flopping open a copy of *Martha Stewart Living*. "Isn't that the most gorgeous thing you ever saw in your life?"

Against a backdrop of ivory satin, a disembodied hand clutched a bouquet of bloodred roses, each velvet bloom a study in symmetry. I could just picture a room full of sweating assistants sorting through bushels of flowers, searching for hours for these perfect blossoms, rearranging each one a degree this way or that for the camera while Martha shrieked orders in the background.

"So, what do you think?" Audrey asked. "It's not that big of a deal, right? We just cancel the gardenias and ask for, what, three, four dozen red roses instead?"

"Sit down." I eased the magazine from her hand and guided her to a stool.

"Now, listen. I agree, this is a beautiful bouquet," I said. "But what about everything else? Starting with the fact that your bridesmaids' dresses are blue."

"They aren't *blue*," she said. "They're aquamarine."

"Well, whatever you call it, it won't go with red flowers."

"Maybe my bouquet could be red and theirs could be white?"

"Honey, you've got to trust me on this. You've already picked the right flowers. I know you're nervous—"

"I'm not nervous!" She began to gnaw at a hangnail on her thumb. Gently, I guided her hand away from her mouth.

"Sure you are. You'd be crazy not to be."

"Were you?"

"Crazy? Probably."

"Nervous, I meant."

"That depends. The first time, I wasn't much older than you are, and I remember walking up the aisle and seeing Mitchell standing at the altar and thinking, *Who is that man?*" I poured myself a cup of coffee. "Come to think of it, that happened the second time, too. I was six months pregnant, and even though I was madly in love and I truly believed Ash and I were set for life, even then, I broke out in a cold sweat standing up in front of the preacher."

"But it goes away, though, right? That feeling?"

I looked at her, this beautiful girl transformed by two-toned hair and eye makeup and love into something wholly her own, and realized I didn't know how to answer her. In my experience, you never knew when you woke up in the morning or came home from work at the end of the day whether the person you shared your bed and your tub and your icebox with would appear to you as the love of your life or a face last seen on the post office wall, wanted for crimes in half a dozen states. One minute you were sure you'd found your soul mate; the next, you wanted to grab the keys and ride as far as the road and your wits would take you. But you tamped it down; you got through it, made your little deals with your partner and the devil, and somehow, if you were lucky, the good stuff trumped the bad, or at least balanced the other out.

I leaned over and smoothed down a strand of Audrey's hair. "Yeah," I said. "It goes away."

After Audrey left for school, I picked up the phone and called the house. The machine picked up, and I left a message for Denny that I didn't really think she'd hear, reminding her to come by the shop and see me. Then I reached into my tote bag and pulled out the paper sack I'd slipped in there early this morning, at home. I opened it and read the directions on the side of the box. It was a lot less messy than it used to be. But where, I wondered, was the red-letter warning that said, "Results guaranteed to change your life," the fine print that motherhood was a job not to be attempted except by professionals? I remembered watching my own future change course some eight years earlier, a few months after I took up with Ash, thanks to a plus sign on a little plastic stick. I didn't regret it, which was not the same thing as saying I wouldn't have done things differently if I'd known what was coming. But then, I wondered if it was ever really possible to plan these things. Did nine months of pregnancy make me any more or less ready than Geneva, whose preparations for her daughters had involved passports and plane tickets? Jude had been an accident: a happy one, but still unexpected. Come to think of it, so had Denny, the day Marlene dropped her off in Ash's front yard, wearing her defenses like a shirt of barbed wire.

I switched on the light in the restroom and studied myself in the mirror over the sink, trying to decide if I looked like somebody's grandma. By East Texas standards, I was more than old enough; plenty of girls I'd gone to high school with had grown kids already, and grandbabies Jude's age.

If Denny planned to have this baby, Ash and I would have to help her. But I'd only arrived at the parent party myself a few years before; I'd barely begun making the mistakes I was entitled to with Jude, that would earn me my stripes and teach me how to do better next time. This, I decided, was the real thrill at the possibility of a baby: the idea that your future could begin over and over again.

I smoothed my hair with my palms, turned off the restroom light, and walked back into the showroom. As the sun slanted in through the plate glass, I enjoyed a fleeting sense of satisfaction that everything in sight was well ordered, in its rightful place. I dusted the leaves of a schefflera that didn't need dusting and straightened a rack of cards that didn't need straightening. It was only a quarter till eight, but I walked to the door and flipped the sign to OPEN. You never knew when somebody might wake up at the crack of dawn and feel like ordering flowers in a burst of affection, or remorse, or just for the heck of it. You never knew if the day might bring a miracle.

CHAPTER 3

Denny

I WOKE UP on the couch in Daddy's studio with a sour stomach and a fuzzy head. I'd been dreaming about Ty, weird, broken dreams that I couldn't hold. I thought about calling him, but I couldn't think what to say, where to begin. He surely knew by now that I was gone, but I couldn't make up my mind how he'd feel about it. I wasn't as good at reading people as I ought to be; I guess Will Culpepper was proof of that.

Both Daddy's truck and Lucy's Blazer were gone, and there was a note on the kitchen table, propped against the sugar bowl, in Daddy's handwriting, with both their cell phone numbers and the number of the flower shop. I went upstairs and shed my clothes in a heap on the bathroom floor and climbed into the shower. Lucy always had great soap and shampoo, stuff that smelled like an African rain forest or a market in Marrakesh,

and the towels were fat and thirsty like the kind in first-class hotels. Not that I'd had much personal experience in first-class
hotels. My band wasn't doing quite *that* well, even though Ty
told us at least once a day that it was only a matter of time.

It occurred to me we might never make it now, that I
might have just turned my back on all that, the way Daddy
had. It seemed to me that once you'd had a taste of the spotlight it left its mark on you forever, like a tattoo. Sure, they
had ways of getting rid of tattoos nowadays, but they supposedly hurt more than the original needle, and the skin looked
weird afterward, pink and tight and shiny. Let's face it, once
you'd done it, you were scarred for life.

I was tugging a comb through my wet hair when the
phone rang in some far-off part of the house. Downstairs, the
answering machine clicked on, and Lucy's recorded voice
floated up the stairs asking the caller to leave a message, followed by a beep, then her voice again, for real this time, saying, "Denny? I don't know if you'll hear this, if you'd even
think to check the machine, but if you do, well, try and come
by the shop today, okay? Maybe for lunch? I really want to—
to get caught up, just the two of us. Love you. 'Bye."

I thought back to the way she'd looked at me the night before, standing in the front yard in the rain. She knew something, or *thought* she knew, which was just as dangerous.
Maybe things had been better when I was fifteen and she and
Daddy were so wrapped up in each other they'd barely have
noticed a marching band parading through the house.

I finished unsnarling my hair, then wrapped myself in a
towel and walked down the hall to their bedroom, leaving

damp footprints on the hardwood floor. I felt sort of bad ri-
fling through Lucy's bureau drawers, but I knew she'd rather
me borrow her underpants than go without. She had nicer
stuff than the last time I'd visited, pastel colors and little bits
of lace. We were pretty much the same size on the bottom but
she was way bigger than me on top, so I decided to skip the
bra. Her shirts were all corny beyond belief, so I went into
Jude's room, where I dug around in the little-boy clutter till I
found a T-shirt that cracked me up; it had Daddy's picture
on it, airbrushed to all get-out—I mean, he's a good-looking
man, but this was silent-movie-star time—and the words
ASH FARRELL COMEBACK SPECIAL, and a date from just a little
over a year before: the famous night he'd busted up the
Round-Up, wrecked a new truck, and then disappeared,
turning up three days later hungover and sorry as hell in
Lucy's mama's backyard. It had been a comeback, all right,
though not the kind anybody expected.

I pulled the shirt on over my head. It was a kid's size extra-
large, so on me it was pretty snug, but in a way that looked
cool and that I thought Lucy would get a kick out of. I went
back to my bedroom and plucked my Levi's off the floor, carried them downstairs and pulled them on with my beat-up
boots in the front hall. The spare key was in the vase on the
hall table, like always, and I locked up and climbed into my
pickup and headed into town.

NOT MUCH HAD changed since the last time I'd been to
Mooney, but then, nothing much ever did. The Food King

had finally gone out of business, and the café had a new neon Lotto Texas sign in the window. An elderly black man with a bucket and a rag was scouring pigeon poop off the bronze statue of Jefferson Davis outside the courthouse. If you ever need proof that the Old South is still alive and well in the twenty-first century, all you'd have to do is come to Mooney. I swear, somebody ought to make a documentary.

I swung by the elementary school hoping to catch a glimpse of Jude on the playground, but the swings and slides and jungle gym were empty, bright metal glaring in the midday sun. I thought about driving around looking for Daddy, but I couldn't remember the name of the lady he was working for, and I didn't really have an excuse, except maybe to show him my T-shirt.

I admit, I was putting off going to see Lucy. I wasn't all that crazy about the thought of sitting across from her at the café or the DQ, eating something fried and smothered in cream gravy while she tried to read my mind with her eagle eyes.

I drove over to Aunt Dove's, hoping she might invite me in for a glass of tea and not ask too many questions. Anyway, I wanted to see her garden, a place that was responsible for some of my first happy memories in Mooney. To say she had a green thumb was an understatement; she could, and did, grow anything from Johnny-jump-ups to watermelons, and everywhere you looked were religious figurines and truck-stop souvenirs and plaques with pithy sayings. It looked like some slightly crazy person's idea of heaven, which, come to think of it, I guess it was.

And there she was, never mind it being more or less high noon, in her polyester pants and straw hat and gardening gloves, plucking salad greens and putting them in a bucket. I slammed the truck door behind me and Dove looked out from under the brim of her hat.

"Well, I'll be danged," she said. That's when I saw her other visitor, unfolding his long legs out of the lotus position and stepping out of the shade into the sun. He was wearing some kind of loose linen pants and sandals that probably cost two hundred bucks, and his hair stuck out in little twists and sprigs in about fifty different directions, but the smile—that was pure back-roads East Texas, that was home.

"Hey, Red," Erasmus said, and reached out to loop a lock of my hair around his finger.

"Hey, Dread," I answered, lifting my hand to tug at one of his sprigs. He'd been my first love and my best friend, and I realized I'd been carrying the thought of him with me all the way from Nashville, tucked back in a corner of my mind, like an old letter you keep folded under your pillow for safe-keeping.

"What are you doing here?" we asked at the same time, and laughed.

"I've got a week off before I go into the studio with Clifton," he said. Clifton Janis was a famous New York jazz trumpeter whose band Erasmus played in—combo, he called it—since he'd graduated from Juilliard. "I decided to come visit the folks, soak up a little down-home culture."

"Come to eat my tomatoes and drink my sweet tea," Dove said, elbowing her way between us. I was startled by how frail she felt, all bone and gristle, but her hug was fierce, her blue eyes gleaming under the brim of her hat like an elf's. The front of her T-shirt read NATALIE FOR PRESIDENT. "You just get in?"

"Last night."

"That good-lookin' boy you married along for the ride?" I don't know why Dove always referred to Will that way. The one and only time she'd seen him, Daddy had just punched him in the nose and he was holding a bloody towel to his face.

"Not this time." The air was hot and still but for the sound of a car passing by one block over and the birds making a ruckus in the backyard.

"Well, come on in, the both of you, 'fore we all die of thirst."

Erasmus held open the screen door and we followed Dove into the house. She still had the same gold velvet couch, the same fake-wood-grain coffee table and bookshelves stuffed with titles I couldn't believe anybody outside a schoolroom ever read. There were pictures all over the room of family members both aboveground and below, including her parents and her big brother Garnett, who'd died in a hunting accident when he was eighteen. The one I loved best was of Lucy and her brothers when they were little, hand in hand on a bridge over a creek in Arkansas, the boys looking scrappy and fearless on either side of their pigtailed sister, whose smile was just the slightest bit lopsided, like she wasn't quite sure the world was a place that deserved smiling at. It had been taken, Dove told me once, right after their daddy left, and I loved looking into Lucy's six-year-old face, hunting for whatever it was that would lead her one day to my own daddy, and to me.

Dove kept up a regular patter as she led us into the kitchen and ordered us to sit at the table while she took a pitcher of tea out of the icebox and poured three Mason jars full. I sat back to listen to Erasmus and Dove's conversation, a lazy back and forth about New York and family and last night's rain and its effect on her tomatoes. I was only half paying attention, sipping my tea, bobbing along on the ebb and flow of their voices and remembering the first time I'd sat across this table from Erasmus King, a skinny, big-eared kid who'd gobbled down three mayonnaise-and-tomato sandwiches in a row. If I looked at him just so, I could still glimpse that boy underneath the big-city spit and shine. It had been half a year since I'd seen him, but to me, he was always here, in Dove's kitchen, his white teeth flashing, wiping tomato seeds off his chin with a handful of paper napkins.

I glanced at the clock and saw that it had gotten to be twenty past twelve. "I better go," I said, polishing off my tea. "Lucy was expecting me at the shop at noon."

"Can I bum a ride?" Erasmus asked. "I left Pop's truck over at the courthouse." We scraped back our chairs and set our empty glasses in the sink.

"You reckon your auntie might like a mess of these greens?" Dove asked.

"Oh, I reckon."

She put the greens in a plastic bag, then led us down the front walk, making Erasmus promise to come back in a day or two to help her with her bean poles.

"I been tryin' to talk Lucy into puttin' in a garden," she said to me, holding on to my arm as I opened the truck door. "Seems like a crime lettin' all that good land go to waste."

"Yes, ma'am."

"She says she gets all the beans and tomatoes she needs from me. I keep tellin' her, that's not the reason why you do it. It's about the doin', not the gettin'."

I kissed her cheek, as brown and crinkly as a paper sack, and climbed into the truck.

"Miss Dove is something else, isn't she?" Erasmus said as I turned the key and fired up the engine. "I've met a lot of New York characters, but nobody that compares to her."

He was all bones and angles, his twiggy hair scraping the headliner. There was a smell about him I didn't recognize, something bottled, spicy.

"You've got A/C, I hope," he said as I put the truck in gear and eased it away from the curb.

I twisted the climate-control dials, and he aimed the vents till cold air was hitting him full in the face. "Ah." He tilted back his chin and closed his eyes.

"What's the matter, Dread? Forgotten how to take the heat?" I said.

"It gets plenty hot in New York."

"Give me a break. When you called me last April, it was *snowing*." He smiled without opening his eyes, and we drove a block or two in silence, me sneaking sideways glances at him with his head against the headrest. When the cab had cooled off some, I turned the fan down, and he sat forward and opened his eyes.

"You're awful quiet," he said. "You mad at me or something?"

"Just surprised to see you, is all."

"Your daddy didn't tell you I was in town?"

"It was pretty late when I got in."

"So, where's the great Will Culpepper?"

"This time yesterday he was in Nashville," I said. "But I guess by now he could be anywhere. Vegas, maybe, or Cancún. One of those places you go to forget your troubles."

I turned onto the courthouse square. Erasmus's daddy's work truck was parked in front of the bank, with its big flatbed and its winch and chain, EXTREME AUTO WHOLESALE in faded paint on the driver's side door.

"How about you?" he asked. The truck seemed suddenly too full of him, his East Coast dress and new smell. I couldn't see the country boy quite so clear anymore.

"Me?" There wasn't an empty parking slot to be found, it being lunchtime on the square, so I pulled in behind the tow truck and kept the motor running.

"You trying to forget your troubles, too?"

"Maybe I just felt like coming home to see the folks, like you."

A fat man in suit pants and suspenders stood on the sidewalk in front of the bank's glass doors with his hands in his pockets, scowling at us like we were about to stick up the place.

"How long are you here for?" Erasmus asked.

"I guess right now it's up in the air."

He opened the door, stepping out into a blast of heat rising off the asphalt and the fried-grease stink of the DQ.

"Well, call me at Pop's," he said. "You know the number."

"Okay." I felt both relieved and guilty that he was out of my truck. Seeing him should have made me glad—Erasmus would always be in my corner, no matter what—but instead it only seemed to shine a light on the distance between who we were now and who we used to be.

I backed out and drove the block and a half to Faye's, where Lucy was sitting at the counter eating a turkey sandwich.

"I like your shirt," she said, pulling out a stool for me.

"Thanks." It didn't seem as funny now as it had back at the house.

"I'd just about given up on you."

"I stopped by Dove's a minute," I said. "Erasmus was there." I picked up a potato chip, put it down again.

"Your daddy said he saw him in town the other day," she said. "I guess nobody thought to tell you last night."

"That's okay. He'll be around awhile."

"Here," she said, handing me half her sandwich. "I haven't seen you eat two bites since you got here."

I took a bite and chewed slowly. It stuck in my throat like cardboard. "Good," I lied.

"I want you to do something for me."

She leaned over and pulled a canvas tote bag from under the counter. She rummaged in it, bringing out a brown paper sack, the kind I used to carry my grade school lunches in. Unfolding the flap, she tilted it so that a small cardboard box slid out next to my sandwich. I picked it up, turned it over, and read the words printed in black letters across the top.

"God!" I said, dropping it onto the countertop.

She pushed the box toward me. "I want you to take this in the bathroom right now, and let's get things out in the open once and for all."

"I won't pee on a stick!"

"Honey, you can't run from this," she said. "Not like you took off and ran from Will Culpepper."

"You think you know everything, but you don't." I picked up my half of the sandwich and threw it in the trash. Why was I being so mean? I was mad at Will, and at myself, and I seemed to be taking it out on all the wrong people.

"I know more than you think I do," she said. "Now, are you going to do this here, or do I have to drag you to Dr. Crawford and let the whole world in on our business?"

I grabbed the box out of her hand and marched back to the bathroom and locked the door. I could argue and stall till the cows came home, but it wouldn't matter. I was no match for Lucy Hatch.

CHAPTER 4

Lucy

"How did you know?" Denny grabbed a handful of Kleenex from the box I'd set on the counter and started to shred it with her fingers. Her nails, I saw, were chewed to stubs, the cuticles bloody and raw. As I'd suspected, the stick had turned blue in no time at all, the time it took for a thing to go from sneaking suspicion to cold, hard fact.

"You look just like me. The way I looked, at first, with Jude. Like somebody's fired a shot at you from a long way off, and you know it's coming but it hasn't quite hit you yet."

I walked over and bolted the front door and turned the sign around to CLOSED, then went to the little icebox in back and fetched two icy bottles of Coca-Cola.

"Look, I know it's a lot to take in at first," I said. "Nobody's asking you to make any decisions on the spot."

Denny closed her eyes and pressed the frosty bottle to her forehead.

"You know, honey," I said, "whatever's going on between you and Will, he needs to know about this."

"Impossible," she said, wiping her nose on the back of her wrist.

"It's his business, too."

"No, it's not."

"What makes you say that?" She didn't answer me. "This— The baby is Will's, isn't it?"

"I can't believe you'd even say that!"

"I'm sorry. I didn't mean—"

"Anyway, it's not even a baby," she said. "It's barely even the *idea* of a baby!"

She sagged forward, laying her head in her arms on the countertop. I didn't blame her for being upset. It didn't seem fair that something so momentous could happen to a person without her knowing, that alarms didn't blare and lights flash in the moment sperm met egg and changed everything.

Abruptly she sat up again, flinging her hair back over her shoulder. There were two bright spots of color high on her cheeks as she pulled in her breath, held it a second, then let it out in a long, fluttering sigh.

"You know Marin?" she said. "Marin Bishop, who plays fiddle in my band?"

"Sure." It would be hard to forget Marin, with her black leather lace-up pants, her long dark hair whipping as her bow sawed wildly across the strings. "Oh, no. You don't mean . . ."

"Right under my nose, it turned out," Denny said. "But I didn't know it till— What day is this?"

"Thursday."

"Tuesday night. Or, Wednesday morning, I guess it was. Will went out, said he was meeting some of the guys for poker. He didn't come home. Not that that's unusual. He's stayed out all night lots of times. But this time, I *knew*. You know what I mean?" I nodded sadly; I knew. "He came sneaking in around daybreak carrying his boots, and I switched on the kitchen light and busted him. It wasn't hard. He had hickeys all over his neck, and he smelled like Fracas. That's the perfume Marin wears. Funny, huh? *Fracas*."

There are so many ways to get your heart broken. Parents leaving. People you love not loving you back, or loving something else—another person, a bottle, a dream—more than they love you. I wanted to protect Denny the way I'd tried when she was fourteen, to say something profound and soothing.

"So, he's in love with Marin?"

"Love? I doubt either one of them knows the meaning of the word. They're just like animals on one of those PBS shows about Africa. Doing what comes naturally."

"Does he want to *be* with Marin?" I asked. "Or does he want you?"

"It's complicated," she said. I nodded in what I hoped was an encouraging way. "Do you remember when I brought Will home last year, when I asked you if it was possible to be in love with two people? Well, it's not. I know that now."

"But I thought you and Erasmus—"

"Not Erasmus. I mean, yeah, I love him, but not like that, not anymore."

"I don't understand," I said.

She sat for a few minutes rolling the Coke bottle between her palms.

"You remember Ty," she said finally.

"Well, sure." Ty Briggs had been Denny's manager for the past three years: tall and broad shouldered, with sandy, side-swept hair and serious gray eyes that followed Denny everywhere. The first time I'd met him, when we'd traveled up to hear Denny sing at the Garland Opry, I'd felt right away that Denny was in good hands. But more than that, I liked how she was with him—her true self, feisty and funny, not the fawning, trembling leaf she turned into next to Will. I remember thinking, without Denny ever saying so, that she and Ty seemed like a good pair, or at least that things might be headed in that direction; but then, the next thing I knew, she'd come home married to Will Culpepper.

"Do you want to tell me about it?" I asked, gently pulling her bitten fingers out of her mouth.

"There's nothing to tell."

"But you just said—"

"It's really stupid, okay? Like something out of junior high."

Most of life is like junior high, I thought, but this didn't seem like the right time to say so.

"Try me," I said.

She just sighed again and buried her head in her arms. I stood beside her awhile and rubbed her neck under her damp, fragrant hair. Contrary to popular belief, being a parent doesn't give you an edge on wisdom, no matter how long you've been doing it. Sometimes there's nothing you can say except, "We're in this together." Having a baby is hard enough when both parents love each other and want to make things work. I tried to think what Dove or Peggy would do in my shoes, but the sages were silent. I was on my own.

The phone rang, and Denny slid off her stool. I said hello into the receiver, motioning that she should sit back down, but she just gave a little wave and mouthed something I couldn't make out and headed for the door. In my ear, Penny Jeanrette, administrator at the Golden Years retirement home, began to explain that she was sorry, but Miss Grace Wick's upcoming ninety-eighth birthday party would have to be canceled due to Miss Wick's having fallen and fractured her tibia.

I covered the mouthpiece with my hand and called, "Wait!," but the bells tied to the knob of the door were already jangling as it slammed shut. Through the glass I watched as Denny climbed into her red pickup and pulled away from the curb.

"Hello? Lucy?" Penny was saying. "Are you there?"

A cloud of exhaust settled over Front Street. I swallowed hard and told Penny that I understood, that things happen sometimes that are nobody's fault at all.

CHAPTER 5

Denny

I KNEW THIS road like the back of my hand, going from sun to dappled shade as it switched back and forth between patches of forest and field, the odd hand-painted sign for a backwoods church, a lean-to beside the road where, in a few weeks, little kids or old ladies would be selling metal buckets full of baseball-size tomatoes and zucchinis as long as your forearm. I passed trailer houses up on cinder blocks, yards full of rusted-out farm equipment and propane tanks alongside brand-new Trans Ams or 4×4s and satellite dishes, old tires planted with marigolds, skinny dogs panting in the shade of chicken coops. The air was muggy, the sky dotted with clouds where it showed between the trees. It was strange country, northeast Texas, prehistoric-seeming in some ways, like time had passed it by. That could be good thing or a bad thing. Like the landscape, it could change on you in a heartbeat.

I set my brain on cruise control and fell into the rhythm of tires on blacktop. Will and Ty and Marin, the mess I'd left behind in Nashville, all of it was just a buzzing in the back of my brain, like a trapped insect I could barely hear. I couldn't think about anything except that stick turning blue in the bathroom light, the way it seemed to pulse and throb with a life of its own. I wondered if it was a bad thing, maybe even a sin, to let yourself get knocked up by a man who was bound to break your heart, even if it hadn't been on purpose, even if you and he'd been fighting like crazy and then just as crazy making up, and maybe there was alcohol involved, and maybe you were too carried away or too lazy or too angry— it was hard to remember now—to get up and get a rubber. Will didn't like them, anyway, even though I tried to make him use them due to his shady past and, as it turned out, his shady present. "Just this time, baby," he'd growl in my ear, which I'd thought at the time was a sexy thing to say, not a prediction of things to come.

Out of the corner of my eye as it zipped by, I saw a road sign reading WHITE PINE 8. I'd been just a few days shy of fifteen the first time I made this trip, a hitchhiker in a milk truck in search of my grandmother, Evelyn LeGrande. At the time she and Daddy hadn't seen each other in thirty-some-odd years, not since she'd had some kind of nervous breakdown when he was a baby and given him up to foster care, and I had no real reason to think she'd take me in. She had, though, and in the years since I'd tried keeping in touch with her, but Evelyn was a slippery character. She wasn't big on visitors, much less telephone chitchat. It had been a couple of years, I guessed, since the last time I'd talked to her. But I'd loved it there at her house on the lake, loved her scrambled eggs with peppers and her old boat with the Evinrude motor, the way we'd stood on the dock singing Brenda Lee. Of everybody I knew, Evelyn might understand the best how it felt to be in my shoes, pregnant and scared out of your mind.

I MISSED THE turnoff and had to circle back, scanning the woods for the old sign to LeGrande's Fish Camp. It took another pass to realize the sign was gone, the entrance hidden deep in an overgrowth of weeds and scrub pine.

I drove slowly up the narrow red-dirt road, low-hanging branches scraping the roof of the pickup and shutting out the sunlight, giving the place a creepy, supernatural feel. I pulled into the yard and shut off the engine, then sat in silence as the sun slid in and out between fast-moving clouds. I tried telling myself that the house looked no different than it ever had. And it's true, the paint had been peeling for years, the windows grimed over, the porch screen saggy. Evelyn had never been much on keeping up appearances.

The shed where she'd always parked her truck was empty. I got out and walked around the house, knocking at the front door and the back, trying to see in the windows, but either the curtains were shut or the glass too dirty to make out much. Out back I found the vegetable garden grown over, the chicken-wire fence falling in on itself.

I strolled down to the dock, past vacant cabins from back in the day when Evelyn's daddy's fishing camp was a going concern. There was no trace of the boat. The only time Daddy and his mama had been within shouting distance of each other in my lifetime had been right here, when he'd come to fetch me and carry me back to Mooney; and I felt a sudden stab of fury at him for his stubbornness, the grudge he'd held against her all these years. If he'd only let bygones be bygones, he'd know why her house was empty, her garden trampled and choked with weeds, her boat and her truck gone. Why had he held on so long to his bitterness, hoarding it like a prize? How could the woman who'd given birth to him, who'd turned him over to a foster family when she couldn't see fit to care for him herself, who'd spent most of her life living not a half hour's drive from him and his family, just fall off the face of the earth?

But it wasn't really possible to disappear, not in this day and age. A person left clues, whether they meant to or not.

The little homegrown gas-and-bait store where I'd stopped years before to ask directions to LeGrande's had been replaced by a Shell station with half a dozen pumps and a minimart that sold everything from Harley caps and cold drinks to Lotto tickets and barbecue sandwiches. The two clerks behind the counter were even younger than the boy who'd been there on my first visit, and neither of them knew a thing about the woman who used to run the old fish camp down the road.

I bought a Coke and drank it in my truck with the A/C going full blast. I'd gone from being pissed off at Daddy to being pissed off at Evelyn. What kind of person lived the way she did, without any ties to the outside world? Not only was I her only blood relation—the only one who would admit to it, anyway—but as far as I knew, she didn't have a single friend. What's more, she liked it that way. It was her prerogative, I guessed, to live like a hermit, but it would have been nice to know there was somebody besides me looking out for her. Maybe, I thought, she'd gone off the deep end again and was locked up someplace. Maybe she'd died.

I finished my Coke and drove into White Pine proper. I'd never been to town before, if "town" is the right word to describe a handful of houses, a post office, a filling station, and a Pik 'n Pak.

I parked in front of the post office and stood for a minute on the steaming asphalt. Across the street in the filling station's single bay a blue Buick was up on the lift, and two men stood underneath it, staring at me. I raised my hand to wave, and they both ducked back under the car like I'd caught them doing something shameful.

The girl reading *US* magazine behind the counter in the post office was about my age, though she wore a cheap polyester blouse that might have been borrowed from her mama. Her skin was dotted with angry-looking pimples, and her hair looked like it hadn't been washed in a week.

"Hep you?" she asked, closing her magazine and sliding it under the counter.

I gazed around the tiny room, one wall covered with metal mailboxes, the counter with its little postal scale and the bulletin board full of notices about rate hikes and wanted criminals. No wonder the girl looked bored to death if this was what she had to stare at day in and day out. I wondered what she did when the office closed, if she went home to her mama and daddy or a husband, maybe a couple of kids. I tried to make it nice for her in my head, to give her a sweet little house with a patch of flowers out front, a good man waiting for her with a kiss and a cold beer in his hand.

"I'm looking for somebody," I said. "She lives around here, or used to. On a fish camp over by the lake. Her name's Evelyn LeGrande."

"We ain't allowed to give out information about customers."

"She's my grandmother," I said. "I went by her place and it's all closed up. I just want to know if maybe she moved or something." The girl continued to stare at me blank-eyed, her mouth set in a straight line. I took back the house and the husband; I put her in a cramped apartment that smelled like cat pee, macaroni and cheese from a box for her supper, and downstairs neighbors who kept her up all night blasting Iron Maiden on the stereo. "I'm the only kin she's got," I said. It wasn't strictly true, but it was my last resort.

"Hang on," the girl said, and got up and went through a door into the back.

While she was gone I amused myself reading the notices on the bulletin board—nobody I was related or married to, fortunately—then looked for a while out the front door, where there wasn't a thing to see but the men across the street under the Buick.

Finally the girl came back, along with a middle-aged black lady wearing a uniform. She had shoulders like a linebacker's, a head full of tiny cornrows, and contact lenses as green as the algae that grew in Daddy's pond.

"Jess here says you're looking for Miz LeGrande."

"Yes, ma'am. I'm her granddaughter."

"Where you been?"

"Excuse me?"

"How come you to come sniffin' around lookin' for her now?"

"I don't know what you mean."

"You after her place, or what? 'Cause I can't think of any reason for you to go showin' up all sudden like this, claimin' to be kin. Not after leavin' her out there by herself all that time, no better'n a dog."

A buzzing started up in my head. It got louder and louder, and the next thing I knew, I was sitting on the floor and the girl and the lady were kneeling over me, fanning my face with a WANTED flyer. An old man in overalls stood gawking just inside the door, a fistful of envelopes dangling from his hand.

"You okay?" the lady said. "Whew. You had us goin' there for a minute." I started to stand up, but she pushed me down again and held me there. I swear, she could've played tackle for the Oakland Raiders. "You just stay put a minute. Last thing I need, somebody passin' out and suin' the U.S. Postal Service."

The girl went behind the counter and brought out a bottle of water. "Go on," she said, twisting off the top and handing it to me. "It's brand-fresh."

I took a drink, mentally giving her back the house and the supper and the husband, adding candles on the table and Harry Connick Jr. on the stereo. The kids, if there were any, were at her mama's for the night, sleeping like little angels.

"I know you," she said suddenly. "I seen you the other night on CMT! That redneck woman—that's you, right? It's her, Lavelle! It's, it's . . ."

"Denny Farrell," I said. I didn't have the heart to point out that "Redneck Woman" was Gretchen Wilson, who was longer legged and darker haired and who'd sold a hell of a lot more records than me. I guessed one country singer was the same as another when you lived in a place like White Pine.

"Right! See!" She nudged the older lady. "She's on there every time you turn it on, just about."

"Well, I'll be." Lavelle put her hand under my elbow and helped me to my feet.

"Redneck woman, huh?" she said. "Lord a mercy, won't the Countess be surprised."

CHAPTER 6

Lucy

MY MAMA'S HOUSE was full of ghosts. I couldn't round a corner without coming up on a photo of myself as a baby, a pigtailed ten-year-old, a high-school track star, a young bride standing fresh-faced and dumb as a post alongside her silent, rugged first husband.

Over the past year Mama's bad hip had gotten worse, and my brothers and their wives and I had divvied up the duty of looking in on her. As luck would have it, today was my day. I pulled up in front of her house and left the motor running. Every single week I sat at the curb giving myself a pep talk, telling myself that maybe this time things wouldn't be so bad. Mama's and my relationship had never been what you could call warm and fuzzy, and the older we both got, the more we seemed to rub against each other like a couple of pieces of sandpaper.

Yet I couldn't ignore the fact that she was the one who'd told me to give Ash another chance, that the great regret in her life was not taking back my daddy, Raymond Hatch, when he'd wanted to try and make one last go of it. It had shaken me to the core, wondering what my brothers' and my life might have been like if she'd set aside her pride and said "Come on home." Even all these years later, I sometimes wondered about that man whose face I could barely recall, wondered if he was still out there in the world somewhere with a bitter tang of regret on the back of his tongue. After Mama's confession, we'd never discussed the subject again; we were bound by an unspoken code of silence, like two people who have buried a body in secret. Every week I thought, *Today is the day I will ask her everything;* and every week she did something mean or maddening and I let another chance go by.

The yard looked terrible, scraggly and overgrown as a beggar-man's beard, and I made a mental note to call my brother Bailey and rag him about it. Mama's Olds sat in the driveway like a beached boat. I wondered if it even ran anymore. She'd pretty much stopped driving herself to church or the store, preferring instead to have somebody pick her up or run her errands for her.

I rang the bell, then took out my key and let myself in the front door. With her hip, it took Mama forever to get from one end of the house to the other, and she refused to leave the door unlocked. You never knew, she claimed, what with the world the way it was, when some psycho might decide to crawl out of the woods and start slashing people's throats—a fear that grew sharper the more time she spent planted in front of the TV watching CNN Headline News.

"Mama? It's me," I called into the dark recesses of the house. She kept the curtains shut 24/7, in winter to keep the house warmer, in summer to try and hold the heat at bay. I switched on the hall lamp and made my way toward the den and the drone of the television. Anderson Cooper was on-screen, talking about some far-off catastrophe, but there was no sign of Mama. That was strange; ordinarily she wouldn't miss Anderson Cooper for all the tea in China. "Such a smart boy—and handsome! His mother was an heiress, you know," she liked to say. I didn't ordinarily pay much attention to the news myself. Keeping my own life from tilting off its axis was enough of a challenge without adding natural disasters and crime sprees and political corruption to the mix.

A small, cool hand grasped my forearm, and I yelled and jumped a foot.

"Lord, Mama! What do you mean, sneaking up on me like that?"

"It's my new duster shoes. See?" She demonstrated, shuffling silently across the parquet to the recliner, where she held out one foot for inspection. Sure enough, there was a paper dust mitt fitted over her sneaker.

"Have you been shopping out of those catalogs again?"

"I tell you, Lucy, it's just amazing the things they come up with." She waggled her foot. "Guaranteed to cut your weekly vacuuming time in half!"

"You don't vacuum, anyway. Heather does."

If you'd told me a year before that Heather Starbird would wind up as my mama's housekeeper, I'd have laughed in your face. All I'd known about Heather then was that she was keeping mysterious company with Ash, paying visits to the trailer he'd set up in our backyard after I banished him from the house for his drinking, riding around town with him in his pickup, her witch-black hair and cigarette smoke streaming out the window. It was only after his worst and last drunken rampage that I learned that they were going to AA meetings together.

I hated to admit it, but part of the reason Ash and I were still together was because of Heather, who was engaged to a former marijuana farmer and small-time dealer named Tripp Redmond doing time at the Hodge Unit down in Cherokee County. They were supposed to have gotten married after Tripp's scheduled release last Christmas; but with that day just weeks away, he'd been caught in the yard with two reefers in his pocket and gotten slapped with another eighteen months. Heather couldn't, or wouldn't, give up on Tripp; she spent half her time driving back and forth between Mooney and Hodge, carrying AA pamphlets and books on the importance of following one's star. As far as I could tell, the only stars Tripp cared about were the ones he saw when he was stoned, but who was I to give advice to a woman in love with a man who seemed to need to get high more than he needed her? Not since Ash had finally gotten sober— eleven months now and counting—had I really understood the meaning of the AA motto, "One day at a time."

"What do you want for supper?" I asked, as Anderson

Cooper handed off the story to a junior reporter and Mama was finally able to tear her eyes from the screen.

"You don't need to bother," she said. "Heather and I had a snack during *General Hospital*."

"What kind of snack?" When it came to nutrition, the main two items in Heather's repertoire were coffee and cigarettes.

"Ritz crackers. With cream cheese on top."

"That won't tide you over till breakfast. How about I fix you a Lean Cuisine?" I started for the kitchen, Mama sliding up the hall behind me in her paper slippers.

Nowhere was Mama's fixation with catalog shopping more evident than in her kitchen. Every time I visited I did a quick scan, tallying up the matching quilted-kitty toaster and can opener covers, the ceramic bread warmer and the lacey-edged, glass-domed cake plate, the Ginsu knife set and the salad spinner and the peel-and-stick spice-jar holders. This from a woman who hadn't fixed a meal from scratch since I entered high school.

"What's this?" I asked. There were packing boxes all over the floor, some stacked and sealed, some open and half-full. I lifted a flap and peered into one, peeling back a corner of newspaper to see a gold-rimmed platter.

"I want you to take that," she said. "Heather spent the whole afternoon boxing it up."

"But this is your wedding china!" Over the years Mama had managed to get shed of just about every physical reminder of my daddy she'd ever had—her wedding ring had disappeared shortly after he did, along with every existing photo of the man—but she'd hung on to that china obstreperously, keeping it locked in a cabinet in a corner of the dining room. Not once had any of us eaten a meal from it, or even seen it on this side of the cabinet's glass doors. To find it wrapped in sheets of last week's *Dallas Morning News* and piled in boxes seemed like some kind of sacrilege.

I lifted the plate free of the paper and held it up to the light. It was thick and heavy, a creamy ivory ringed with burnished gold. And just like that, I was back inside one of my ghost lives: the little girl who used to climb up on a chair and gaze into the corner cabinet, believing in a way she couldn't put into words that, so long as that china stayed locked up in the corner cabinet, the daddy she could barely remember had once been real, and might someday be again.

"It's not doing me a bit of good," Mama said. "Seems like somebody ought to get some use out of it."

"What am I going to do with twelve place settings of china?" The boxes took up half the floor space in her kitchen.

"Fine. I'll let Heather have it, then. Somebody who doesn't take nice things for granted. Who hasn't already got a house stuffed to the rafters with this and that."

I pressed the back of my hand over my eyes. "I just think you should keep it for yourself, is all. You might decide you want it someday."

"What for? It hasn't been out of that cabinet in forty years."

I watched her hobble over to the sink. All during my growing-up years, my mama had prided herself on keeping up appearances. Never mind that her husband had run out and left her with three kids under the age of ten to raise; she wouldn't set foot out of the house, not even a trip to the Food King for a gallon of milk, without her hair set and sprayed, panty hose, red lips and nails to match.

But now that she didn't get out as much as she used to—she refused to let the doctors do anything about her hip—she was starting to look less like her former self and more like her big sister, Dove. But whereas Dove had always worn her lack of vanity like a banner, my mama seemed to be caving in on herself, shrinking every time I saw her. Her hair hadn't been styled in weeks, the seat of her stretch pants was pilled and sagging, and she'd evidently misplaced her once-trademark Fire and Ice lipstick. What if Raymond Hatch *did* suddenly appear out of nowhere and ring the doorbell? He'd find not just his wedding china in boxes on the floor, but the woman he'd married looking like she'd been digging in the Dumpster behind the Greyhound station.

She turned on the hot water tap and squirted a stream of Joy into the sink. "Ash was by here earlier," she said as the lemony scent of bubbles filled the kitchen.

"He was? What for?"

"Oh, he didn't stop. I just saw him out the front window. Heading over to Vergie Humphries's, it looked like, the back of his truck all loaded up. I said to Heather, 'There goes trouble.' "

"What do you mean? He's putting in kitchen cabinets. It's his job."

"Heather says he's in denial." Mama began to scrub the coffeepot.

"Oh, so that's Heather's professional opinion?" I didn't know why I was biting Mama's head off. Personally, I thought Heather was right.

"No, it's Heather's opinion as a . . ."

"A drunk?"

"A concerned friend. Who has had troubles of her own in the past, and who knows the signs."

I stepped over to the icebox and opened the freezer compartment. It was stuffed full of frozen dinners, and I pulled one out at random and set it on the drain board.

"I know the signs, too, Mama, believe me." Like Ash spending all winter on that studio, making sure every board and nail was perfect, but never laying down a single track of music; taking one dead-end carpentry job after the next, a steady stream of deck construction and kitchen remodeling, keeping his hands busy so that his heart and his brain wouldn't have to do the heavy lifting. I knew denial, too, when I saw it, and it seemed to me that, like grief, the only way through it was straight down the middle. So far Ash had been content to skirt the edges, like a deer dipping its nose into frigid water and then scurrying away. But the last thing he needed was to feel like the woods were full of hunters taking aim at him down the sights of their rifles. The last thing I wanted was to be one of them.

"How's this?" I asked Mama, holding up a frozen fettuccine Alfredo.

"Put that back," she said, swabbing the clean coffeepot with a dish towel. "I'll fix something later if I get hungry. Last time I checked I still knew how to run the microwave. Now, are you taking this china, or should I call Heather and tell her she can have it?"

I SWUNG BY Dove's to pick up Jude and Lily and headed home with the boxes rattling in the back of the Blazer, thinking about what Mama had said about Ash and denial. When he first came back to Mooney, all I cared about was seeing him get sober. It was only lately, sitting across from him in silence at the supper table or reaching across the bed in the middle of the night to find his side empty, that I'd started to wonder just how much the life he was living now was costing him.

Music had always come as naturally to Ash as breathing; I'd just assumed that the ability, along with the desire, was present but dormant, like an idling engine, waiting for the gentle pressure of foot to pedal to bring it surging back to life.

But the truth was, Ash had been coasting for a long time now. The Ash I'd first known hadn't needed a special room or a dozen rare guitars to make music. He'd written songs sitting on the edge of the bed, the front porch, the tailgate of his truck. He'd kept notebooks on the night table and in the glove compartment; the words and melodies had seemed to run through him day and night, as rich and constant as his blood, and out through his fingers.

Then Arcadia Records called, and the line had gotten blurred between art and commerce. After they canceled his contract, in the worst of his drinking days, he used to roam around the house cursing the guys in the industry who'd strung him up and left him for dead.

But what it really came down to was that he'd lost faith in himself. "You've still got talent," I said. "Nobody in a suit can take that away from you." He used to argue about it with me, saying that I wasn't an artist and wouldn't understand, but lately he didn't even bother, just shook his head in stony silence, or got up and left the room. I'd hear him later on the phone with Heather, and even though I knew she was his AA sponsor, I felt a blistering heat in the middle of my chest every time, like a cigarette burn.

"Mama!"

I looked at Jude in the rearview mirror. "What, baby?"

"I'm trying to *tell* you something. It's very important!"

"Sorry. What is it?"

"Did you know that a great white shark isn't really white? It's gray!"

"Is that so."

"Jared Miller got a hermit crab at the beach. It's painted like a rainbow, and it eats lettuce and cooked carrots, and he gives it a bath in the sink every day. How come we never get to go to the beach, anyway? Jared Miller goes every year with his mama and his daddy and his baby sister, and they stay in a room that looks out at the ocean, and there's snakes in the grass, and big machines with, like, shovels to take the seaweed away. It stinks, Jared says, and his sister stepped on a jellyfish and they took her to the doctor and she got a shot and a sucker."

My cell phone rang. I flipped it open and saw Ash's number on the display.

"I was just thinking about you," I said.

"Guess where I am."

"The Piney View Motor Court?"

He laughed. One of our favorite things to do when we were first courting had been to check into the Piney View for a long lunch hour or a midday coffee break, though we'd seldom gotten around to the lunch or the coffee.

"Try the next best thing," he said. "I'm up at Willie B.'s. Want to meet me for some supper?"

"I've got the kids with me," I said regretfully. "We're almost home now. Why don't you pick up a couple pounds of ribs and meet us there?"

I pressed the phone hard against my ear, hearing only the crisp, crackling sound that meant the call was breaking up. Jude was kicking the back of my seat rhythmically with the soles of his tennis shoes. "Quit!" Lily said, reaching over to give Jude a shove. "Mama!" Jude cried. "Lily's pushing me!"

Wait, I wanted to say to Ash. There's so much more I want to know. Where do you go when you wander off in the middle of the night? Why is there never time, between our work and the kids and the everyday business that makes up our lives, for us to talk about what we really feel? And oh, by the way, how would you feel about being a granddaddy?

There was a click and a beep, and the line went dead. I flipped the phone shut and dropped it on the seat beside me as I slowed to make the turn off the highway onto Bates Road. It wasn't the first time I'd had to trust that Ash understood what I meant, even when he couldn't hear me.

CHAPTER 7

Denny

Y OU WANT TO slow down when you get to the sign
that says JESUS DIED FOR YOUR SINS—that's the
turnoff to Mt. Sinai Baptist." Lavelle was drawing
me a map on the back of the old WANTED flyer. "If you
come to the old Gulf station with the school bus out front,
you've gone too far. And whatever you do, don't stop at the
church and ask directions! Reverend Willy gets his hooks
in you, you'll wind up gettin' saved whether you want to
or not."

I found the place without much trouble, on an unpaved
red-dirt road just west of Hughes Springs. I idled in front of
the mailbox and double-checked the address on the paper in
my hand. It was an ordinary yellow-brick ranch house, with
an old Ford van in the driveway and barrels full of striped
petunias on either side of the front door.

I shut off the engine and climbed out, stretching my legs in the sun. Somewhere behind the house a dog barked.

A short black man came around the corner of the house pushing an old-fashioned lawn mower, the kind it took muscle rather than gasoline to power. Seeing me, he stopped and pulled a bandanna out of the pocket of his overalls and mopped his head, which was slick as a peeled egg, shiny with sweat.

"Scorcher, ain't it?" he said. "Don't usually see this kinda heat till July. Almanac says this summer's gonna be hotter than normal. Wetter, too."

"Yes, sir," I said, to be polite. Texans are always telling you it's too hot for May, or October, or whenever. The fact is, it's mostly *always* too hot, regardless of the month or season. I don't know why we even bother with it as a topic of conversation.

"You lost, or you here on purpose?" The man had a lazy eye, which made me nervous; I couldn't be sure where he was looking.

"The lady at the post office in White Pine sent me." I held out the map Lavelle had drawn me, but it was wrong side up, displaying the face of Curtis Wayne Price, wanted on two counts of burglary of a motor vehicle. I flipped it over. "I'm supposed to ask for Contessa."

"Hold on, I'll fetch her for you." Stuffing the bandanna in his pocket, the man crossed to the front door and disappeared inside.

Some time passed before he reappeared. "The Countess says come on in. She's been 'specting you."

A small entryway opened onto a living room full of couches and overstuffed chairs and a big color TV going full blast, that silver-haired CNN reporter gazing into the camera with his famous puppy-dog eyes, even though no one was watching. From the back of the house I could smell something like meat loaf cooking, but it wasn't exactly a good smell, or comforting, like you might expect. There were other smells besides the meat loaf: laundry soap, for one, and Pine-Sol, which anybody who's ever spent any time in an actual forest knows is a shoddy imitation of the real thing. Mixed together, I can't say it was exactly a heady bouquet. My stomach started to churn, and I was just about to head for the door when a lady appeared from the rear of the house, dressed in a flower-print dress with a patent leather belt and white crepe-soled shoes.

She took me by the arm and steered me to one of the couches, telling me to put my head between my knees.

"That's it. Breathe now, nice and slow," she said. Her hand was cool on the back of my neck, and slowly but surely my insides began to settle.

I lifted my head and looked at her. "Better?" she asked. I nodded, not quite trusting my voice. She was broad shouldered and big hipped, with skin the color of ginger, an all-over spattering of cinnamon-colored freckles. "Sure? I can holler at Joyner to fetch you a bucket."

"Yes. I mean, no. I'm okay now, I think. I'm just—"

"Pregnant. I know. I'm a nurse, honey. That, and I got four kids of my own. It don't take a genie to recognize the signs."

"Oh, God." I covered my face with my hands.

"Don't worry, I ain't gonna say nothin'. Mind your business and I'll mind mine is my motto."

"Are you the Countess?"

"Contessa Jones. You'd be Evelyn's granddaughter. Lavelle called and told me you was on your way."

"Yes, ma'am. Denny Farrell," I said, holding out my hand. "I mean, Culpepper."

"You don't know your own name?"

"I've got a husband. Sometimes I forget."

"Ha! I got one, too, but I can't hardly forget him, not with him underfoot the livelong day. Don't get me wrong, Joyner's a good man, but he wouldn't think to put his pants on in the morning without me tellin' him to. How long's it been since you seen your granny?" she asked.

"I can't recall for sure. A couple of years?"

"Well, let me bring you up to speed on what's goin' on here. This is an assisted-living facility. A home for folks who can't take care of themselves."

"Did Evelyn have an accident?"

Contessa studied me closely. "You favor her. I take it that means you don't need your horse manure sugarcoated."

"No, ma'am."

"Your granny has senile dementia. Do you know what that is?"

Before I could answer, a voice came from the back of the house, not small and feeble like you might expect, but a full-throated roar: "Annie Childs! Where's my meat loaf?"

"She calls me Annie," Contessa said. "Danged if I know why."

"Annie Childs was her housekeeper," I said, surprised at the memory, one of the tidbits about her life Evelyn had doled out to me like penny candy during our visits over the few years I'd known her. After her mama died, when it was just her daddy and her brothers and Evelyn living out on the lake, Annie took care of the cooking and cleaning. Later on, when the others were gone and Evelyn moved back to the lake house, Annie came back to work for a while, but it got to be too much for her—she was even older than Evelyn, and she had a bad heart—and she had to quit.

"Well, that makes more sense than half the stuff I've heard today," Contessa said. "You want to sit a spell and get your legs back, or you ready to see her?"

I took one more deep breath and stood up slowly. "Ready."

We passed doors opening onto a series of small bedrooms. I saw folks sitting in chairs next to windows, or lying in bed with the covers pulled up to their chins, their eyes fixed on the ceiling, or heaven, or nothing at all. The house was plain but tidy, and the smell wasn't so bad once you got used to it.

"She's down here," Contessa said as we reached the end of the hallway. "Nothin' but the best room in the house for Miss Evelyn."

"Annie Childs! What's been keeping you? You told me an hour ago that meat loaf was about to come out of the oven."

People change; I know that. But I swear, if I'd walked past my grandmother on the street in White Pine, I wouldn't have known her. She'd never been what you'd call fat, but she'd been sturdy, solid through the hips and shoulders; and I'd barely known her to go five minutes without lighting up a

Lucky, the red-and-black bull's-eye on the pack showing through the pockets of the men's shirts she favored. The woman in the chair next to the window looked like a puff of wind might carry her away, her arms and legs spindly as pipe cleaners in a gray sweat suit, her hair thin and white against her skull. I tried to find one thing to focus on, one familiar thing, so that I wouldn't get dizzy and end up on the floor like I had in the post office, but the only thing that reminded me of the old Evelyn was her fierce black eyes. Daddy's eyes.

"Look here, Miss Evelyn, who's come to see you," Contessa said, moving into the room. "It's your granddaughter! Ain't this the nicest surprise?"

"I have a granddaughter," Evelyn said, lifting her chin.

"You do indeed, and here she is."

Contessa gave me a nudge, and I lurched forward and knelt in front of my grandmother.

"Hey, Evelyn," I said. "It's Denny. Remember me?"

"Where's my meat loaf?" she asked. "Annie here's trying to starve me to death. I should've had my supper hours ago."

"We'll eat when we always eat," Contessa said. "Five thirty on the dot, and not a minute sooner. Maybe you and Miss Denny can sit and visit while I go finish up in the kitchen. I'm guessin' y'all have some catching up to do."

As soon as Contessa left, Evelyn turned her face to the window and sat staring out, humming and tapping her fingers on the arms of the rocker. She seemed to have forgotten I was there, and I started wondering if there was a back door I could sneak out and just drive away and pretend all of this had never happened.

My knees hurt, so I got up and perched on the edge of the bed. It was pretty, white wrought iron with a pattern of little birds worked into the headboard. I thought the quilt looked familiar, but then, everybody and their cousin in this corner of the world had a whole trunkful just like it. On the wall over the bed was a framed picture of Jesus with flowing locks and foggy blue eyes, looking like he should be playing lead guitar for Pearl Jam. The old Evelyn would have pitched a fit about that picture, would have chucked it across the room and then chewed the ears off whoever hung it there. It made me sad to think that that person was gone for good, sadder still to know that I was probably the only person on earth who remembered how she used to be, or cared.

Then I noticed a small silver frame on the night table. It held a photo of a young woman in a cotton dress and sneakers, her face squinched up in the sun and cradling a baby against her hip, one of his little white hands spread like a starfish toward the lens. I'd seen the picture before, on the bedside table at Evelyn's lake house the summer I turned fifteen.

She was watching me out of the corner of her eye. I picked up the frame and turned it so she could see.

"Do you know who this is?" I said. Slowly Evelyn nodded. "Who?" I asked. "Can you tell me?"

"You." Her voice was shy, halting. "Lynette."

A shiver crept up my spine. Lynette was the name Evelyn had called herself by back when she was a just-married woman with ambitions to be a nightclub singer. I remembered Dove had told me once that I resembled my grandmother, that when I got older and taller and lost my baby fat, I might be as pretty as she'd been. I wasn't, but glancing at the frame again, I saw that the likeness was real, and strong.

"What happened to you, Lynette?"

I looked up. In the middle of that strange, sunken face, my grandmother's eyes were sharp and searching.

"Where did you go?" she asked. "What did you do with the baby?"

CHAPTER 8

Lucy

ARE YOU SURE Denny didn't call? I thought for sure she'd be home by now." I went over and checked the machine, but the red light was steady, the display reading 0.

Ash was unloading the boxes of Mama's china from the back of my Blazer and stacking them in the front hallway. "Haven't we got enough dishes already?" he grumbled. "What do we need with twelve place settings of something that's too fancy to even eat off of?"

"That's what I said. But she said if I didn't take it, she'd give it to Heather."

"Well, that might not have been such a bad idea, seeing's how Heather's idea of fine dining is Styrofoam instead of paper. Damn it, I took a shower when I got home from Mrs. Humphries's and now I'm all sweaty again."

"I like you sweaty." I wrapped my arms around him from behind, pressing my cheek between his shoulder blades. In spite of his complaining, he smelled like bar soap and the clean T-shirt he'd changed into. "It reminds me of when I first met you," I said. "You were sweaty quite a bit in those days, I recall."

"That was your fault. You kept me in a lather."

We stood facing the screen door. Out on the deck the table was set for supper, and beyond it, Jude and Lily ran along the pier in their swimsuits and life preservers, throwing sticks into the water for the dogs to retrieve. I lifted the tail of Ash's T-shirt and slid my palm across the plane of his belly. He covered my hand with his, ran his thumb absently over my wedding band.

"What's going on, Lucy?"

"What are you talking about?"

"Something's got you all jacked up. I could hear it in your voice a while ago, on the phone."

I sighed and rested my cheek against his back. "I guess I was just thinking about how we never seem to talk about what's really going on anymore."

"Like what? Are you talking about Denny?" It was more than that, I wanted to say, but I guessed Denny was as good a place as any to start. "Because I hate to tell you, this may be her first broken heart, but it won't be her last."

"It's not just a broken heart, Ash."

"Will Culpepper's a no-account scoundrel, and the sooner she's shed of him, the better."

"It's not that simple."

"Why not? They got married in Vegas, for Christ's sake."

I was saved from having to answer by Denny's pickup rolling into the yard.

"Here she is," I said, easing my thumbs out of Ash's belt loops, relief flooding my voice.

Jude and Lily ran toward the pickup, the dogs barking excitedly as they trailed behind; and for a minute, as their voices carried, mingling with their laughter in the dusky twilight, I had one of those rare flashes where life suddenly seems to click into focus, everything lining up as neatly as ducks in a row.

Then Denny came into the house, easing the screen door shut behind her. Her face was splotched, like she had a fever.

"Are you okay?" I asked. "Where've you been?"

"Hughes Springs." She aimed a loaded glance at her daddy.

"What were you doing up there?" I asked.

"Evelyn's there," she said. "My grandma, remember? In a *home*. An 'assisted-living facility,' they call it. She's got senile dementia."

The kids came scrambling onto the porch, the dogs still barking up a storm. Ash stepped over to the screen door and stuck out his head.

"Leave those dogs alone!" he shouted. "How would you feel if somebody was chasing you with a stick?"

Jude and Lily froze. "We're not chasing them, Daddy," Jude said in a small voice. "They're chasing *us*."

"Well, cut it out, before somebody gets hurt!" He let the door bang shut.

"Ash," I said.

He wheeled toward Denny. "What were you doing there, anyway? Why is everybody in this family always sticking their noses where they don't belong?"

"How can you say it's none of my business? It's your business, too, even if you act like it isn't!"

"I'm not having this conversation with you, Denise," Ash said. A vein pulsed in his temple. "I told you years ago, that woman is dead to me. I won't discuss it."

For a long moment they stared at each other, not flinching or even blinking.

"I'm going to lie down," Denny said. Gripping the banister, she made her way slowly up the stairs.

With one foot Ash pushed a box of Mama's china hard against the wall.

"Ash," I began. "I really think you—" But he'd already turned and stomped off down the back hall.

I carried a pitcher of Kool-Aid out to the kids, then went upstairs and tapped on Denny's door. When she didn't answer, I twisted the knob and felt it give under my hand.

"Can I come in?" I asked.

"This has been the worst day of my life." Her voice was muffled by a pillow. "I thought yesterday was as bad as it could get, but I was wrong."

I crossed the room and sat down at the edge of the bed. "It's a lot to take in, I can see that."

She sat up, pushing her hair out of her face.

"How can he just not care?" she said. "Evelyn's like a, a ghost! She doesn't even know me. She thinks I'm her! That

I'm Lynette LeGrande! She wanted to know what I'd done with the baby. It totally freaked me out."

"Well, what do you expect him to do, honey?" I asked. "He and his mama haven't had a thing to do with each other in forty years."

She flopped back against the mattress. "I should have known you'd take his side."

"I'm not taking anybody's side. I'm just saying this is not news. He's been this way since before either of us knew him. To expect him to do a hundred percent about-face—" She pulled the pillow over her head, and I reached out and gently retracted it. "Look, I know you've got a lot on your plate right now. But keep in mind, your daddy hasn't got it easy, either. He hasn't been sober a year, even. And what happened in Nashville— He acts like he never gives it a thought, but you know it still eats at him."

Scents and sounds drifted in through the open window: lighter fluid, citronella, Lily saying to Jude "The fork goes on the *left*!" in an imperious voice.

"I know you think you ought to be able to make your daddy act the way you think he should," I said. "But nobody ever changed another person by trying to shame them, or bully them."

"That is *so* not true."

"Okay, maybe so. But you can't force somebody to feel something they don't feel. Sometimes you have to stand back, give them some room to let them work things out for them-selves, on the inside."

"So, that's what you're doing?" she said. "Letting him work things out on the inside?"

"I'm trying."

"Well, it makes me crazy. I just feel like grabbing him and shaking him, hollering in his ear."

"I do, too, sometimes."

She rolled off the mattress and went over to the bureau, where she stood staring at her reflection in the small framed mirror. "Did you tell him about me? About—you know."

"I didn't think it was mine to tell."

"The lady who runs the place where Evelyn is said she could see it just by looking at me."

"Honey, your daddy and I lived together for three months without him ever once guessing I was pregnant, not even after I knew it myself."

From below came the sound of a vehicle pulling into the yard. A car door opened, then slammed. The dogs started to bark, and Ash said loudly, "What the hell are *you* doing here?"

Denny and I looked at each other, then pushed past each other to the window.

"Oh, shit!" she said.

I didn't recognize the car—a tiny dark-blue foreign thing—but I knew the man standing beside it, all right, just like I knew that the worst day of Denny's life was a long way from over yet.

CHAPTER 9

Denny

"OH, SHIT!" I drew back from the window and grabbed Lucy's arm. "You've got to go down there and cover for me!"

"Cover for you, how?"

"Say I'm not here. Say you haven't heard from me since yesterday!"

"But your truck's right there, big as life."

I couldn't believe it. Just when you thought things were about as bad as they could get, God decided to play another one of his tricks on you, just to remind you who was running the show.

"Do you believe in karma?" I asked.

"What kind of question is that?"

"I'm just trying to figure out if I'm being punished for something I did in a past life." As we looked on, Daddy transferred the tongs to his left hand and slowly put out his right for Will to shake. Even from a distance, I could see how much it pained him.

"We'd better get down there, don't you think?" Lucy said. "Before the fur starts flying?"

"You go. Please?" I said as she gave me a look that said she knew what I was up to and that I better not think for a minute I could get away with it. "I'll be down in a minute, I promise."

After she left, I sat for a while on the edge of the bed, chewing my thumbnail and trying to make sense of what was happening downstairs. I wanted to believe in forgiveness and second chances, but I was pretty sure that Will and I had passed salvation a long time ago—no passing go, no collecting two hundred dollars.

I changed my shirt and ran a brush through my hair, then dragged myself downstairs just in time to meet Will coming in through the screen door.

"Hey, there," he said in his slow, supple Mississippi drawl. He looked like hell, his eyes bloodshot, his skin the sickly blue-white of skim milk. I could smell the sharp, familiar man smells of him, of sweat and hair pomade and Tennessee whiskey, and I took a step backward, away from him. I didn't want to be alone with Will. I didn't trust him or myself, either one.

"What are you doing here?"

I tried not to flinch at the sight of his hand coming toward my face, but he just brushed the backs of his fingers gently against my cheek. "I got worried about you. You didn't answer your phone, and I didn't like how we left things."

"Are you insane, Will? Do you remember anything I said to you?"

"I've been a bad boy. I know that."

"You're screwing my fiddle player! You've been screwing her for months!"

Daddy appeared on the other side of the screen. I'd never been so glad to see anyone in my life.

"Everything okay here?" he asked as he came inside, carrying an empty pitcher in his hands.

"Yes, sir," I said. He gave Will a look that would have scared the bejesus out of any other guy, then headed down the hall to the kitchen. I brushed past Will and opened the screen door, stepping out onto the porch.

"I broke it off with Marin," Will said as he followed me outside.

"Not on my account, I hope," I said. "I'm not coming back. I already told you that, in case you don't remember."

He smiled lazily. "I don't believe you."

"You're pathological, you know that?" I said. "You need professional help."

"Why? Just because I care about holding on to what's mine?"

He reached down and circled my wrist with his hand. The smile was still in place, but his eyes were like marbles, blue and hard, as his fingers slowly tightened, pressing into my skin. Will never left a mark; he was careful that way. The fear he created was never from what he'd done but from what he might do, the suggestion, always hovering just above his shoulder, that next time might be the time I would push him too far.

Daddy came back out through the screen door then, saying, "Soup's on," and Will grinned and let me go. He'd rattled me, but I knew better than to let it show. The truth was that, even though he scared me sometimes, with his wild highs and deep-blue lows, it was familiar to me, being loved like that. With Will, like my daddy, their attention was a spotlight. I'd planted myself in its center while I could because, sooner or later, it would swing off in search of something new to focus on. What I'd never expected was that one day I might find myself trapped in the spotlight's beam, wishing for the safety of the dark.

He followed me across the yard at an easy saunter. The table was laid out with platters of meat and bowls of potato salad and beans and coleslaw, pickles and onions, a loaf of Wonder bread.

"Hey, little brother," Will said, reaching out to ruffle Jude's hair as we climbed onto the deck.

"Who are you?" Jude asked.

"I'm your brother-in-law."

"You're a policeman?"

"I'm married to your sister. I saw you last Christmas, remember?"

"My birthday," Jude said.

"Right. We brought you a pair of cowboy boots from Nashville."

"They're too little," Jude said. He stuck out one of his bare feet. "My feet are almost as big as my mama's, and I'm only seven!"

"You sit over here, Will," Lucy said. "Can I get you a glass of tea?"

"It sure looks good. Thank you, ma'am."

"How many times have I asked you not to call me 'ma'am'?" Lucy said. "You make me feel like an old crone."

"You're not a crow, Mama!" Jude exclaimed. Daddy turned around and started cawing and flapping his arms like wings, making Lucy smile and the kids crack up laughing.

We sat down at the table, and Lucy asked Lily if she wanted to say grace.

"I can't," Lily said. "I don't believe in Jesus anymore."

Lucy and Daddy looked at each other across the table.

"How come, Lily Belle?" Lucy asked.

She shrugged, playing with her fork. "I don't know. I like the other guy better."

"What other guy?"

"The little brown man. The one who smiles all the time, and you can send him an e-mail. Jesus doesn't have e-mail."

Daddy was biting his lip, trying not to laugh.

"How about it, then—Jude? Can you do the honors?"

Jude bowed his head and the rest of us bowed ours. "For what we are about to receive let us give thanks," he said, all in a rush, like if he didn't get it out fast enough, Jesus might clap his hands and shout out, "Next!"

We got through supper thanks to Lucy's good manners and a long, drawn-out argument between Jude and Lily over some movie they'd seen at school. Will picked at his supper and drank his tea, glancing at me now and then across the table with his hooded blue eyes. Daddy was acting nicer than I expected, but I could see him keeping an eye on Will, like if he let his guard down even for a second Will might make off with everything that wasn't nailed down.

After supper Lucy took the kids inside to get them ready for bed, and I carried an armload of dishes into the kitchen. Upstairs I could hear bathwater running, and Jude singing, and Lucy saying something I couldn't make out. *How do you do it?*, I wanted to say. *How do you give and give and never ask for anything back, how do you fill up the empty place in your stomach in the middle of the night?* I envied her. Lucy had learned to embrace the ordinary, the way she set a pot of bare bulbs and stones in a window and waited patiently, on nothing but faith, for it to bloom. But I was beginning to think I wasn't wired that way, for everyday happiness.

As I watched out the window, Daddy stood up from the table, and Will got up and followed him across the yard to the studio. I shut off the tap, leaving a sink full of forks and sticky cups, and ran out the front door.

I DON T KNOW what I thought Daddy was up to—that he was going to tie Will to a chair and pistol-whip him, maybe. But he was giving him the same tour he'd given me the night before, showing off his guitars and demonstrating the sound system. He slipped a cassette into the tape deck and a jazzy number flowed from the speakers, horn and bass and a sweet, lively fiddle I'd have recognized anywhere.

I picked up one of Daddy's guitars, the 1960s Gibson with a sunburst finish and a Hummingbird pick guard, and started playing along. Will fell into the easy chair, stretching out his long legs and watching me from under the black wing of his hair.

"Nice," Daddy said after the song ended, switching off the tape deck. "Maybe if your gig doesn't work out, Erasmus can get you a job."

I gestured that he should pick up a guitar. I could see he didn't really want to, but he reached for his black Martin and sat down beside me.

I started to play "Flyin' Shoes" by Townes Van Zandt, a song whose message about hitting the road as a cure for the blues fit my state of mind pretty much exactly, just in case some mopey-eyed boy in the corner might actually happen to be listening. Daddy fell in on the second bar, his voice plucking out the harmony, winding itself in and out, following mine.

And for a while it was like it had been back when we used to sit out on the front porch of Daddy's old house, swapping songs back and forth, jumping in whether we knew the words and melodies or not. We moved from Townes to Slim Harpo to John Prine to Hank Thompson, barely pausing between songs.

Finally Daddy started in on something I'd never heard before. I picked up the melody in the middle of the first verse, working my voice around Daddy's silky tenor. It was a quiet, pretty song about losing love, with a chorus that went, *And you know that it's all over but the crying.*

"Is that one of yours?" I asked when we'd reached the end.

"I wish. It's by a fellow down in Austin, name of Bruce Robison. Know him?"

"Not personally. I know his stuff, though. He married one of the Dixie Chicks, didn't he?"

"That's his brother, Charlie. They cut a couple of Bruce's songs, though. So have Tim McGraw and George Strait. Shit, if I had Bruce's luck, I'd be running out to the mailbox every morning with a big old grin on my face, papering the walls with royalty checks."

"It's not luck," I said. "You're every bit as good as he is."

Daddy set down the guitar. I knew I was stepping into a minefield, but I couldn't seem to stop myself.

"How about the new stuff we talked about last night?" I said. "You said you'd let me hear some."

"I told you, I haven't really got anything. Just odds and ends."

"Oh, come on. I bet if you—"

"Damn it, Denise!" Daddy jumped to his feet. The Martin started to tip and he grabbed for it, the strings echoing in a rude, complaining chord as he caught it and set it in its stand.

"Did you hear what I said?" he asked, his voice shaking. "I haven't got anything."

His eyes were terrible, dark and hunted. I looked down at the guitar in my hands like I had no idea how it got there. Daddy circled around behind the couch and, without another word or even a backward glance, went out and shut the door with a soft, firm click behind him.

"Nice job," Will said. I hated the smirk on his face, the way he looked like not only had he expected this but that he was enjoying it.

He hoisted himself out of the chair and walked over to the little icebox.

"Shit. There's nothing in here but water and Coca-Cola."

"Don't be an ass, Will. You know he quit drinking."

I stood up and put the Gibson back in its stand. Will came up behind me and put his hands on my shoulders. Under his palms I could feel myself trembling.

"That beer joint your daddy took me to last year—it's not far from here, is it?" His voice was husky against my ear. "How about we go have us a drink, for old time's sake."

I wish I could say I wasn't tempted. Will and I had always been at our best when alcohol was involved. A couple of beers and a shot of whiskey were usually enough to carry us the distance from our two separate poles to a sweet common ground. Probably, if we'd been sober that night in Vegas, I would never have let him talk me into the Happy Together wedding chapel.

And afterward, on more nights than I care to confess, I drank with Will instead of fighting with him. But that had been in Nashville or out on the road, where liquor and pot and pills flowed around us in constant, lazy rivers. Here now, in Daddy's studio and sober as a judge, the memory of those nights scared me a little. Because of them I was married to a man I didn't trust, with a secret or two of my own that I didn't begin to know how to tell him.

Will slid his hands under my hair. "How 'bout it, hm?"

"I'm mad at you, remember?"

"I know how to make you forget." He put his thumbs against the base of my skull and worked them in slow circles, and I felt the familiar loosening of muscle and bone, animal heat spreading from my shoulders downward. Thirty seconds more, and saying yes would have been the easiest thing in the world.

Outside I heard Daddy's truck start up. It was one of those moments you don't see for what they are until later, when you look back and say, "There," laying your finger on the spot where things go a different way from the one you expected and everything that follows changes direction.

I slipped out of Will's grasp and rushed over to open the door. I was too late, though. The pickup shot out of the yard and onto the road, kicking up a cloud of dust that hung in the air for a long time after the sound of the engine had died.

A minute later Will came out and joined me in the yard, easing a hand under my hair.

"I just know there's a cold beer up the road a piece with my name written on it. What do you say?"

I stepped back and turned to face him. "Go right at the highway a couple of miles, then hang a left at the Miracle Mart. The Tap's about a mile up on the right. You can't miss it."

His eyes narrowed, two slits of blue flame, as he reached into his pocket and produced the keys to his little Audi.

"If that's the way you're gonna be," he said. "I don't guess you've got a twenty on you?"

I stood in the yard for a while after Will drove off. The moon hung like a yellowware plate in the inky sky. Lightning bugs winked among the trees, and frogs called back and forth to each other like opera singers across the pond. I thought back to the first summer I'd spent with Daddy and Lucy in the country, how the quiet had spooked me so bad that I'd kept my Walkman headphones on all the time. I'd gotten used to it eventually, though I wasn't sure I'd ever be able to really appreciate it, not like they did. I wasn't all that wild about Nashville, but I missed the road like I guessed Daddy must miss drinking, an empty echo in my heart and my head. I thought I might go inside and give Ty a call. Of everybody I knew, Ty was the one who understood best the need to feel wheels turning under you, mile after mile of blacktop unraveling in the rearview while you slept, that little white-hot thrill when you woke up and didn't know where you were, an atom floating free in the universe, when you could be absolutely anywhere.

I took care to shut the front door quietly behind me, mindful that folks were sleeping. I figured I'd use the cordless phone in the kitchen, maybe carry it out on the front porch and sit awhile if the mosquitoes weren't too bad.

There was Lucy at the kitchen table, with a cup of tea she wasn't drinking and a magazine she wasn't reading.

"Have a seat," she said. "There's some decaf chai stuff Geneva bought in Dallas. It's pretty good, if you add a little milk and sugar."

"No, thanks," I said. "I've got to make a phone call."

"Hold up a minute. I want to talk to you."

I could count on one hand the number of times Lucy'd been mad at me. Usually it was me and her against the world. But now her face was funny, a look I couldn't quite read.

"You want to tell me what happened with your daddy just now?" she asked as I poured myself a cup of tea and took a seat at the table.

"I'm not real sure," I said. "I mean, we were just sitting there playing, swapping songs like we used to. Everything was fine. Good, even. Then . . ." I stopped to think, trying to untangle the threads of what had happened. "I asked him if he'd play me some of the new stuff he'd written. He was acting kind of funny, and I guess I pushed him too hard, and he snapped." Lucy nodded into her cup, like this explained everything. "What did I do?" I asked.

"I know you meant well," she said. "But you touched on a real sore spot with your daddy. He doesn't even talk to me about it. Well, almost never."

"I don't get it. I thought he was writing again."

"I think he wants to, but he can't figure out how. It's like every time he gets an idea or a tune in his head, all that business about Nashville starts up, whispering in his ear, telling him he's no good, that he hasn't got what it takes."

"But that's crazy! Just because he had some bad luck, that doesn't mean he hasn't still got the stuff."

"You know that and I know it. But he seems to feel like he only got one shot and he blew it. I wouldn't care if he never made another record again. I just keep thinking about how he used to be when I first met him, when I'd wake up in the middle of the night and find him sitting on the edge of the bed, scribbling away. Record deals and crowds and all are nice, but they were never really what it was about for your daddy. Making up the songs—that was the part that made him happy.

"It's different, for you," she said. "You're tougher than he is. Things bounce off you, and you keep on going. But Ash's hide's not that thick, even though he'd die before he'd admit it."

"I'm not that tough," I said.

"Sure you are. You're the Bionic Woman. You're like Marlene that way."

I took a sip of my tea; it was thin and sweet, like something you'd feed a sick kid. I hated being reminded of my real mama, who flitted among jobs and towns and men the way bees flit among flowers, sucking out the sweetness, then moving on. Last I'd heard, she was living in Santa Fe with a painter of cheesy desert landscapes fifteen years younger than she was and selling ski lodges to rich retirees.

"Not many folks have what you've got," Lucy went on. "Guts and brains and talent. Some get one or two of those, but hardly anybody gets all three. I used to think talent was the thing that mattered most. But I was wrong, I know that now. You have to be able to keep coming at a thing, keep punching away. Even when it seems the whole world is lined up against you.

"Anyway, I guess what I'm saying is, try to cut your daddy a little slack, okay? He worships the ground you walk on, but he envies you, too."

"Me? What for?"

"You make it look so easy, what's like pulling teeth for him. And I know you think that if you try hard enough, you can get him to do what you think he ought to do. I used to think that, too. But men can be funny that way. You've got to sort of sneak up on them, plant the notion in their head, then stand back and let them figure it out for themselves. So that in the end they wind up thinking it was theirs all along."

"That is *so* twentieth century," I said.

"I guess it is." Lucy pushed back her chair and set her cup in the sink. "Look, I'm not trying to tell you how to live your life," she said. "I'm just trying to make things a little easier between you and your daddy. Or, I don't know. Maybe I'm just trying to make things easier on myself. Wanting everybody to get along."

She leaned over and slipped an arm around my shoulders and rested her chin on top of my head. I could smell the Ivory soap she washed her face with and the lavender water she used to iron her nightgowns.

"Go ahead and make your call," she said. "But think about what I said, okay? And try getting to bed at a decent hour, for once. You might be surprised what a good night's sleep can do." She kissed my hair and went on up to bed.

I lifted the phone out of its cradle and carried it out onto the deck, punching in Ty's number in Nashville, a number I knew by heart. The phone rang two times, three, and then his recorded voice said, "This is Tyler Briggs. Leave a message and I'll get back to you when I can."

I disconnected the call and sank down at the picnic table with the phone in my lap. There was a weight in my chest as heavy and strange as the yellow spring moon. I was too young to remember the Bionic Woman except from reruns, but I knew you'd never find her sitting around waiting for the Six-Million-Dollar Man to rescue her. I was going to have to start figuring things out for myself.

CHAPTER 10

Lucy

I T WAS A restless night. First, the kids kept me hopping, wanting stories and pillows and glasses of water. I finally settled in bed and tried losing myself in the pages of my Michelin Green Guide to Italy, but I just kept skimming the same descriptions of ancient churches and four-star restaurants over and over again. All I could think of was the look on Ash's face when he'd come inside to get his keys and said, "Don't wait up."

A little past one, I heard his truck pull in. In the beginning I always used to get up and turn on the light when he came in from meetings, ask him how it had gone; but one night, when he was just a few months sober, we'd had a big fight, him accusing me of staying awake to make sure he hadn't been out drinking. After that, I'd learned to pretend I was asleep, even though his suspicions about my motives were at least partly true. Like a bad tire, trust is something you can patch up, maybe even get some more good miles out of; but once there's been a blowout, you're always, in the back of your mind, waiting for the next one.

I turned toward the window, listening to Ash's footfalls on the stair, the bedroom door easing open and shut, water running in the bathroom, the sounds of him undressing in the dark. I felt a gust of cool air as he lifted the sheet, followed by the heat of his body as he lay down next to me. I pantomimed the routine I'd perfected over the past several months: murmur, shift, then settle back into the bedclothes, making my breath deep and even. After a few minutes he got up and dressed and went downstairs again, the screen door opening and closing, followed by a soft, sharp whistle as he called the dogs and set off on another one of his mysterious night ramblings.

IN THE MORNING everybody was out of sorts. We were out of Froot Loops and Jude didn't want cornflakes. Lily had forgotten her backpack. Ash came into the kitchen looking hollow-eyed—I guessed he'd spent the night in the studio— pausing just long enough to grab a glass of orange juice and say he'd see us for supper. Denny's bedroom door was closed and I figured she and Will were sleeping in, but when I herded the kids out to the Blazer, Jude whining about not being allowed to ride to town with his daddy, there was Will stretched out, sound asleep, on top of the picnic table. I was just about to wake him up and tell him to go inside and get comfortable when Lily brought me back to reality, saying, "I don't like him, Aunt Lucy."

"No? How come?"

"I just don't think he's good for Denny, that's all."

So I'd left Will where I'd found him, reminding myself that, hard as it was to accept, some things just weren't mine to fix.

I SAT AT my desk with a cup of industrial-strength coffee in my hand and a lump in the pit of my stomach, watching the numbers flicker on my computer screen. When I'd first started keeping the books at Faye's, I used to live in fear of making a mistake, of forgetting to record a sale or putting the profits in the expenditures column. This morning I was actually hoping to come across such an error, some excuse for the fact that, for the third month in a row, our losses had exceeded our profits by more than twenty percent. It would be a lot easier to confess to Peggy that I'd messed up the accounting than to have to admit that the shop, her birthright and family business, was in the red.

The bells on the front door jingled. I leaped up, jittery with panic and caffeine, and hurried out to the showroom, thinking that if I sold just one potted plant or five-dollar carnation bouquet, it would be something I could hold up to show Peggy, proof that things weren't really as bad as they seemed.

It wasn't a customer, though, but Peggy herself, carrying a white bakery box from the café.

"I got doughnuts." She set the box on the counter and pushed it toward me. "I thought you could use something sweet."

I plucked out a lemon cream and bit into it, savoring for a second the explosion of gooey tartness on my tongue. Peggy poured herself a cup of coffee and took an exploratory sip.

"This tastes like it would strip paint." She dumped out the contents of the coffeepot and measured grounds into a paper filter and filled the carafe with water. "You look all nerved up," she said. I shook my head, chewing slowly, postponing the inevitable. "I hear Denny's home."

"Mm," I said around a mouthful of fried dough.

"Well, come on. Tell."

The words started and then just kept spilling out, like water over a dam, as Peggy stood murmuring and nodding, interjecting a comment or a word of advice, pushing the coffee and pastries at me. I realized we were trying to reconstruct the old days, back when we'd worked side by side and told each other everything. I missed that time. Audrey was good company and comic relief, but she was too young, too green in the ways of life and love, to be any real comfort. She'd figure it out for herself a few years down the road, when she had kids of her own and was, as Dove called it, payin' for her raisin'. But Peggy had always known the importance of everyday things.

"That's enough." She closed the bakery box and tucked in the flap. "Let's save a couple for Audrey. Besides, I don't need you going into sugar shock." Peggy hardly touched sweets herself anymore, not since her heart bypass six years before. I wondered if I would ever learn to adapt to my losses as grace-fully as she had.

"So," she said, stirring Sweet'n Low into her coffee, "are the books done?" I said they were. "How bad?" she asked.

I brought out the spreadsheet I'd printed that morning and laid it on the counter. For a few minutes Peggy studied it silently, running her thumbnail over the rows of numbers and chewing her bottom lip.

Finally she sighed and picked up her mug and stepped around the counter. I watched as she moved slowly up the cen-ter aisle of the shop her mama had built, where she'd learned to wrap stems as soon as she could walk, where she'd raised her own two kids practically underfoot after her husband, Duane, had died. It scared me, how self-possessed she was, when I could hardly bear what I felt for the light streaming through the plate-glass window, the mingled scents of brewed coffee and rose petals and greenery, the colorful scatter of ribbons and greeting cards, the blast of chill when the cooler door was opened. It was hopeless. You could hang on to things till your arms came out of their sockets, but that wouldn't keep them from changing. No matter how many times I'd had that lesson hammered home, it still kept creeping up and blindsiding me.

"Oh, Lord, don't you start," Peggy said, seeing me blinking back tears. "If both of us get going, they'll have to carry us out of here in a padded wagon."

"It's all my fault."

"Lucy, we've had this conversation a hundred times. Things have been headed south for a long time. I guess I'm just an old fool for trying to hold on as long as I did."

"The last thing you are is a fool. Old or otherwise."

"You know, it's funny," she said, setting her mug on the counter. "I've been talking a lot to Duane lately. And him gone near twenty years. I never thought I'd be one of those women who swears she can feel her dead husband at the foot of the bed or any of that nonsense. But here recently, we've been having us some interesting conversations, him and me."

"What about?" The notion that Mitchell might suddenly find the urge to speak to me, after all these years behaving himself the way dead husbands should, put the fear of Jesus in me in a way not even my mama could manage.

"Oh, just regular stuff. Whether or not it's time to get the tires rotated on the Plymouth. If the Mavs really have a shot at the NBA title." She saw the look on my face and laughed. "I'm kidding, sort of. It's different from that. More like what we'd have done with our lives if we had more time. Like whether I should have let him buy that RV he wanted, back in '67. Whether we should have tried harder to convince Kelly to go to nursing school, like her guidance counselor said, instead of letting her marry Bob Broyles and move to Florida."

"But Kelly loves Florida. They've been there—what? Fourteen, fifteen years?"

"Uh-huh."

"They're not having problems, are they?"

"Just the usual stuff. The boys are growing up, starting to run a little wild." She turned the mug around and around in her hands. "I think Kelly's got a little too much time on her hands. She's got her book club and her volunteer job at the food pantry, and the boys keep her on the go, but Bob's away so much on business—"

Peggy's voice broke, revealing a truth that hours and days of talk might not have gotten out of her. The older I got, the more I was starting to understand that home was not so much about place as about people; that if you had to, you'd live in a cardboard box under a bridge, even in Florida, if it meant having your loved ones nearby.

"I've had an offer," she said.

"What kind of offer?"

"Burton wants to expand the café."

"But—isn't this place a little out of his way? I thought the whole point of the café was to be on the courthouse square."

"Oh, he's not moving. He's buying out the barbershop next door. So you'd think old Wendell Hayes would just take the money and move out to the lake, right? He's got to be seventy if he's a day. But he claims he's not ready to retire. And I guess there's still enough men in this town needing their ears lowered on a regular basis to keep him in business. Even if most of them quit buying their wives flowers a long time ago, the cheap sons of bitches."

Any other day I would have laughed. Peggy hardly ever cussed.

"You've made up your mind, sounds like," I said.

"This town is shrinking faster than an icicle in July. Wendell's offer is like some kind of a miracle, considering."

"What if you got a better one?" The notion seemed to come out of nowhere, but the minute it was out, it seemed like the perfect solution.

"I'd say no, ma'am. No way, no how."

"I've got some money in the bank."

"That money is for your retirement someday, for Jude's college. It's rainy-day money, not lose-your-shirt-in-Reno money. I won't stand by and watch you flush it away on a thing that can't be saved."

"But what if—"

Peggy held up her hand. "Lucy. You know I love you, but you've got to face facts. Towns like this one are drying up right and left. Pretty soon there won't be a thing left but a speck on the map to show where Mooney used to be."

I could see my reflection in the door of the cooler. For eight years, I'd watched myself in that glass: a young widow who didn't know a hibiscus from a hydrangea, a pregnant bride, a scared single mom, to the person I was today—or at least who I'd been till a couple of days ago, a woman grounded in her marriage, her work, her home, and her family. Now it all seemed to be coming loose, like an old tree in a gale-force wind, roots that have taken years to establish ripped out and sent flying, and who knew, in the end, where it would land?

"You've lived in this town your whole life," I said.

"My whole life so far." Peggy smiled. "Maybe me and Duane didn't get the chance we deserved. But there's still time to watch my grandkids grow up. Besides, I can think of worse ways to get old than sitting on the beach watching the sunset with a piña colada in your hand."

"They have hurricanes in Florida," I said. "And alligators. And sharks!"

"I'd rather be shark bait than shrivel up to nothing in this old town."

I opened my mouth to disagree, then snapped it shut again. I could argue with Peggy till I was blue in the face, but I knew her well enough to realize when she'd made up her mind. Wendell Hayes would come in with his swivel chairs and his scissors and his combs in antiseptic, and there wasn't a thing I could do about it.

And she had a point. As much as things seemed never to change in Mooney, slowly but surely the outside world was taking over. Farms were going belly-up, huge patches of the piney woods being clear-cut. Kids almost never stuck around after high school—Audrey and Joe were planning to move to Dallas in the fall—and now their parents were packing up and heading out, too, in search of greener pastures, or rather its opposite: steel and asphalt and traffic and crowds. It took a certain kind of person to stay and fight. I'd always thought I was that kind of person; but I'd thought Peggy was one, too.

"Why don't you pack up early and get out of here," she said. "Run over and help Geneva get set up for the party."

"How long?" I asked.

"How long what?"

"Before Wendell wants to move in?"

"I told him June first," she said. "That'll give us a few weeks to sort things out, pack up what we can send back for credit, sell off what we can't. I'll pay you till the end of the summer. Give you time to find something else."

Something like what? I wondered as I gathered up my things and walked out to the Blazer. Sliding behind the wheel,

I tried to picture myself in a white polyester uniform and squeaky-soled shoes, enduring snide remarks as I poured coffee and doled out blue plate specials at the café. All the other jobs in town were either locked up tight or required skills I didn't have. Even the family business, Hatch Brothers Contracting, had had the same bookkeeper, a stout, pink-haired lady named Orvetta Stiles, since they'd cut the ribbon on their first job twenty-five years before.

This wasn't about money; we had enough in the bank from the sale of our Nashville house to keep us afloat for a while, and my paycheck had never been much to brag about to begin with. But it had never been about the income. Faye's gave my life a shape and a purpose, a sense of belonging that I'd never felt the same way anywhere else. I loved the flowers, but more than that, I loved the way the job kept me anchored, not just to the community, but to the earth, the little corner of northeast Texas I called home.

As I saw it, I had two choices. I could go home and sit by the phone and wait for some TV psychic to call and tell me what to do; or I could do what I usually did in times of trouble: wrap myself in the safe, if slightly irritating, blanket of my family.

No contest. I put the Blazer in gear and headed for Bailey and Geneva's.

CHAPTER 11

Denny

I GUESS I was supposed to feel all gooey with forgiveness when I found Will asleep on the picnic table the next morning, but we'd done this scene too many times before. He'd expect me to be grateful that he'd made it home in one piece, instead of passing out in a holding cell, or some ditch. In spite of the fact that he looked so pitiful, with his hair flopped over his eyes and his mouth gaping open, I felt the iron bars sliding shut over my heart.

Besides, what would I say to Erasmus, who'd called an hour earlier asking me to meet him in town for breakfast? The girl he remembered, the one he thought he knew, had more backbone than to be taken in by the likes of a snake charmer like Will Culpepper.

Erasmus was already waiting by the time I got there, in a booth by the window at the café. Even in New York he would have stood out in a crowd, a head taller than anybody else, with his coffee-colored skin and the gold stud in his ear. The room, empty at that hour except for the usual suspects, got quiet as a church when I walked in. Erasmus rose as I approached, his good East Texas upbringing on display for all to see, but he made his face a careful blank as I slid into the bench across from him and picked up a menu.

"Wow," I said. "Just like old times."

"I hope not." The first time we ever appeared in public together in Mooney, we'd been terrorized by a bunch of rednecks at the Dairy Queen. Things had changed since then, but not much. Besides Erasmus, the only other black person in the café was the cook behind the pickup window. But a framed picture of me hung behind the cash register, alongside one of my daddy, and everybody knew about the King boy who'd gone off to music school in New York City. They say you never stop being who you started out as in a small town, but maybe because Erasmus and I weren't natives, we were excused, at least partly, from the usual rules.

That didn't mean folks wouldn't talk, though. One of the men at the counter cut his eyes our way and muttered something under his breath, and the whole bunch of them, including Carol, the waitress, burst out laughing.

"This was your idea," I reminded Erasmus.

He scanned the laminated menu. "The ham and redeye gravy sounds good, don't you think?"

"I thought you were a vegetarian."

"When I come home, something takes over my brain. Starts demanding I eat meat."

Carol came over and, without lifting her eyes from her pad, asked what she could bring us. We ordered the breakfast special even though it was almost noon: ham and eggs and hash browns with coffee. "Comin' right up," Carol said, sticking her pencil behind her ear and sauntering off toward the kitchen, hips swinging in her white uniform.

We were quiet for a few minutes, looking out at the square. Cade County had one of the oldest courthouses in Texas, but it wasn't pretty or picturesque, just a big white-washed box. From the looks of things, about half the shops surrounding it had gone out of business, including the video store where Erasmus and I had finally had a run-in with the Butler brothers, who'd tossed him into the front window hard enough to smash the glass. They'd gotten caught, eventually, but disappeared before the case could come to trial. Good riddance, Daddy said, but everybody knew there were plenty more where they'd come from.

In spite of what had happened with Seth and Sean Butler, my memories of that summer were mostly sweet ones. I thought I'd go crazy at first in this sleepy little town, where the biggest thing happening was my daddy taking up with the new widow Lucy Hatch. Then I'd met Erasmus, and my grandmother, Evelyn, and my life began to unfurl, slow at first and then faster and faster, like a bright-colored pinwheel.

"Earth to Denny," Erasmus said.

"Sorry. I was just thinking."

"I could see that."

Carol plopped down a couple of mugs of coffee and sashayed off again.

"I've got an idea," I said.

"Yeah?" Erasmus poured sugar into his coffee from a glass shaker and stirred it intently.

Keeping my voice low, I told him about what had been going on between Will and Marin. "So, it looks like I'm gonna be needing a new fiddle player," I said.

Erasmus shook his head. "You need more than a new fiddle player. You need a new husband. Or at least get rid of the one you've got." He took a sip of coffee. "The guy's bad news, Denny. I thought so from the first time I heard his name. Love's supposed to bring out the best in people. Do I really have to tell you that?"

Carol slapped down our breakfast platters, then spun on her heel and waltzed over to the counter and started whispering with the regulars. I lowered my voice. "Look, it's not like you think, with me and Will."

"So, explain it to me."

I watched Erasmus saw off a bite of meat and gravy.

"How come you wanted to see me?" I asked.

"You're changing the subject."

"Yeah, I am."

He took his time chewing and swallowing, then dabbed his mouth carefully with a paper napkin. "You remember Camille," he said.

The last time I'd seen Erasmus, back in the fall, in a waffle house on the interstate in Colorado one morning after his and my band's gigs had overlapped, he'd showed me a picture of a girl he was supposedly dating in New York, a grad student at Columbia. I'd accused him of cutting the picture out of a magazine, that nobody in real life had cheekbones like that.

"The supermodel? Sure."

"I told you a hundred times—she's getting her Ph.D. in women's studies."

"So you say. What about her?"

"Well, she's been applying for fellowships. And the one she really wanted, she got. It starts in September."

"Great. I'm really happy for her."

"The thing is, it's in Paris. And I'm going with her."

"Paris? Paris, *France*?"

"I've done a ton of gigs in Europe already. Jazz is a much bigger scene over there than it is here. Cliff says I'll be able to work as much as I want." Erasmus pushed his plate aside and folded his hands on the table. "Stop looking at me like that."

"Like what?"

"Like I'm, I don't know, speaking in tongues or something. Of everybody I know, I thought you'd understand. Why I'm going. Why I *have* to go."

"Because of Camille," I said. My voice was croaky. Maybe I was coming down with something. Maybe I could lie in bed for a week and Lucy would bring me chicken soup and magazines, and the rest of the world could go to hell.

"Partly, yeah. But this is a big deal for me. Once in a lifetime, maybe. Like when you went to Nashville."

"But Nashville's only five hundred miles from here," I said. "Not five thousand. And I didn't have to learn a whole new language to move there."

"*Je parle déjà français,*" he replied breezily. "*Vous ne savez pas tout.*"

"Shut up! Whatever it was you just said." I threw a plastic straw at him and it bounced off his chest.

Erasmus leaned toward me across the table. "What do you want me to say? That I still want to be with you? Even if it was true, what difference would it make? You've never known a good thing when you had it, not even when it was staring you right in the face."

I sat back against the vinyl bench and turned my face to the window. Sunlight bounced off chrome from the cars parked across the street, giving me an excuse to squint, to hide the sting of tears. It seemed to me that men felt like it was some kind of moral victory to make women cry, and I wasn't about to give Erasmus, or anybody, that kind of leverage.

"I thought we were supposed to be best friends," I said.

"We are," he said. "Or at least we used to be. I'm not sure I feel like I really know you anymore."

"What kind of a thing is that to say?"

"Look. I know as well as anybody what it's like to take up with somebody just for— For a good time." The rims of his ears were red; it had always tickled me, how prudish Erasmus could get. "But, Denny, you spend a night or two with those people and then you move on. You don't marry them! Marriage is supposed to be about the real thing."

"Like what you have with Camille?" I asked.

"Yeah," he said, "I think so, anyway. That's why I'm going to France with her. To find out."

"Fine. So, you're moving to France with Camille. Congratulations. I hope you live happily ever after." I balled up my napkin and dropped it on the table. "I have to go. I've got an errand to run."

Erasmus turned and waved at Carol and asked for the check. She tore a slip off her pad, set it next to his plate, and walked away without comment.

Erasmus took out his wallet and laid down a twenty. We got up and threaded our way between the tables, ignoring the men lined up along the counter bright-eyed and watchful as grackles on a wire. Nobody said a word as we pushed out the front door, no "thanks, folks" or "y'all come again."

Heat rose off the sidewalk in waves, along with the stink of exhaust and asphalt.

"You know," Erasmus said, "you never used to bullshit me like this."

"What are you talking about?"

"You always were a straight shooter. Now you're lying about having errands to do, and you can't even look me in the eye."

"I'm not lying! I need to go see my grandmother."

Erasmus narrowed one eye and squinted at me, like he was trying to make up his mind whether or not to believe me.

"I'm not kidding. She's in real bad shape. She's in a home up near Hughes Springs."

"Jesus," he said, "that's rough."

"She thinks I'm her, if you can believe that. The way she was when she was younger. Daddy won't even talk about it, so I'm all she's got."

"I'll go with you, if you want."

"You'd do that?"

"If I take the truck back, Pop'll put me to work replacing transmissions or something."

I could picture Erasmus performing brain surgery more easily than I could see him under a car, up to his elbows in sweat and axle grease.

"Okay," I said. "But no lectures, okay? I mean about anything."

It was a steamy morning promising a steamier afternoon, the sky a chalky blue full of cotton-ball clouds as we made our way around the square and onto the FM road that led north out of town. Beyond the city limits sign, woods and fields flew by, a blur of green and gold broken by the occasional house or church. We passed a stooped figure in overalls and a sunbonnet spearing trash with a stick in the bar ditch, face as brown and wrinkled as a shelled pecan, male or female impossible to tell, just a streak, then gone.

It was rest time when we arrived at the house outside Hughes Springs, Contessa told us sternly; didn't I know better than to visit between twelve and two? When I said I didn't, some of the sourness went out of her face and she said, "Y'all come on in out of the sun. I'll see if Evelyn's up for comp'ny."

I introduced Erasmus as we followed Contessa into the living room where, like before, the TV played to an audience of no one. "Uh-huh," Contessa said, trying to pretend she wasn't looking him over out of the corner of her eye. I doubted they saw the likes of Erasmus King very often around Hughes Springs.

My grandmother was sitting in the same chair by the window as the day before, wearing a bright flowered muumuu the old Evelyn wouldn't have been caught dead in.

"Hey, Evelyn," I said. "It's me, Denny. I was here yesterday, remember?"

She frowned at her hands in her lap.

"This is my friend Erasmus King," I said. "Erasmus, this is my grandmother, Evelyn LeGrande."

"How do you do, Miss LeGrande," Erasmus said, stepping forward and offering his hand. Evelyn took it, gazing at his long, graceful fingers. "How are you feeling today?" he asked. He was using what I called his Barry White voice, deep and smooth as melted chocolate.

"I'm fine, thank you." She patted her head self-consciously. "Annie washed my hair this morning. Here, feel."

Erasmus touched her fleecy hair. "Soft as silk," he said.

"I've used Prell my whole life. I think it brings out the shine, don't you?"

"Yes, ma'am, I surely do."

"Are you going to get that cat out of the yard, like I asked you?"

"Ma'am?"

"I told you yesterday, that orange cat is stalking the birds when they come to the feeder. You said you'd do something about it, but I saw him out there again this morning. We wouldn't want the baby birds to lose their mamas, now would we?"

"No, ma'am, we wouldn't."

"You'll take care of it, then?" she asked.

"I'll see what I can do."

I stepped forward and knelt in front of my grandmother's chair. "Is there anything we can get you, Evelyn? Anything you'd like to have?"

She looked at me for a long time with that same confused look. It made me want to scream, or cry. What kind of God would invent a disease that left your body intact but your mind a spider's web, nothing left of who you'd been but bits and pieces of silvery thread?

"Frank," she said.

"Excuse me?"

"Bring me Frank."

A lump rose in my throat. "Frank is dead, Evelyn."

"Don't be silly," she said. "I saw him last night. You were singing in that little club, you know the one over by the Stockyards, and he was standing at the bar and listening. His hair was as shiny as shoe polish. You teased him about it, and he bought you a drink, the kind with the cherries you love so much."

I looked at Erasmus, who shook his head. So I said to her the same thing he'd said: "I'll see what I can do."

FRANK WAS HER husband?"

"Yeah. Who ran out on her and Daddy when he was, like, two years old."

We were quiet awhile, the same scenery as before zipping by backward, like a film in reverse. JESUS DIED FOR YOUR SINS, proclaimed the sign outside the Mt. Sinai Baptist Church.

"I don't believe that for a minute," I said, watching the words shrink in the rearview mirror. "It was Hank."

Erasmus rested his hand lightly on the seatback behind my head.

"Hank?"

"Hank Williams."

"HANK WILLIAMS DIED FOR YOUR SINS," he said. "Good name for a song. Pull in here a minute, would you?" We were coming up on the Miracle Mart.

"What for?"

"Does everything have to be twenty questions with you? Just stop."

I waited in the truck while he went inside and came out carrying a paper sack tucked under his arm. He reached inside and pulled out a Miller longneck.

"No, thanks," I said as he offered it to me.

He shrugged. "Suit yourself."

He brought the bottle to his lips, swallowing a long draught, then tilted his head against the headrest and started to sing.

Oh, he rose to the top of the charts
With a voice that could break people's hearts
But he threw it away
For the bottle, they say
Hank Williams died for your sins.

I'd forgotten how it felt to be so easy in somebody's company, to not have to pretend to be something you weren't. We made up verse after verse, howling like lunatics as we navigated the winding back roads of Cade County. With each mile that passed, it felt like we were shedding our shiny new selves, going back to who we'd been before New York and Nashville, back to the pine and red dirt that had always been our common ground.

At the Corners, Erasmus directed me to head south. "Slow down," he said as we approached the turnoff to Daddy's. "Take a left."

"Left?" The home place was to the right, at the end of Bates Road. Left was Little Hope Road, where Daddy's old house stood empty with a Realtor's padlock on the front door. As far as I knew there hadn't been one potential buyer in a whole year. The place was just too far off the beaten path for anybody other than hillbilly drug dealers or pipe bomb makers who, as a general rule, couldn't afford that kind of real estate.

"Just turn," Erasmus said.

I eased up on the gas as we left the hardtop and began to bump slowly up the unpaved county road. It had rained just enough that spring to carve deep grooves in the red clay, and I had to fight to keep the truck out of the ditch. We drove in and out of a canopy of shade, pine and oak and cypress, and I hit the button to roll the windows down and breathe in the dense, green smell.

Coming up were the ruins of the Little Hope cemetery, a place I'd visited regularly that first summer I'd spent with Daddy and Lucy, the times we weren't getting along so great and I needed somewhere I could breathe. Lucy always claimed it creeped her out to be living next door to all those

ghosts, but I liked it there, sitting among the toppling headstones with a peanut butter sandwich and my Walkman. I
liked reading the names and dates and making up stories
about the people whose bones lay beneath them. I'd brought
Erasmus here, once he'd recovered from the knock on the
head the Butler brothers had given him, and we'd gone back a
few more times that summer, taking his fiddle and my guitar,
sitting on the old stone wall and serenading the dead.

"Stop here," he said, and I eased the truck off the road and
parked under the leafy spread of a pecan tree.

"I dream about this place sometimes." He reached between his feet for the six-pack. "Want to get out for a while?
Cool your heels?"

My heels were a lot cooler in the air-conditioned pickup
than they would be in the blazing sun, but I followed him
anyway as he gathered the brown paper sack and swung nim-
bly over the low rock wall into the cemetery. Daddy claimed
that what kin was left of the folks buried here still held Re-
membrance Day twice a year, to tidy the grounds, cut the
grass, and prop up the crumbling headstones, but to my eye,
the place looked even more unkempt than ever. Dandelions
and chickweed grew taller than the grass, which was littered
with beer cans and plastic soda bottles. I stopped to stare at a
shriveled condom.

"This is awful," I said, but Erasmus was forging among the
headstones, his voice trailing him loud and off-key:

He had the whole world by the tail
But he fucked up and landed in jail

And he croaked in the back
Of a white Cadillac
Yes sir, Hank Williams died for your sins.

"Here's a good spot," he called out, and I followed him over to a shady patch under a live oak tree. The Johnson grass was sparse and dry, but at least there was no trace of vandalism. What kind of a person, I wondered out loud, would trash a cemetery?

"I'm serious," I said. "It's bad karma or something."

"You know what your problem is?" Erasmus plunked himself down under the tree, reached into the paper sack and brought out another beer and twisted off the cap. "You can't see why the whole world doesn't share your view of things. Did it ever occur to you that some people don't give a shit about karma?"

"I bet they'll care a lot when they come back as a tree roach."

"Why don't you just try living in the present, for once?" he said. "Be here now, like your aunt Dove would say." He put the bottle to his mouth and drank.

I rambled off among the headstones, reacquainting myself with old friends. There was a man here who'd lived to be a hundred and four, and twins who'd died just two days after they were born. "Hello," I whispered, tracing my finger along their carved names, Effraim and Germaine Cotton. "Can you hear me?"

"Talking to ghosts?" Erasmus had snuck up behind me, giving me a start. "Relax," he said, putting his hands on my shoulders. "You're jumpy as a cat."

"You know what we should do?" I said. "We should get some trash bags and clean this place up a little. Has your daddy got a lawn mower we could borrow?"

"Denny."

I turned and looked up at him. His face was like one of those postcard holograms, where if you turn it one way you see the sweet country boy, the other and you see the grown man. The girl I'd been had loved that boy the way you maybe only get to love somebody once in your life. But I wasn't that girl anymore.

A gust of wind moved through the trees, and in spite of the heat I got a chill. Erasmus had been right that morning, outside the café. I'd always been a straight shooter. It was time to get that back again, before it was too late, before I'd turned, like Evelyn, into somebody who couldn't recognize herself.

"I need to get home," I said. There was a conversation I needed to have with Will Culpepper.

CHAPTER 12

Lucy

THE GAZEBO IN Bailey and Geneva's backyard was strung with strands of pink and white lights and matching paper streamers, like a giant peppermint drop. I sat beneath it stuffing goody bags—pink for the girl guests, white for the boys—with candy and trinkets and listening to the members of the Methodist Ladies' Guild as they fussed over the long tables set up on the lawn and loaded with covered dishes.

"... beautiful service, just beautiful. Every last one of his kids and grandkids got up there and said a few words about their daddy, even Danny's girls, the little ones. They say there wasn't a dry eye ..."

"... spent the whole thing on scratch-off tickets. Didn't win a penny, and now Junie doesn't know how they're supposed to pay the bills. Said she'd like to put his La-Z-Boy out in the shed and ask him how he . . ."

". . . cut her open and sewed her right back up again. Her cousin's over there at the house, the one from Carthage, looking after things. Poor Tom, ever since they got the diagnosis he just can't seem to . . ."

". . . eighty-one years old and still working thirty hours a week in the cosmetics department at Wal-Mart. Lou Ann can't get her to quit. You know how it is with Germans and their work ethnic."

I smiled to myself, letting the talk spill in and out of my head like waves breaking, soothing me with its gentle, predictable rhythm. This is what I'd missed in Nashville: the overheard conversations of women whose histories were so closely interwoven they spoke in a kind of shorthand, no last names or identifying characteristics necessary.

Geneva came out of the house in pedal pushers and a bandanna-print blouse, carrying a big white bakery box. The Guild ladies stepped aside and ooh'd and ahh'd as she set it on the table and lifted an edge of the lid so everybody could get a good look. A local lady named Priscilla Swinton, famous for her cakes, had baked it, layers of angel food with strawberry filling in between and decorated with candy-striped frosting and the words WELCOME HOME EMMALEE! in sugar-pink script four inches high.

"Whew," Geneva said, coming over to check on the goody bags. "I was starting to think I might have to send Bailey to Wal-Mart after a cake." We both waved to Bailey, happily tending the grill on the other side of the yard,. "Pris's great, but man, she dances to her own drummer sometimes, you know?"

"Well, she hasn't been the same since Eddie died," I said. "He used to drive her everywhere, and now she has to wait on that good-for-nothing daughter of hers to get off work at the . . ." I dropped a handful of fruit chews into a bag and laughed as I tied the top shut. "Listen to me," I said. "I sound just like one of them."

"Who?"

I nodded at the Methodist ladies, who'd moved on from the cake to investigate Florence Binder's home-style baked beans, smothered in brown sugar and layered with bacon. Twenty years ago they'd dressed in polyester dresses and heels, with frosted hair and pearls to match, and now they wore flowered capri pants outfits and had short, stylish hair-cuts, but underneath, nothing had changed and never would, not until Mooney, Texas, was nothing but a memory.

"What's the matter?" Geneva said as I pushed my hair off my sticky face.

"Nothing. Just hot, that's all."

"You look like you're fixing to bust out crying."

"I guess I just—" I glanced again at the ladies and shook my head. "I'll tell you later. Emmy still sleeping?"

"Yeah. I better get inside and get myself dressed before she wakes up."

"Did you know Lily doesn't believe in Jesus?" I asked. "She said there's somebody else she likes better—a little brown man? It had something to do with e-mail . . . I didn't get it."

Geneva started laughing. "The Dalai Lama," she said. "We saw a special about him on PBS. She liked how he smiles all the time, even when he's talking about stuff like war and hunger. And he has an e-mail address. It bothers her that Jesus hardly ever smiles, and you can't send him e-mail."

"You don't sound too worried about her immortal soul."

"She's seven. I think Jesus would understand. Anyway, maybe Jesus needs to take the hint. Get himself a website if he wants to keep up with the competition."

"Better watch your mouth. The Guild ladies might hear."

"Their tongues'll be wagging soon enough, when Kit gets here with the keg."

I stacked the finished goody bags carefully inside an empty cardboard box, then dug my cell phone out of my tote and flipped it open. It worried me a little that I hadn't seen or heard from Denny all day. I called her cell but got a recording that the phone wasn't in service. Come to think of it, I hadn't seen her use it since she'd arrived two nights before. I called the house and left a message on the machine, telling her that she should come over and meet the newest member of the family, that Will was welcome to tag along if she wanted him to. Unease nagged at me as I disconnected the call and dialed Ash. I hadn't figured out yet what Will Culpepper was doing in Mooney, but I had a hunch his intentions weren't a hundred percent honorable.

Ash picked up on the second ring. I could barely hear him over the sweep and swell of classical music in the background.

"What's that racket?" I asked, raising my voice.

"Vivaldi. Vergie's got her speakers hooked up, and we're out on the sun porch, drinking lemonade and shooting the breeze."

It cheered me up a little, reminding me of the early days of our courtship, when Ash's woodworking and remodeling business had been in great demand by Mooney's old guard. He did beautiful, painstaking work, but I'd always suspected it was his company the ladies enjoyed as much as their new cupboards.

"I'm just calling to remind you about Emmy's party," I said.

"I didn't forget. I need to run by the Sav-Mor and pick up Vergie's prescriptions, and then I'll be over directly."

So you're a delivery service now, too? I nearly said, but stopped myself in time. I had a bad habit of trying to make other people unhappy when I was, as if to prove the saying that misery loved company was true.

"Just hurry," I said. "I need to talk to you."

"See you in a few," he shouted, and hung up.

Dove arrived a few minutes later with Jude and Lily, and my brother Kit showed up right behind them with the keg, along with a handful of guys from his crew. Some were kids, stopping off in town just long enough to earn a few bucks before they moved on up the road in search of more lucrative opportunities, but many had been with Kit and Bailey since the beginning, men I'd known most of my life. I let one of them, Pete Ruscheka, pour me a plastic cup of beer and was standing in the shade of a crape myrtle listening to a story about his teenage daughters and their various boy problems when Mrs. Florence Binder sidled up to me, balancing a Chinet plate loaded with sausage and potato salad and beans.

"Hey there, Miz Binder," Pete said. "Get you a beer?"

"Oh, heavens, no! I've never been much of a drinker. I might have a sip of brandy before bed at night, but never in the daytime. Now my Arthur, when he was alive, he loved a Pabst Blue Ribbon . . ." Her voice trailed. "I will take a Coca-Cola out of that cooler over there, though, if it isn't too much trouble."

Pete winked at me over her head and set off across the yard.

"How are you, Mrs. Binder?" I said, taking a furtive sip of beer. I hardly drank at all myself anymore, especially since Ash had given it up, but today I needed a touch of the medicinal myself.

"Well, my shoulder's been bothering me some, but all in all, I can't complain." She stood peering up at me through her rhinestone-framed glasses. "You know, I was out watering my caladiums the other day and I saw Wendell Hayes talking to Peggy outside the shop." Mrs. Binder lived catty-corner to Faye's, and little that went on there escaped her attention.

"Is that right?" I took another sip of beer. "Well, maybe Wendell needed some flowers."

"Now, Lucy, you know as well as I do, there isn't a man in Cade County who has less need of flowers than Wendell Hayes." It was true; Wendell, who had to be pushing seventy, was not just a lifelong bachelor but, as far as the citizens of Mooney knew, hadn't even dated a woman ever since he'd been thrown over at the senior prom by Marguerite

Saunders for a guy whose daddy owned a Pontiac dealership in Texarkana. Wendell had become a barber and a famous grouch, the kind of person who might steal bouquets off the headstones of strangers to leave for his own mama and daddy, if he ever bothered visiting their final resting places at all.

I was saved from having to answer by the appearance of the guest of honor, resplendent in pink taffeta with a candy-striped bow in her feathery black hair, smiling her Buddha smile as she sailed through the crowd in the arms of her tall, blond mama. I don't know what Gen was thinking with that getup; anybody could see that Emmalee Hatch was never going to be a pink-ribbons kind of girl. There was something smug and knowing in the expression on her face. As the Methodist ladies began to gang up, jockeying to touch and hold her, I half expected her to wink at me over their heads the way Pete Ruscheka had and offer to get me another beer.

I T W A S A good party, or it would have been if I hadn't been so distracted by the imminent prospects of joblessness and grandparenthood. Geneva and Bailey had a way of bringing together the most motley assortment of people in a way that might seem ruinous in theory but that always seemed to work like a charm when put into play. Children chased one another through the grass, their voices piercing the air over the blues music that spilled out of speakers on the patio, where the church ladies sat with their plates balanced on their knees, gossiping and eyeing the construction workers.

Before long one of the men would ask one of the ladies to dance, and even though she'd blush and stammer, eventually she'd set down her plate and get up and take his hand, and the next thing you knew, there'd be Methodists and heathens side by side, shaking their tail feathers all over the backyard.

I was holding Emmy while Geneva heaped her plate with beans and chicken when a ripple of noise started up and made its way, like cascading water, across the yard. I didn't even have to turn around to know what it meant: Ash was here.

Jiggling Emmy on my hip, I watched him come. He still knew how to work a crowd, dispensing greetings like benedictions, pausing to brush the back of a craggy old hand with his calloused fingertips. Sometimes, I actually forgot that he was my husband, and felt the same ache of longing that I imagined most of the Methodist ladies felt, waiting with held breath for the magic moment that his roving smile would light on me.

"Here comes your uncle Ash," I said to Emmy, who was gazing at him with the same look of bewitchment as everybody else.

"Taw!" she cried, surging forward with her whole little body, and fell with a happy sigh into his arms.

"Hey there, princess," he said, rubbing his chin over the top of her satiny head. "Man. I'd forgotten how good babies smell." Emmy reached up and grabbed a hank of his hair in her fist, and he laughed and leaned over and kissed me. "Maybe we should get us another one, what do you think?"

I gave him a little push, and he stepped back and looked at me.

"What? What'd I say?"

"Peggy's closing the shop," I announced, then dropped my voice and looked around to see if anybody besides Ash had heard me. "She's selling out to Wendell Hayes and moving to Florida."

"What the hell does Wendell want with a flower shop?"

"He doesn't. He's moving the barbershop. Burton's buying him out to expand the café. I guess flowers are a luxury these days, but folks still need lunch and haircuts."

Emmy patted Ash's face with the palm of her hand, as if to say, *There, there.* He smiled indulgently and ran his fingertip across the frilly top of her sock.

"You wouldn't have to work, you know," he said. "You could take some time off, stay home. Take it easy."

"And do what? Vacuum the living room? Bake pies all day long?" I'd tried that, in Nashville, and just about lost my mind.

"We could have another baby."

"Why is that your solution to everything?"

"Calm down. I didn't say it was."

"Having a baby isn't something you do just because you don't know what else to do with yourself!" No, in this family, it was what you did because you were too lazy or foolish or just plain ignorant to practice birth control.

"Now, Lucy, I think you're getting a little too—"

"Ash," I blurted out, "Denny's pregnant."

The words seemed to hover between us like a soap bubble. I hadn't known I was going to tell him, until suddenly it seemed I couldn't *not.*

"What did you say?" He was smiling like you do when you think you might be the victim of some elaborate practical joke.

"You heard me."

He looked at me for a minute, then shifted his gaze to Emmy. "Doe?" she asked.

With a shake of his head, he handed her back to me and strode toward the patio. I watched as he passed the guys grouped around the beer keg and got himself a Coke out of the cooler. Instead of opening it, he stood to one side, looking over at the men joking and laughing and guzzling beer without a care in the world. Even from this distance I could feel the heat of his gaze on them. I knew what he was thinking: life was hard and it wasn't fair, and why shouldn't he be allowed to take the edge off like everybody else? How much could it hurt, just this once?

I handed Emmy to Mrs. Binder and took off across the yard, pretending I didn't hear the buzz of the Guild ladies trailing me like a swarm of bees as Ash set the Coke can on top of the cooler and walked around the corner of the house. I caught up with him just as he was unlocking his pickup.

"Ash, wait," I said. "I'm sorry. I shouldn't have sprung everything on you like that, all at once, in the middle of a party. I just— I'm scared. I don't know what to do."

I reached for his hand, turning it over in mine, studying the branched lines, the ridge of calluses along the base of his fingers. This, at least, was familiar, something to hang on to.

"I wish you'd talk to me," I said. "Instead of just going off like you do. Shutting down."

He took a breath and held it, then let it slowly out again.

"We're getting old, Lucy," he said. "This is what it's gonna be like from here on out. Shit you can't do anything about. The old giving way to the new. It's the way of the world, I guess. I just didn't expect it to come up on me all at once."

"What's gotten into you? I'm the one who's supposed to be having the bad day here."

"Sorry. My back is killing me. I must've pulled something at the lumberyard."

"Well, why didn't you say something? We could have gone home and gotten you a heat wrap and some Advil."

The sun was going down, reflected in the windows of the houses across the street, making the sidewalk under my feet look like the proverbial Yellow Brick Road. I wondered, idly, what had happened to Dorothy after the movie ended, once she was home in Kansas. Was it the happy place she remembered, or had everything changed, not just there but inside her, because of what happened in Oz? Probably she learned that there really *was* no place like home, not even home itself; probably she ended up wandering the dusty roads of the old farm raving about talking apple trees and flying monkeys while folks shook their heads and whispered behind their hands.

"I hate this," Ash said.

"Hate what?"

"I don't know what good I am to you, sometimes. When it gets like this, I feel like I can't see anything but this, this fog."

"Have you tried talking to Punch about it?"

"Yeah. He says I've hit a bump in the road."

"Well, did he have any advice?"

"He said give it over to God. I told him that hasn't been working too well lately."

"That's it?"

"The phone number of some doctor down in Marshall. A headshrinker."

I tipped back my chin and saw the clench of Ash's jaw, the gleam of held-back tears in his eyes.

"Well, maybe that wouldn't be a bad idea," I said. "I mean, maybe it would be good to at least hear what this doctor, whoever he is, has to say."

He reached into his pocket and pulled out his work bandanna and blew his nose into it.

"What are we gonna do about Denny?" he asked.

"I don't know."

"The baby—it's Culpepper's?"

"She says she hasn't been with anybody but Will."

"What was she doing having unprotected sex with the guy, anyway? He's practically got 'sexually transmitted disease' carved into his forehead."

"We were young and stupid once, too," I said.

"Not that young, and not that stupid," he said. "Anyway, we thought you couldn't get pregnant. It's not the same."

"We were in love. It makes you do things you wouldn't ordinarily do."

"We were grown-ups. Not twenty-some-year-old idiots."

"We were grown-up idiots."

"Anyway, you stayed home with Jude. The road is no place for a baby."

"Lots of women in the music business have kids," I said. "Look at Faith Hill and Martina McBride. Shania Twain."

"You're talking about folks who are at the top of the heap already, not still making the climb. They can afford to hire help when they're on the road, or take time off when the kids are little. Do you know what a year off would cost Denny at this point in her career?"

"So you think she shouldn't have it."

"I didn't say that."

"What, then? You want her to give up everything she's worked for the past few years, be a full-time mommy?"

He shook his head. I knew we were picturing the same thing: a dingy apartment reeking of diapers, the TV running night and day, Denny growing slow and heavy and resentful as the baby screamed and Will stayed away and her life got smaller and smaller.

The sounds of the party drifted over and around the house, filtering down around us in the gathering dark: the chatter of conversation, laughter, Bobby "Blue" Bland singing "I'm not ashamed 'cause you saw me crying."

"I want you to listen to me," I said to Ash. "Just listen, now, and don't say anything until I'm through."

CHAPTER 13

Denny

FTER I TOOK Erasmus back to town I drove around for a while trying to work up my nerve. But Will wasn't at the house when I got there, and neither was anybody else, plus my head hurt, and I was starving.

I let myself in with the spare key and went straight to the kitchen, where I dug through the icebox, scrounging for leftovers. I made myself a plate of cold meat loaf, cabbage slaw, dill pickles, and cling peaches and carried it onto the front porch.

The sun was setting, a fireball in the flamingo-pink sky. I ate with my fingers, wiping my plate clean with a piece of loaf bread and finishing things off with a big glass of cherry Kool-Aid. Daddy's black mutt, Booker T., and Lucy's heeler, Steve Cropper, came loping around the side of the house, and I gave them my plate to lick, even though I knew Lucy would die if she saw. If there was such a thing as karma, I thought, there were worse things to come back as than a dog. I leaned over and looked into Steve Cropper's eyes, trying to see if there was some old soul in there, but he just kept yipping at me with his dumb doggy grin and dancing away. I picked up the plate and carried it inside and put it in the dishwasher, then went upstairs and fell across my bed, where I lay watching the pink light fade against the walls until I couldn't keep my eyes open another second.

Two women stood onstage in a dim blue light, wearing spangled jackets and boots decorated with curlicues. *Ladies and gentlemen,* a voice boomed out of the dark, *please welcome, live and in person, the one, the only Stardust Cowgirl!*

My head filled with the sound of chanting: *Lynette! Lynette!* I turned to the other woman. Her smile blinded me, and I threw up a hand to shield myself. What was I doing here? Who was Lynette?

"Denny!" Hot breath brushed my face.

"Let her alone, Jude. She's sleeping."

I sat up and switched on the bedside lamp, the room slowly swimming into focus.

"No, she's not! Her eyes are open, see?"

I shifted to make room for Jude. His brown legs were nearly as long as mine, and that sweet little-boy smell I remembered was gone, replaced by the scented gel he'd taken to using in his hair. He'd told me he had a girlfriend named

Ruth Ann Painter—an older woman, a second grader—whose daddy was an orthodontist and who lived in a big ranch-style house complete with a Shetland pony, a pet crow that did tricks, and a paved outdoor basketball court. Everybody seemed to think this little romance was harmless except for Lucy, who worried that being known as a ladies' man was possibly not in a seven-year-old's best interest.

"I'm going to run your bath, Jude," she said from the doorway. "You've got a game tomorrow, remember?"

"Our team is the champions!" he said to me.

"Not yet, you're not. You've got one more team to beat first," Lucy reminded him.

"We'll beat 'em." Jude fitted his head under my chin. For all his long legs and sharp angles, he was a surprisingly snuggly child. "Where's the guy from the picnic table?" he asked as the sound of running water came up the hall.

"I don't know."

"Maybe he went home," Jude said.

"Maybe so."

"Then you could stay here with us, right?"

"Not for long, I couldn't."

"How come?"

"Because I've got to go out on the road with my band, that's how come."

"Daddy used to do that," Jude said. "But not anymore."

"He might again, someday."

Jude lifted his head and looked at me. "He told you?"

"No." I thought back to the night before. "Just wishful thinking, I guess."

Lucy reappeared in the doorway. "Let's go, champ. Bath time, then a story, then bed."

I gave him a pat on the hip, and he slid off the bed. "Daddy's going back on the road!" I heard him tell Lucy as she steered him toward the bathroom.

"He is? How do you know?"

"Just wistful thinking," he said.

I stood and stretched and went to the window. My pickup and Daddy's were there, along with Lucy's Blazer, but still no sign of Will's Audi.

"How was your day?" Lucy stood in the doorway holding Jude's pajamas.

"Okay. I had breakfast with Erasmus. We went to visit Evelyn."

She nodded, but I could tell her mind was somewhere else. "Is Will around?"

"Haven't seen him since this morning."

"We've all been over at Bailey and Geneva's," she said. "A party for the new baby. I left you a message on the machine, but I guess you didn't get it." I shook my head; I hadn't thought to check. "Have you had your supper?"

"Some meat loaf from the icebox."

"I'm going to get Jude into bed. Why don't you come on downstairs and have a cup of tea with your daddy and me?"

Here it was, finally: the talk I'd been dreading. I sat on the bed for a while and tried to come up with something to say in my own defense, but it was hopeless.

As I passed Jude's door, Lucy was reading to him from *Charlie and the Chocolate Factory*. The phone rang, and I paused halfway down the stairs as Daddy answered in the kitchen, but I couldn't make out what he was saying, just the soft rise and fall of his voice.

I walked in as he was setting the handset back in its cradle. He gave me a long look, head to toe.

"Shit," I said. "Lucy told you, didn't she?"

"Didn't I tell you that man would leave you in a world of hurt?"

"It's not like I'm the first person in this family to get pregnant without meaning to," I said.

"Even more reason to make sure it doesn't happen to you."

"Shouldn't we wait for Lucy, so the two of you can gang up on me?"

He turned to look at me across the table, a look that implied I was personally liable for every gray hair on his head. "What do you aim to do, Denise?" he asked.

"I don't know yet."

"How far along are you?"

"About eight weeks, I think."

"Does Will know?"

"We haven't been getting along too great lately, in case you hadn't noticed."

"You must've been getting along fine eight weeks ago."

I felt the heat rise to my face. I had a pretty open relationship with my daddy, but not *that* open.

"Never mind," he said. "What I want to know is, do you mean to stay with this man?"

Lucy came in carrying an armload of towels for the

washer. She sized up what was going on in about two seconds and gave Daddy a sharp look. "Didn't I ask you to wait so we could have this discussion together, all three of us?"

"I was just getting Denise to bring me up to speed," Daddy said, "seeing's how I'm arriving a little late at this particular party."

"Well, sit down and hush, both of you," Lucy said. "I'll start this laundry, and then we'll talk."

By the time she came back the kettle was whistling, and Daddy lifted it off the stove and filled three mugs, and dropped in bags of Constant Comment. They had a whole cupboard full of teas in dozens of flavors, but Daddy always came back to this old-time brand. It was one of those little quirks about a person that can either touch your heart or drive you nuts, depending on your mood.

"Look," Lucy said, motioning that we should all sit down, "I don't know what your daddy has said to you. But we talked this over earlier tonight, and . . ." She paused to stir some honey into her tea. "I know it might feel like now isn't the right time or place for you to be having a baby. But we want you to know that we're here for you, whatever you decide."

"Thanks," I said. I wished I'd just pretended to stay asleep when Jude came in earlier. I didn't think I could stand the way Daddy was looking at me.

"I'm not saying it right," Lucy went on. "What I mean is—" She looked at Daddy, who looked into his cup. "If you decide you want to have this baby, we'll help you out."

"Help me, how?"

"Well, you can't very well take a baby on the road, can you?"

"You take a year off now, you'll never get it back," Daddy said.

"So, let's see if I've got this straight," I said. "I get rid of the baby and keep my career, or I have the kid and wind up a has-been at twenty-two."

"No, that's what I've been trying to say," Lucy said. "I think there's another way to do it, if you want."

"How?" Honestly, it was like pulling teeth sometimes, getting folks to come to the point.

"Leave the baby with us."

"You mean—to raise? Like it was yours?"

"Not ours. But we'd give it—that is, him, or her—a home while you're on the road. You'd visit when you could, or we'd bring the baby to you. And maybe by the time he's a little older, you'll be in a better place to take him along."

For the first time since I'd first guessed I might be pregnant, I let myself picture it: a baby, fat and smelling of sweet pink lotion, waving its little fists in the air. Loretta Lynn Farrell. Technically, I guessed her last name would be Culpepper, but I didn't want to get tripped up by that now. I wanted to hold the image of her in my head and see if it was real or just some trick, like the faces you think you see by the side of the road when you've been driving all night on nothing but cigarettes and talk radio.

Lights swung across the kitchen window and went out.

"Denny," Lucy said, "you've got to tell Will. He has a say in this, too, whether you like it or not."

A car door opened and shut, then someone was knocking at the front door.

"For goodness' sake, go let him in."

I dragged myself down the hall and switched on the porch light. I'd been bracing myself for Will's bedraggled ass, so the sight of the person standing on the other side of the screen, shielding his eyes from the glare, just about knocked me sideways.

"Ty!" My heart shot up and off the top of my skull like a pinball, ricocheted down my throat and made a few loops in my chest and my stomach, caromed down to my toes. "What are you doing here?"

"I've come a damn long way to be left standing on the front step like some Jehovah's Witness with a suitcase full of pamphlets. Come on, ask me in," he said. "I won't preach at you, I promise."

I unlatched the screen and stepped aside. I caught a whiff of him as he squeezed past, the leathery aftershave he always wore, the smell of a just-smoked cigarette.

"You drove here from Nashville?"

"Straight through. Had to stop about half a dozen times to get directions to your daddy's place, though. Man, folks around here are choosy who they talk to. Why aren't you answering your cell?"

"I lost it." It was only partly a lie.

"Tyler Briggs." Daddy came up behind me and stuck out his hand. "Good to see you, old son. We've been expecting you."

"You have?" Ty asked as they shook.

"No such thing as a secret in this town. I've had three calls in the past hour telling me some stranger's been driving around, asking how to get here."

I followed them to the kitchen, where Lucy was running the coffeepot full of water, shaking grounds into a paper filter. She'd either guessed or remembered that Ty was a hardcore caffeine addict.

"How've you been, man?" Ty asked as he took the chair Daddy offered. "You look in fighting trim."

"Don't be fooled. I threw my back out. Occupational hazard."

"Damn," Ty said. "Being a songwriter's a harder job than I thought it was."

I tried to signal him that this was a sore subject, but he just sat there wearing his easygoing smile.

"Ash, you'll have to take Ty out and show him your studio," Lucy said. "He spent all last winter building it," she told Ty as she took a coffeecake out of the microwave and placed it on the table. "It's really something. State of the art."

"I don't believe Ty came all the way down here to see my studio," Daddy said.

Everybody looked at me. "What?" I said. I got up and set my teacup in the sink.

"You must be hungry, Ty," Lucy said. "Can I fix you some eggs or something?"

"Oh, no, thank you, ma'am," he said. "I ate a couple hours ago, in Texarkana. This cake looks good, though."

She handed around plates and forks and cut the coffeecake into generous slices. I picked at mine while the others made small talk about weather—hot and getting hotter—and the price of gasoline—high and going higher. I snuck glances at Ty when I could. His hair was longer than I remembered, combed to one side. As always, his shirt was long-sleeved, the collar buttoned to his throat and pressed, like his jeans, to within an inch of its life. If you happened to pass him on the street, you'd never guess he was in the music business. Instead of partying all night and sleeping all day, he played golf, something I and the rest of the band found hilarious.

Every now and then he'd glance over at me and give me a careful half smile. Most of the time Ty was an open book, but tonight I found I couldn't read him. I felt the way I had in grade school when I was about to be called to the principal's office and needed to come up with some pretty fancy excuses pretty fast.

Lucy began to load the dishwasher, and Daddy said he was going upstairs to soak his back in the tub. "Sure I can't get you anything else?" Lucy asked. "I could start another pot of coffee."

"I'm good, thanks," Ty said.

"Have you got a place to stay? We'd be glad to put you in the guest room for the night."

"I found myself a motel not too far from here. The Piney View, I think it's called?"

Daddy and Lucy traded a glance, and I laughed out loud.

"What's so funny?" Ty asked with a puzzled smile.

"Not a thing," Lucy said. "I'm sure you'll find it very comfortable."

"How would you know? It's not like you ever actually slept there," I said.

"That's enough, Denise," Daddy said. "Try not to scare the man off so fast, huh? Let's at least try and pretend we're civilized."

Good-night kisses and handshakes were exchanged, and Ty and I sat in silence as Lucy and Daddy went upstairs. I asked Ty if he wanted what was left of the coffee.

"Hit me," he said. I got up and poured the last couple of inches into his cup, then unplugged the machine, rinsed out the pot, and set it upside down on a dish towel. I stared out the window over the sink, but there was nothing to see but woods and water against a moonless sky.

"So," he said, "you want to tell me what's going on? What was so all-fired important that you just took off without telling anybody?" I turned to look at him. "Don't yank my chain, Denny," he said. "You owe me that. Anyhow, I'll know if you do, so save us both the trouble."

"Well, for starters," I said, "we have to find a new fiddle player."

"I know all about it."

"You do?"

"Nashville's a pretty small town," he said. Like I needed reminding. "So we're out a fiddle player. So what? Fiddle players are a dime a dozen."

I started playing with the fringe on the dish towel. "What about bass players? Are they a dime a dozen, too?"

Ty set down his cup. "Didn't I tell you when you first started making goo-goo eyes at Will Culpepper that there was nothing but bad news down that road?"

"Have you been talking to my daddy?"

"No. What are you talking about?"

"Never mind. So, are you happy now? You had to drive five hundred miles to rub my face in it?"

"That's not why I'm here, and you know it."

"Then why? Why are you here?"

The icemaker came on with a click and a hum.

"Because," Ty said quietly, "you are my business."

"Yeah, 'business,' as in 'meal ticket.'" I knew I ought to stop, but I couldn't seem to help myself. I never had been able to leave well enough alone.

"Don't put words in my mouth," he said. "I mean 'business' as in 'concern.' As in, I think you've gotten yourself in a mess, and I might be able to help you out of it."

He had no idea how right he was, about the mess part.

"Maybe I just needed a break and missed my family," I said.

"Even if I bought that, which I don't, it isn't like you to just up and disappear. Not without letting me know."

"Hey, I'm off the clock, aren't I? We don't go out on the road again for six weeks."

"That doesn't mean a six-week vacation. You have obligations." I turned back to the window, but the view was the same as it had been two minutes before. "The least you could have done was let me know," he said.

"Because I'm your 'business'?"

"Goddamn it, girl! Why are you making this harder than it has to be?"

He looked bone-tired in the glare of the kitchen light, the lines around his mouth and eyes deeper than I remembered. Maybe I ought to suggest that Daddy replace the fixtures, install some of those pink bulbs that make everybody look like an old-time movie star.

"How are Tina and the kids?" I asked, to change the subject.

"The kids are fine. I had them last weekend. We went to Graceland." Ty laughed, rubbing his eyes with the backs of his wrists. "Jeremy's idea. Lately he's been obsessed with the King. Grace, on the other hand, seemed to think the place was some kind of amusement park named after her. She was pretty pissed to find out it's just a big, tacky house full of some dead guy's gold records."

He pulled an envelope out of his shirt pocket and took out a handful of photos, fanning them across the tabletop. There was Jeremy, twelve years old, outside Graceland's famous gates, another of him and Grace, his eight-year-old sister, next to one of the stone lions that flanked the house's front door. Jeremy again, this time in front of a mannequin modeling the black leather suit worn by Elvis on his '68 Comeback Special. A shot of both kids in the Memory Garden, Elvis's tomb in the background surrounded by gaudy wreaths and throngs of Japanese tourists. Finally a group portrait outside the Heartbreak Hotel, Ty and Jeremy grinning, Grace looking like somebody was holding a gun at her back.

"You really stayed there—Heartbreak Hotel?"

"It was fun. Even Grace got into it once she found out we had pay-per-view and room service." Ty shuffled the snapshots into a stack.

"Where are they now?"

"Back home in Nashville, with the queen of the hell-bitches."

So much for my question about Tina. Ty had gotten involved with her when Jeremy and Grace were six and two,

right after her husband, Gary, dumped her. Their relationship had been trouble from the start—Tina had problems
with cocaine and credit cards—and they'd split up after
eighteen months, but Ty had continued to be there for her
kids, not just trips to Graceland, but parent-teacher meetings
and soccer games and college funds. It killed him when Tina
went on one of her rants and talked about getting back together with Gary and moving them all to California, something she did periodically when she wanted to shake Ty down
for a trip to Neiman's or a spa weekend with her girlfriends.
Never mind that Gary had remarried and had two more kids
out in L.A., that he'd never paid a lick of alimony or child support, that he never called or even sent cards on Grace's and
Jeremy's birthdays. Tina had Ty by the short hairs and they
both knew it. Like a priest or a prisoner, he was in for life.

"You know who you remind me of?" I said. "The guy in
the cowboy movie who always comes riding in at the last
minute and saves the day."

"I don't know about that," Ty answered. "I think I may
have finally learned my lesson."

"Keep clear of bitches from hell?"

"Keep clear of women with kids," he said, slipping the
photographs back in his pocket. "One trip to Heartbreak
Hotel is enough for me."

The phone rang. Probably another good citizen of
Mooney, wanting to let us know about the stranger sniffing
around town.

"Miz Farrell?" It was a man's voice, roughened by cigarettes.

"This is Denny Farrell," I said. "Ash's daughter."

"It's the wife," the man said to somebody on his end.

"Excuse me? Hello?" I said. Ty was miming at me to tell him what was going on. I turned to the window and ignored him.

"This is Leon Yancy. I run a place called the Tap."

"I know your place." I also knew that nothing good ever happened there, unless you were a fan of hangovers and fist-fights.

"I got a feller here says he's your husband. Found him passed out in the back of my barman's truck."

"Oh, God."

"Now, I can call the sheriff and have her run him in, let him sleep it off downtown. Or you can come fetch him. It's your call."

Ty stood up and took the receiver from my hand. He was silent for a minute, listening, and then I heard his voice, steady as a judge, thanking Mr. Yancy for calling and saying we were on our way.

HOW COME YOU didn't tell me he was here?"

Ty fumbled with the dashboard lighter, firing up a Marlboro. He inhaled hungrily, then blew the smoke out the crack in the window and mashed down on the accelerator of his big Dodge 4x4 with the trailer hitch and the Bambi bumper.

"You better slow down," I said. "There's a mean cop who likes to lay back in the woods Friday nights with a radar gun."

Ty acted like he hadn't heard me, clenching the cigarette between his lips, his left hand loose on the wheel.

"I wasn't hiding it or anything," I said. "I just hadn't got around to it yet."

"How long has he been here?" Ty jerked his head around. "Jesus. Did you bring him *with* you?"

"No! He followed me." It took a lot to get Ty riled up, but when he did, look out.

"How far is this place? I thought you said it was just a few miles."

"It's up ahead, on the right."

In a clearing a few feet off the road stood a small, square building of concrete blocks, strung year-round with Christmas lights. A handful of vehicles was strewn willy-nilly across the gravel parking lot, like dice tossed from a giant's hand. Will's little blue Audi two-seater looked as out of place among the rusty pickups and ancient sedans as a sapphire in a box full of junk jewelry.

"Thank God he didn't try and drive," Ty said as we pulled in. "I can just imagine trying to get him off a DUI down here."

"You don't have to deal with this," I reminded him. "Just drop me off. I can take him home."

Ty shut off the engine and sat staring out the windshield, his face rainbow streaked by the Christmas lights. "Let me do the talking," he said as he got out, dropping his cigarette and grinding it out with his heel.

The room was dim and smoke filled, only a couple of patrons at the bar. A jukebox stood silent along one wall, and a small color TV over the bar was showing a basketball game, the volume turned low. A fat man with a bald head and a goatee stood beneath it, polishing glasses with a rag and watching us.

"Mr. Yancy?" Ty strode forward, his voice a little too loud for the room.

"In back," the barman said. "I'll get him."

The regulars sat hunched over their beer bottles, glassy-eyed, like a museum exhibit. I was grateful for Ty's unwavering confidence as he folded his hands on the bar, propping one boot on the rail, and turned his face toward the TV.

"Who's ahead?" he asked.

"Pistons up by six at the half," one of the men grunted. "But the Bulls gonna come out on top."

"Got anything riding on it?" Ty asked.

"Not this time. Lost a shitload the first time, though, back in '92."

The bald guy reappeared along with a small, neat man in a black western shirt and the kind of crew cut once favored by the likes of George Jones. "Y'all here about the drunk feller?"

Ty pulled himself up straight. He was half a head taller than the other customers and had a foot, maybe, on the owner. "Yes, sir, we are."

"He's out back, by the Dumpster," the man said. "He can puke all he wants in them bushes, but I won't have Art here swabbin' up the men's room after the likes a him."

"We appreciate you calling us, Mr. Yancy," Ty said.

"Well. I got no more use for the law than the next man."

Ty's hand went to his hip pocket. "What do we owe you for your trouble, sir?"

"I reckon you can settle his tab," Mr. Yancy said. "Twenty dollars orter cover it."

Ty pushed thirty across the bar, and Mr. Yancy folded the bills into his palm.

"I reckon you can tell him he ain't welcome here no more, neither, once he comes to. These big-city fellers, waltzin' in here actin' like their shit don't stink . . ." Mr. Yancy glanced at me. " 'Scuse me, missy. I best keep my trap shut. Just take him on home and put him to bed, hear? And see that he don't come back."

Ty jabbed his thumb into the small of my back. "Yes, sir," I said. "Thank you, sir."

We followed Mr. Yancy through an office with a big metal desk covered in papers, an overflowing ashtray, and an old-fashioned hand-crank adding machine, liquor boxes stacked against the walls practically to the ceiling. He pushed open a heavy metal door and, with a jerk of his head, indicated that we should step outside.

Will sat against the rear of the building on an empty beer keg, his head propped against the wall. I said his name, and he opened one eye and squinted at me.

"Oh boy," he said. He reeked of whiskey and cigarette smoke, but then, that was pretty much Will's standard aroma.

"You sorry sack of shit," Ty said. "I ought to break your legs right here, you know that?"

Will swiveled his head to peer at Ty. "Ho," he said. "Look who's here. The fuckin' cavalry."

"Get up," Ty nudged Will's foot with his. "We're taking you home."

"Don' wanna go home," Will said. "Like it here. Nice out. Stars." He waved a hand toward the sky. I guess he was too far gone to appreciate the Eau de Dumpster.

Ty leaned forward and grasped Will by the shoulders, jerking him upright. "Listen up. Mr. Yancy here has offered us two options. You can either come with us, or he'll call the sheriff. You want to sleep this off at home, or in a jail cell? Because it's the same to me either way."

"Lady sheriff," Will mumbled. "Big broad. Scary. Eat you alive."

"Fine," Ty said, reaching into his pocket for his cell phone. "I'll give her a call."

"Put that away." I leaned toward Will, my face close to his. "Will, get up. I need to talk to you."

Will laughed, his head swaying on his neck like a flower too heavy for its stalk. "Chicks," he said. "Never give ya a break. Always wanna *talk*."

"Will, come on. This is serious."

"Ooh, *serious*." He fluttered his fingers mockingly in the air.

"I'm pregnant."

For a second his eyes opened wide. Then his head drooped forward and he slid in a boneless heap to the ground.

"Will!" I crouched beside him and grabbed his arm. "Goddamn it." I twisted my head to look at Ty. "I think he fainted."

"No kidding. Jesus, Denny."

"Remember how you said you thought I was in trouble and you wanted to help me?" I said. "Well, you were right."

Ty prodded Will's leg with the toe of his boot.

"Let's see if we can get him to the truck."

Mr. Yancy called his barman, and together they and Ty wrangled Will into the backseat of Ty's pickup. We found the keys to the Audi in Will's pocket, and it was decided that I'd drive it home, leading the way.

The bullet-shaped little car cut a neat swath in the dark, Ty's headlights bouncing like twin moons in my rearview mirror. The air was damp and heavy, the stars Will claimed to be admiring earlier obscured by a low scrim of cloud. From the CD player Johnny Cash sang, "Sooner or later God'll cut you down." What would it be like, I wondered, to live your life unencumbered by expectation, folks prodding and pushing at you to see things their way? I envied Aunt Dove, who never seemed to give a rat's ass what anybody else thought, who for seventy-some-odd years had been making up her own rules as she went along. I even envied Evelyn a little bit—not the wasting away and totally dependent part, but the part that allowed her mind to shift through the hodgepodge of her life like a miner panning for gold, washing away the grit, hanging on to the shiny pieces.

The house was dark when we pulled in. I cut the headlights and the engine, but climbing out from behind the wheel suddenly felt like more effort than I could muster.

Ty rapped on the window with his knuckles.

"Help me get him out," he said.

"Can't we just leave him here?" Will lay on the backseat of Ty's pickup, still as a dead man.

"And take a chance on him puking up my truck? Not on your life."

"Well, what are we gonna do with him?"

"We can dump him in the pond for all I care. Where's he *been* sleeping?"

The screen door opened and Lucy stepped outside in her nightgown and bare feet.

"Is everything all right?" she called.

"Will passed out at Leon Yancy's place," I answered.

"Oh, Lord. Marjo didn't arrest him, did she?"

"No, ma'am," Ty said. "We've got him right here, in my truck."

Lucy came over and looked into the back of the pickup. "Oh," she said again in a faraway voice. I guessed she must have been thinking about Daddy, all those nights before he'd sobered up.

"Ty's afraid he'll get sick if we leave him here," I said, "but I can't think where else to put him."

"I would say the couch, but I don't know that I want him getting sick all over my living room, either," she said.

"How about the picnic table?" I said. "That seemed to suit him fine last night." *There,* I thought, answering Ty's question without admitting I was doing it.

"We could put him in the trailer."

"The trailer?" Ty and I said in unison.

"That little trailer of your daddy's," Lucy said. "The one he lived in last year, remember, over at the old house? I've been after him to sell it, but he won't do it. It's around back, behind the house. No lights or water or anything, but the furniture's still in it. We could take Will out there. If he does get sick— Well, he couldn't make the place any worse than it already is."

"Like hell he couldn't," Daddy said from the porch. I guess he'd heard enough and figured out the rest.

"Have you got a better suggestion?" I could tell Lucy was wishing he'd stayed inside. Five minutes more and we'd have had Will bedded down and Daddy would never have been the wiser.

"What's wrong with the drunk tank downtown? If it was good enough for me, it's good enough for Will Culpepper."

"I would think—no offense, sir—that you wouldn't want your daughter's husband and the father of her child having to go to court for public intoxication," Ty said.

Daddy opened his mouth, then shut it again. I could tell he had something else to say, along the lines of that being just what Will deserved, but "father of her child" seemed to have brought him up short.

"All right," he said. "Let's make it quick."

"Ash, don't you even think about trying to lift him," Lucy said. "You won't be able to get out of bed for a week."

"I'll do it," Ty said. "Lead the way."

"Denny, run inside and get some sheets from the linen closet," Lucy said. "And stop by the laundry room and grab the bucket."

By the time I got out to the trailer, Ty had managed to get Will up the cinder-block steps and into the living room, where he sat on the threadbare couch, moaning softly into his hands. Daddy had brought a little Coleman lantern from the shed and set it on the coffee table, where it threw off soft shadows. The place smelled like Lysol and kerosene and was stuffy as hell, even though Lucy was going around opening windows. In the past few minutes Daddy had stopped being mad and decided to treat the whole thing like some big joke.

"I told you this place would come in handy," he said to Lucy. "A flophouse for drunks. Fitting, when you think about it."

"I wish you'd go back to bed, both of you," I said. "Really. Ty and I can take it from here."

Lucy insisted on helping me make up the bed, then she and Daddy left, kissing me good-night for the second time. Ty and I steered Will into the bedroom, where he fell face-down on the mattress. I set the bucket next to the bed.

"Shouldn't we take off his boots or something?" Ty said. "That's what they always do in the movies."

I knelt on the carpet and lifted one of Will's feet in my hands. He and I had courted shamelessly in public and in private, pawing and fawning all over each other everywhere we went; but somehow, the act of pulling off his boots as Ty watched from the doorway felt more personal than making out with him in front of my whole band.

"What are you gonna do?" Ty asked as I set the boots in the corner.

"You mean for now?" I asked. "Or, like, permanently?" I couldn't read his face, and he didn't answer me. "I ought to stay with him, don't you think?"

"You mean for now? Or, like, permanently?" Ty's voice was lightly mocking. He took two steps forward and put his hand on my shoulder. "This is no good, Denny," he said. "It's one thing to have a husband who's catting around on you, but a baby—"

"I haven't made up my mind about that yet."

"Just answer me one thing," he said. "Do you want me to leave and let you deal with this on your own? Because if you do, say so and I'll turn around and head on home."

The lantern cast flickering shadows on the wall while outside a moth threw itself, over and over, against the screen.

"It seems like a shame to miss spending the night at the Piney View Motor Court," I said.

"Don't joke. And don't try and act like you don't know what I'm saying, because you do." Will thrashed for a minute on the mattress, then lay still. "Okay," Ty said. "I guess I'll go back to the motel. But I'm offering you a deal here, girl. I want you to think about that while you're sitting here holding his head over that bucket. See you tomorrow."

Ty left, the whole trailer shaking as the door slammed behind him. Quiet moved in to fill the space where he'd stood, the words he'd said. In it, I could hear Will snoring softly, the moth at the screen, and underneath it all, the watery beating of my heart, being pulled in so many different directions at once.

CHAPTER 14

Lucy

"I'M TELLING YOU, Lucy Bird, what you need is a garden."

Dove and I sat on the porch swing drinking coffee and shelling black-eyed peas. At ten in the morning it was already muggy, the air shimmering thickly over the pond. Ash and Jude were inside oiling Jude's glove for his Little League game. Denny's bed upstairs hadn't been slept in; I guessed she'd spent the night out back with Will.

"At least you didn't say what I need is a baby," I said. "You get points for that."

"I reckon you got enough on your plate without adding more human beans to the mix." I'd called her at dawn and spilled the whole story, and she'd driven out toting two paper sacks full of vegetables and a quart of berries from her deep freeze. "Lookit that spot yonder," she said, pointing with her chin. "It's a good size, and the light's just right. Seems a crime letting it run wild like that."

"Isn't it a little late to be putting in a garden?"

"How many times do I have to say it? It's never too late. You work with what you have. And what you have is time and talent."

"Talent?"

"You got able-bodied men, sounds like, comin' out the doors and windows."

I laughed; this much was true.

"What I haven't got is your green thumb." I was remembering the spring after Mitchell died, how the tomato plants I'd set out behind my rent house in a burst of optimism had washed away in a three-day flood, how once Ash started coming around I'd never gotten around to replanting.

"No such thing as a green thumb, you ask me," she said. "Mostly what it takes is frame of mind. You got to say to yourself, 'Doggone it, I'm a gardener.' You don't even got to b'lieve it. You just got to think it, and do the work, and before you know it, it's true."

"Like magic!"

"You want to know how come I ain't ever gotten old?" Dove asked. I looked over at her as she sipped her coffee, her snow-white hair and skin like a leather satchel, and smiled. "It's because I got something needs tendin'. Ever single day I hafta get up and see to my garden. And ever single day I learn somethin' I didn't know the day before." She reached over and patted my arm. "You get yourself some stuff that's green and growin', Lucy Bird, you got no time for worryin' about the stuff you can't do nothin' about. Anyhow, it's just a little patch of dirt. What've you got to lose?"

I had a retort in mind concerning heatstroke and sunburn, but I kept it to myself as a battered Chevelle pulled into the yard, royal blue metal-flake with patches of primer on the doors and hood. "Who in the world?" I said. Surely Denny had already exceeded her quota for gentlemen callers.

It was one of her long-timers, though, I saw as Erasmus King unfolded his lanky frame from the beat-up car. Even as a boy Erasmus had had a natural majesty, and at the sight of him standing next to the Chevelle in his loose linen pants and leather slippers, I wanted to laugh out loud.

"That's some chariot, Mr. King," I said, getting up to give him a hug.

"One thing about having a mechanic for a daddy," he said. "You get the pick of the fleet."

"Your daddy got me my first car," I said. "The first one I ever owned outright."

"I remember that car. Big old green Buick, right? Looked like a Sherman tank. Noisy as all get-out, too."

"Sometimes I wish I'd never let J.D. buy it back from me."

"Shoot, it's probably still sitting out behind the shop somewhere," Erasmus said. "I could check if you want."

He accepted my offer of coffee, and I went inside to fetch more cups and start a fresh pot. When I got back, he and Dove were discussing the garden. My enthusiasm or consent, it appeared, were not necessary for this venture, which in the past few minutes seemed to have taken on a life of its own.

"I'm not sure you're getting the whole picture," I told

Erasmus once I could get a word in edgewise. "She's talking about you laying the groundwork."

"Me?"

"Among others."

"What others?"

Before I could start to explain, a black Dodge 4x4 came jouncing up the road and parked behind the Chevelle. Erasmus turned, shading his eyes with his hand as Ty Briggs climbed down from the cab and came ambling onto the porch looking fresh scrubbed and buttoned down, smelling pleasantly of cigarette smoke and aftershave.

Erasmus got to his feet and I introduced them. "Ty's Denny's manager," I offered, not sure how much either of them knew about the other. "Raz is an old friend of Denny's. You remember my aunt Dove, from our trip to Garland a while back."

"Oh, yes, ma'am." As Ty leaned forward to grasp Dove's hand, I was astonished to see her cheeks turn pink. "I've heard of you," Ty said, turning to Erasmus. "The fiddle player. Old boyfriend, right?"

"Ancient history," Raz said breezily.

I poured Ty a cup of coffee, and he took a drink. "Thanks. This is a sight better than that swill they charge a buck for at the café downtown."

"Burton charged you a dollar?" The usual cost for coffee at the café was fifty cents.

"The eggs were cold, too."

"Sounds like you got the out-of-towner's special," I said. "You should've come here straight off, let me make you breakfast. Especially considering what we put you through last night."

"What happened last night?" Erasmus asked.

"Will got himself in a little trouble at Leon Yancy's place. Ty and Denny bailed him out."

"Not literally," Ty added. "So, he still out back sleeping it off?"

"As far as I know. I haven't heard a peep out of either one of them this morning. You know, maybe I ought to run and check."

I carried an armload of cups to the kitchen, then walked up the back hall and down the steps. As I crossed the backyard, I could hear Denny's voice through the trailer's open windows.

"Come on, Will, cut it out."

I froze, trying to decide what to do. She didn't sound particularly angry, or in distress. Will laughed then, low and throaty, and Denny's voice dropped to a murmur. I stood there another minute or so, my feelings in an uneasy tangle, before I returned to the front porch.

Erasmus sat on the top step sipping his coffee while Dove and Ty strolled through the field below the house, Ty blocking out measurements with his hands.

"Miss Dove seems to be entertaining a little infatuation," Erasmus said.

"Raz, can I ask you a personal question?"

"Shoot."

"Do you ever think about what might have happened if you and Denny had— If things had been different, and you'd stayed together?"

He and I'd never had what you'd call a close relationship, but the question didn't seem to faze him. "Sure," he said. "All the time."

"But?"

"It wouldn't have worked out. She's in love with somebody else, for starters."

We looked at each other. "You know this for a fact?" I said.

"No, but I know her pretty well. She didn't have to spell it out for me." He leaned back against the porch rail, hugging his knees to his chest. "Anyway, I'm moving to Paris in September."

"Paris, France?"

"My girlfriend, Camille, got a graduate fellowship over there. We decided it was time to take it to the next level."

"Wow," I said, "I'm impressed by your definition of 'the next level.'"

"Like I said. It's time."

"But meanwhile, here you are."

"Yeah. It's crazy, isn't it? Denny's like this, this force field, sucking in everything in its path. I don't even think she does it on purpose. In her head she's just this pissed-off little girl trying to figure out how to make people love her.

"But it's different, knowing I'm going away. I can be around her and still breathe, if you know what I mean. And her life is complicated enough without me," Raz said as Ty Briggs came out of Ash's toolshed dragging the rototiller, squatting to fill it from a red gas can. I didn't even know if the thing still worked, but he gave the cord a couple of hard yanks and it roared to life. Ty peeled off his long-sleeved shirt and tossed it on the woodpile, then set to work in his under-shirt.

Erasmus glanced at me, and we started to laugh. This was starting to seem like one of those TV shows where male contestants compete to win the hand of the bachelor girl—never mind that the girl in question was nowhere in sight. Dove gave a sharp whistle and waved Erasmus over.

"Uh-oh," he said. "Here we go."

"You don't have to do this, you know."

"What, and let some Nashville hot dog show me up?"

Minutes later Erasmus was hauling lumber out of the shed, his hundred-dollar shirt tied around his waist. Dove came back onto the porch and sank onto the swing, fanning herself with her garden hat.

"You shouldn't be out in the hot sun like that," I chided her.

"Shoot, this is nothin'. Wait'll July rolls around and you're out there tryin' to keep your tomatoes from shrivelin' up."

"I haven't got tomatoes."

"You didn't have no garden, neither, ten minutes ago." She grinned. "Face it, Lucy Bird. Sometimes other folks know better 'n you do what you need. You just got to sit back and let 'em do for you."

"Where will those folks be in July, when everything's shriveling up?"

Just then Denny came out the front door onto the porch. Her hair was twisted into a messy topknot, and she wore a pair of my cutoffs and one of her daddy's wash-worn T-shirts.

She paused to watch Raz stack timber rails and Ty maneuver the heavy tiller.

"What's going on?"

"Dove decided I need a garden."

Denny nodded, like this made perfect sense.

"Everything okay?" I asked, remembering what I'd overheard a little while earlier outside the trailer.

She looked at me sideways. "Why wouldn't it be?"

Will appeared inside the screen door, his wet hair slicked back. "Is that coffee I smell?"

"Will, I'd like you to meet my aunt, Dove Munroe," I said.

"Get yourself out here, son," Dove said. "There's work to be done."

"Work?" His voice was wobbly.

Dove sprang to her feet. "Sweat!" she declared. "Guaranteed to cure what ails you."

I poured myself the last of the coffee as Denny sat down beside me on the swing.

"Somebody's gonna have a heatstroke," Denny said.

"I tried to warn Dove, but she wasn't having any of it. Anyway, she's tough as a field hand."

"It's not Dove I'm talking about."

"Want to make a bet?" I said.

"On what?"

"Who'll be the last man standing."

"Well, I don't think Will's got much of a shot."

"No?"

"Look at him," she said as he staggered out of the shed toting a roll of chicken wire. "He can barely hold his head up."

"What about Raz?"

"Erasmus is a wild card," she said. "He's tougher than he looks."

"I don't think his heart's in it, though."

She nodded slowly. I noted how the blue of her eyes changed like water tumbling over rocks, dark in places, alive in others with runnels of light. Her nose was sunburned; wisps of hair clung damply to the back of her neck. What Erasmus had said about her was true; she had something that, like it or not, drew you in and wouldn't let go.

"That leaves Ty," I said.

She slapped her notebook against her thigh.

"Yeah," she said, and smiled a small, secret smile, like the madonnas in all those Italian portraits in my Michelin Green Guide. "It does."

IT'S NOT TRUE, what Tom Hanks said in that movie. There *is* crying in baseball, especially when a team of seven-year-olds loses the division championship by one run to their archrivals, the White Pine Bulldogs. Not even the second-place trophy or a trip to Pizza Rita's complete with unlimited sodas and video games could console them. Back home, Jude shut himself in his room and wouldn't come out for supper, or answer me when I asked through the door if he didn't want to ride down to Palestine the next morning with Dove and me to buy plants for the garden.

"Let him be, Lucy," Ash said as we were scraping the plates

and loading the dishwasher. "He'll work it out his own way, in his own time."

"Because he's a Farrell, you mean?" My tone was sharper than I intended, and Ash looked over his shoulder at me.

"Because he's his own person," he said. "Not some miniature carbon copy of you or me."

"He's a little boy, Ash. How's he supposed to learn how to deal with stuff like this if somebody doesn't teach him?"

He slammed the dishwasher door and locked it. "I just don't see what good there is in sugarcoating things."

"What makes you think that's what I want to do? Maybe I just want to feed him a hot dog and read him a story." Ash shook his head, looking out the window toward the pond. "You know," I said, "not everybody deals with life the way you do. Some people need comfort. And some of us need to give it."

I followed him as he turned and walked into the living room, where he dropped onto the sectional and aimed the remote at the TV, punching the volume button until the roar of stock cars filled the room.

"This is not comfort!" I shouted. "This is escape!" He tossed the remote onto the coffee table and sat back, folding his arms across his chest. "You don't even like NASCAR," I added, but the TV was so loud he couldn't hear me.

I went out onto the porch, where Denny sat in the swing, picking listlessly at the strings of one of her daddy's guitars. The sun had dropped below the tree line and a breeze had come up, bringing on it the scent of a far-off rain shower.

"I guess you probably want to be left alone, too," I said. "Like everybody else under this roof."

"I was just wishing for some company, actually." She scooted over, making a space for me. Even out here, the TV was audible.

"Lord," I said, easing myself down beside her, twisting my hair off my neck. "I'd cut off my arm for a beer. Where's Will?"

"Out back, sleeping off his hangover. That business with the garden this morning just about did him in." She set down the guitar. "Sounds like Daddy's got a bee up his butt," she said.

"You know, if you or I were acting this way, the guys would be blaming it on PMS."

"It's PMS, all right," she said. "Pissy Man Syndrome."

We laughed. It felt good to laugh with Denny, took me back to a time when things between us were always loose and easy.

"So, how're you doing?" I asked. "Any interesting developments you want to talk about?"

"Can I ask you something?" She plucked idly at the strings of the guitar.

"Sure."

"How long does it take to feel married?"

I pondered her question for a minute. "I don't think there's a regular time line. Sometimes I felt married to your daddy before we were truly married—legally, I mean. Then for a while, when things got really bad in Nashville, I didn't feel married to him at all. Then we came back home and started over, and it came back again, that feeling. Stronger than before."

"What about now?"

"Oh, yeah. Of course. You mean, just because he's in there acting like a pissy man? If anything, it makes me realize just how married I am. Being pissed off is a good thing. It's when you don't feel anything at all that you're in trouble."

"Did having a baby make it better?"

"Oh, honey. It changes things, that's for sure. But I think— I'm not sure how to say this. You shouldn't have a baby because you think it might make things right with Will, and you shouldn't *not* have it just because you think it won't.

"You know, your daddy and I barely knew each other when we found out I was pregnant. I didn't know whether he'd be glad about it or catch the next bus out of town, but I told myself that at least I'd have something of my own to love always, no matter what. But it doesn't work that way. A baby doesn't belong to you, even if it does seem that way for a little while. A baby belongs to the world. No less. The minute they cut the cord, both of you are on your own."

"That's pretty depressing," she said.

"I'm just trying to say that, no matter how much you love him, you can't lose sight of the fact that, from his very first breath, he's his own person. Not a— Oh, Lord."

"What?"

"I almost said 'a carbon copy of you.' It's what your daddy said to me about Jude, not five minutes ago. I guess I ought to start practicing what I preach, huh?"

Denny got up and walked over to the porch rail.

"Have you told Will yet?" I asked.

"Last night, when he was drunk off his ass at Yancy's," she

said. "I tried talking to him about it again this morning, but he wasn't really in the mood to discuss it."

"Well, some folks need more time than others to get used to new things," I said. "Remember how your daddy acted when he found out I was expecting Jude?"

"I don't want my baby growing up without a daddy," Denny said.

"I know," I said. "It's why I tried so hard to make things work with your daddy. For Jude's sake and yours, as much as my own."

"So you're saying I should stick it out with Will? Try harder?"

I could feel her eyes on me, but I couldn't make myself say what I was really thinking: that I believed Ash was a good man who would try to do the right thing, as much as it was in his power, even if he didn't always get it right on the first try; whereas Will Culpepper, from what I'd seen of him, would forever put his own interests ahead of everybody else's, no matter how hard you twisted his arm or how much slack you cut him.

"I don't think I can tell you that," I said. "But there's all kinds of ways to make a family. Blood's not the only way. It's not even always the best. You know that."

She sat down beside me and let her head drop onto my shoulder. I reached for her hand, wove her fingers through mine. Her fingertips were ridged with calluses, like her daddy's. If you listened hard, you could hear birds crying to one another in the woods, a car moving north along the FM road. A thin white sickle of moon was just visible beyond the tops of the pines across the pond. I smelled the heavy fragrance of Denny's hair, felt her soft, shallow breathing in my ear. Daughter of my heart, no two ways about it.

"Thanks," she said, wiping her nose on her wrist.

"I didn't do a thing."

"I think I'll go for a drive," she said. "Try and clear my head a little."

"Okay."

She went inside, came back out again with her keys in her hand.

"You be careful. You know how wild things get around here on Saturday nights," I said, and she laughed. "What do you want me to tell Will if he wakes up?"

"Tell him I'll see him when I see him."

I sat in the swing as the dust settled and her taillights vanished between the trees. Inside, the house was quiet. I stood and stretched, working a crick out of my neck. I thought of what Ash had said the night before, about the old giving way to the new, shit you couldn't do anything about. It wasn't in me to accept that. I was the daughter of Dove Munroe's heart, not Patsy Hatch's; and if being married to Ash had taught me anything, it was that trouble wasn't something you ran from, that sometimes it was worth it to turn around and stare it down.

I let myself in through the screen door. In the living room, Jude sat limp in Ash's lap, the two of them staring glassy-eyed at an old episode of *Star Trek*.

Ash gave Jude a nudge.

"Hi, Mama," he said.

"Hey there. How about a hot dog?"

"Okay." Ash murmured something in Jude's ear. "I mean, yes, please."

"You want mustard?"

"And relish!"

Ash and I looked at each other over Jude's head, a long look, weighted with history, shaded with dark and light. "Maintain thrust, Scotty," Captain Kirk said as under my feet something in the foundation of the house seemed to shift, the beams realigning along some invisible plane, slowly but surely bringing us back to the center.

CHAPTER 15

Denny

THERE WERE TWO girls in front of me at the Miracle Mart buying a six-pack of wine coolers, all decked out like drugstore cowgirls: Cruel Girl jeans, snap-button shirts, tooled belts, and polished Ropers. They caught me staring and gave me the kind of look that used to wilt me back in high school, a slow head-to-toe taking-in of my tank top and Levi's with the knees out, my scuffed-up, pointy-toed boots.

"Where're y'all headed?" I asked, flashing my teeth. I wasn't in high school anymore.

"The Round-Up," one of the girls, the blonde, said.

"Yeah? Who's playing?"

She pushed some money at the leering old guy behind the register.

"The Lonesome Pines. Just like every other damn Saturday night since the beginning of time." She gave the old man a look just to let him know she was on to him, and he rang her up and put the six-pack in a bag.

"Ash Farrell used to play at the Round-Up, didn't he?"

"So the story goes. Now it's just his lame-ass backup band. But what else you gonna do for fun in a town like this?"

"I might could hep you out there, honey," said the guy behind the register. A front tooth was missing, and he had about four strands of hair, grown long and combed in whorls on top of his head. He wore a greasy apron tied around his waist and a T-shirt that read SOUTH PADRE SPRING BREAK 1997.

"In your dreams, Klaus." The girls rolled their eyes at each other and headed out to a silver Toyota Tundra.

I stepped up and set my bottle of spring water on the counter, scanning the rows of cigarettes behind the register. A little voice seemed to whisper in my ear, teasing me with the memory of nicotine, that first sweet rush as the smoke hits your lungs.

"We got a sale on Merits," the man behind the counter said helpfully.

"Just a second." I was thinking about the conversation Will and I'd had that morning in the trailer. I'd been trying to explain to him that actions had consequences, that he needed to step up to the plate and help me face what we'd done. That was as far as I'd gotten before he started kissing my neck and groping me through my shirt, and I'd pushed him away and gone back to the house.

"Hey. I know you," the counterman suddenly said.

"No, sir. I'm not from around here."

"I seen you someplace before. On the TV, could be."

"Well, you never know. *America's Most Wanted,* maybe?"

I paid for my water, stuck the change in the Lung Cancer Association can next to the register, and walked back out to my truck, wondering why it was that I always had so much trouble taking my own advice.

MY HEART SKIPPED a beat at the sight of the neon lasso blinking against the night sky, pickups and cars jammed in tight against one another in the oyster-shell parking lot. I climbed out of the truck and stood for a minute listening to the sad, slithering wail of a steel guitar. My band had played here once a couple of years earlier, but my memories of the Round-Up were mostly from my first summer in Mooney, when Daddy sang here every Wednesday and Saturday night. Music was the way he and I found each other after so many years apart, two strangers at the opposite ends of a rope working their way toward the middle; and as I made my way toward the entrance, I found that, in spite of how crazy and impossible life could feel, I could still work up some anticipation for the good things that might still be in front of me.

Instead of old, blind Arless Cooper, who'd worked the door for about a hundred years, there was a thick-necked, bored-looking kid. He didn't have any idea who I was as I fished in my pocket and handed over the five-dollar cover charge. That suited me fine as I made my way through the crowd to the bar and bought a Coke from a guy with a blond crew cut.

While he counted out my change, I studied the photo of me that hung alongside one of Daddy, in matching frames, over the bar. I remembered that girl, with her sassy smile and fire-engine-red guitar, but I didn't feel like her. I wondered if I'd left her back in Nashville, or if she was gone for good. I knew I couldn't stay this way forever, one foot in that world and another in this one. Choose, or the world chooses for you. I couldn't remember who said that. Probably some dead Frenchman.

I stood for a while at the end of the bar, sipping my Coke and watching the dancers. A couple of guys ambled over, gave me the once-over, and sidled away. I guess, in my torn jeans and broken-down boots, I wasn't what they were used to, and I didn't much care.

Someone nudged my shoulder, and I turned to see Dub Crookshank, the Round-Up's owner, grinning at me over the bar.

"Hey, little girl," he said. "Thought you could sneak in here without anybody noticin', did ya?"

"I'm off duty tonight," I told him. "Don't blow my cover."

"You don't want to sit in? The boys'd get a kick out of it." I shook my head. "All right, then," he said. "You let me know if you need anything. And say hey to your daddy for me. I don't hardly never see him no more. It don't seem right, him livin' just up the road and all. Tell him I said don't be a stranger."

"Yes, sir. I'll do that."

The band came out and started strapping on their instruments. The jukebox fell silent, and after a quick three-count, they launched into Bob Wills's "Right or Wrong."

The music seemed to flip a switch inside me. I felt a tap on my shoulder, and looked around to see a gentleman in a pearl-snap shirt and a creased white Stetson. He touched the brim and gestured toward the dance floor. I nodded and set my bottle on the bar, and together we eased into the flow of dancers moving around the floor in the smoky light.

I hadn't done this in a long time, but before long my feet recalled the old rhythms and I found myself drifting into a daydream in which I was married, not to Will, but to this nice, soap-smelling, barrel-bellied man. He'd go off every morning to his job, selling cars or life insurance, and I would stay home and scrub the countertops, and every Wednesday and Saturday night we would come here and dance our boot leather off. His name was Bud, I decided. He liked fishing and baseball, and he was Baptist, but not the hard-shell kind. I would never have to pretend to be happy with Bud, because I would be, and never miss for a minute the life I'd left behind.

We danced to three songs, and by the end of the last one, a waltz, I was ready to follow him home, no questions asked. So it came as a shock when he escorted me back to the bar, smiled pleasantly, touched his hat brim again, and walked away. Two minutes later I saw him scoot by with a husky blonde in his arms. In spite of the fact that the band was playing "White Lightning," one of my favorite songs of all time, I felt defeated. Happiness was so damned hard to hang on to. Something was always waiting to trip you up.

I turned around to flag down the barman and there beside me, from out of nowhere, was Ty.

The barman pointed at him with his thumb and Ty held up my empty Coke bottle.

"Make it two," he shouted over the music.

"What are you doing here?" My heart was tripping in a way that I knew wasn't completely due to dancing or caffeine.

"I called the house. Lucy said you'd gone out. This was the first place I thought to look."

The barman pushed two frosty green bottles across the bar, and Ty handed him a five.

"Maybe you should just hire me a bodyguard," I said. "Or put one of those electronic things around my ankle, so you'll know where I am and what I'm doing every minute of the day."

He acted like he hadn't heard me, just stood there tapping his toe to the band. "You having a good time?"

"Yeah, I am. As a matter of fact, I'm in love."

"Is that so. Who with?"

"There," I said, pointing as the white-hatted man twirled by with another partner, a tiny lady with a stiff beehive and a full, swishy skirt. "His name's Bud. We're getting married and living happily ever after."

"Does Bud know you're already married?"

"We haven't actually discussed the marriage part yet. I just thought it up a minute ago, on the dance floor."

"I've got a feeling it's a good thing I showed up when I did."

I plucked the Coke out of Ty's hand and set it on the bar. "You dance with me, then."

"Whoa, now," he said as I took his arm and dragged him toward the floor. "I never claimed to be any kind of dancer."

"Come on, it's easy," I told him as we merged into the crowd. Couples swerved around us like cars trying to miss a jackknifed semi as I tried coaching him in the two-step. It didn't take long to figure out that Ty wasn't kidding about his lack of dance skills. He kept lurching the wrong direction, tromping on my toes. When people started piling into us and giving us dirty looks, I led him back to the bar, out of harm's way.

"That was pitiful," I said. "How can you spend so much time around this kind of music and not know how to dance to it?"

"I grew up in Connecticut, remember?" he said. "Anyway, I'm the business guy. If it's fancy footwork you want, better stick with old Bud."

He polished off his Coke and set the empty on the bar. "Let's get the hell out of here before I hurt somebody."

HALF AN HOUR later we were winding along the back roads of Cade County in Ty's pickup, the Burrito Brothers on the CD player. The windows were down and the cab smelled of night and woods and the smoke from Ty's cigarette. Our conversation was spotty and rambling, about not much in particular. I'd probably spent a hundred nights riding around with Ty in the three years I'd known him, smoking and talking, listening to music, but this felt different. There was an undercurrent of something, a taut, thrumming wire between us that scared me to think about it too hard.

"Hot Burrito #1" came on—Daddy's all-time favorite song, and one of mine—and Ty turned the volume up a notch. The highway unfurled black and endless in our headlights, boxed in on either side by tall pines, now and then a winking light from some trailer house, a floating poker chip of moon overhead. I leaned my head against the seatback and closed my eyes and let Gram Parsons's voice work its long, unearthly tendrils into me. "I'm your toy, I'm your old boy," he sang, his voice cracking along the fault line in his heart, and I felt myself sliding down into a place I didn't like to go. That was the thing about music; you never knew whether it was going to lift you up on its shoulders or drag you down into a sinkhole of blue.

"Hey," Ty said. The tip of his cigarette glowed in the dark. He'd always been like a bird dog, able to sniff out my darkest moods. "Talk to me."

But it was too late; I'd started to cry, ugly crying, the kind with hiccups and snot. I didn't care. I hoped he dumped me by the side of the road and drove off. Anything would be better than the way he was looking at me now. Couldn't he see that I didn't deserve his caring? It was too big for me, too fragile and unwieldy. I would trip under its weight, and it would shatter, and I would never be able to live with myself again.

He steered the truck onto the shoulder and set the parking brake.

"Come here," he said, leaning over and pulling me to him with one arm. I resisted and then I didn't; I went limp and sobbed into his shirtfront as he rubbed me between the shoulder blades and murmured things I couldn't make out in my ear.

A car approached from the opposite direction, slowed, then sped up as it passed. Ty reached into his pocket and handed me a white cotton handkerchief, and I used it to wipe my eyes and blow my nose.

"I don't know what you want from me," I said. "I used to, but I don't anymore."

"What I want hasn't changed. You're the one who keeps shuffling the deck."

I scooted back across the seat, folding my arms over my chest.

"Look, you've always known how I felt about you," Ty said. "If you'd just held your horses a little while instead of running off and getting mixed up with Will Culpepper— Did you think I didn't know what you were doing? Did you think I'd come riding in at the last second and stop you? Jesus, Denny! This is real life, not some, some show on TV."

"I didn't think Tina'd let you go." It might have been the most honest thing I'd ever said to him.

"I told you, I had to wait till the papers were filed. I was afraid she'd try to keep me from seeing the kids. Why couldn't you trust me?"

I didn't know how to answer him. The truth was, I'd been scared: scared he'd never get loose from Tina's clutches, but scared, too, that I didn't deserve someone like Ty, someone good and kind and steady. When Will came along I thought he was my kind, that choosing him would be better than being alone. I hadn't known then that the worst kind of loneliness is the kind you feel when you're with another person but your heart and your head belong somewhere else.

"You want to know what I want?" Ty said. "I want you to make up your mind." He put the truck in gear and eased back onto the blacktop.

A few minutes later we were back at the Round-Up. Ty left the engine idling while I found my keys. The air throbbed with backbeat; inside, the band was still going strong.

I looked over at him, his face flashing red to green and back again as the neon cowboy's lasso went round and round. It's true that some mistakes you have to live with, but other times, for reasons nobody knows, you get another chance. Here was Ty, offering me that chance, and I didn't know how to take it. I'd thought the only kind of love I ever understood was the kind Will Culpepper had to give, slippery as a ball of mercury, hard to catch, impossible to hold. But Lucy and Daddy had shown me something different. I wanted what they had, even if it meant that to get it I had to find my own way out of all the messes I'd made.

I was lost in thought, thinking about what I'd say to Will, when Ty spoke. "I wonder if maybe what we need is a break."

"What are you talking about?"

"I mean, maybe you need another manager. Somebody who could take care of your business without letting his feelings get tangled up in it."

A hard lump worked itself up against the base of my throat.

"I don't know how long I can keep chasing around after you, bailing out your bad boys when they get in trouble, keeping you from hurting yourself. It seems like it might be better to hand things off to somebody who could stand back from it a little. Who maybe doesn't care so much."

There hadn't been many times in my life that I was at a loss for words, but then again, there hadn't been that many times when I'd been so close to losing so much. What was wrong with me, that I didn't know how to say the simplest things, like, "I'm sorry," or "Don't go"?

"All right, then," Ty said, breaking the silence. "I'm gonna head back to the motel, try and get some sleep. I'll come by tomorrow. If you still can't tell me what you want by then, I guess I'll take that as a sign that I should boogie on up the road. Fair enough?"

"Tonight?" I said. "You expect me to make up my mind to-night?"

"I think you've already made up your mind. I'm giving you a chance to decide whether or not you've got the guts to do anything about it."

He reached across me, his starched cuff grazing my arm, and opened the passenger-side door.

"Wait," I said, and put my hand on his sleeve. I could see the feelings warring in his face, doubt and hope duking it out for first place. "I'll do it," I said. "I'll go home and do it now."

I climbed out of his truck and into mine. Always the gentleman, Ty waited until I'd started my engine and backed out.

At the highway, I pulled away slowly and turned south, toward Daddy's house, watching Ty's taillights disappear in the opposite direction.

I N T H E K I T C H E N I poured myself a glass of milk. There was a note from Lucy on the table, telling me to come up when I got in. But I didn't want to lose my nerve.

I carried my milk down the back hall and stood inside the screen porch drinking it and looking at the trailer. All the way home I'd rehearsed what I might say, but everything came out sounding like soap-opera dialog: "We've made a mistake." "I need my space." "It's time we went our separate ways." One thing about Will, he could sniff out bullshit like a coon dog, probably because he was such a master of it himself. But up till now, telling him the truth had been impossible, too.

As I unlatched the door and headed across the yard, I understood that space was not what I needed, but a different kind of space. Space to strip through all the layers of varnish I'd built up, down below the bone, where I could see and hear what was really in my heart.

CHAPTER 16

Lucy

THE SCREEN DOOR woke me, squealing back on its
hinges, then clicking shut.

I sat up in bed, switching on the lamp on the night
table, everything inside me vibrating high and fast, like a
tuning fork in my skull. It was after midnight. Where was
Ash? Where was Denny? Why didn't anyone in this house
sleep at night, instead of tramping around the countryside
like a bunch of vampires? I looked out the window and saw
Denny's and Ash's trucks along with my Blazer and Will
Culpepper's little blue Audi. Everybody was accounted for.
That should have made me feel better, but it didn't.

I stuck my head into Jude's room. He lay sprawled on the
bottom bunk, one arm thrown over his head and his knee
twisted at a sharp angle, like one of the tortured figures in
those friezes in my picture books of Italy. I crept over and put

the back of my hand against his forehead. He'd gone to bed earlier complaining of a stomachache, but his skin felt cool and dry.

Downstairs the kitchen was empty, the note I'd left for Denny still propped against the sugar bowl. Inside the back door I found a drinking glass coated with milk foam. I thought about what I'd heard that morning, Denny saying, "Cut it out," then silence. *She's a big girl,* I thought, *she can take care of herself.* But the humming in my head was getting louder.

A puddle of lantern light spilled from one of the trailer's windows, and I stood in the yard in my rubber garden clogs with my ears pricked up, listening. A radio was playing somewhere, Hank Williams singing, *Why don't you love me like you used to do?* I couldn't help but think of Ash's drinking days in Nashville, when this music had been a soundtrack for the ugly movie that had become our life. After I got back to Mooney, I didn't care if I never heard Hank Williams again.

I was just about to turn around and go back inside when a sound came from the trailer, a sharp, keening cry like nothing human I'd ever heard. I dropped the glass in the dirt, ran up the steps, and threw open the door.

Denny sat rocking on the edge of the couch, her hair hiding her face as Will stood over her, a cigarette dangling from the corner of his mouth. I had a sudden memory of the first time she'd brought him home with her last spring, when, after mixing it up with Ash, Will had badgered her into leaving with him. Why hadn't I paid attention to what I'd felt then? Why hadn't I gone after her? Ash had told me then that I had to leave her alone, to let her get wise to Will on her own; but did that mean I ought to ignore my instincts, to stand by while he held her feet to the fire?

I rushed inside, crowding Will out of the way, and knelt in front of Denny. When I reached for her hands she howled and doubled over.

I looked over my shoulder at Will. "What's going on?" The lantern light shuddered and danced, throwing his shadow tall and jagged against the wall.

"Aw, for Christ's sake," he said. "Can't two people have a conversation without it turning into a three-ring circus around here?"

As I slowly unfurled Denny's fingers, she moaned, a low, animal sound from deep in her throat. The little finger on her right hand stuck out at a peculiar angle, and her face was white with pain.

"My Lord," I said as Will took a drag off his cigarette, his eyes veiled by smoke. "What did you do?"

"How about you just butt out and let us finish this in private?"

"Are you crazy? So you can break the rest of her fingers and Lord knows what else?"

I got to my feet. Will Culpepper was not a big man, but like most bullies, he had a way of taking up more space than he truly occupied. My heart was pumping hard. For the first time in my life, I believed I might have what it took to kill somebody with my bare hands.

But before I could move, Ash came charging in, grabbing

Will's arm and jerking it around behind him, the cigarette falling from Will's mouth. Both of them were yelling as Ash wrenched Will's arm until he gave a shout and dropped onto the carpet.

Ash fell with him, and together they rolled, grunting and swearing. Anybody who's ever lived in the country knows that when two dogs fight, you don't try to break it up, or you could get yourself mauled in the process. I got Denny on her feet and tried to steer her to the door as Ash and Will grappled and swayed like dancers in some drunken, slow-motion square dance, the light from the lantern playing against the walls. They slipped and smacked and pummeled at each other without either of them ever seeming to land an actual punch. There was something primitive about it, something old and ugly that seemed to go back a long time before Ash and Will's own particular history.

Then Will caught his foot on the strip of metal that divided the living room carpet from the kitchen linoleum and went crashing headlong into the table. It was the kind that folded out from the wall, and it collapsed under his weight, sending him sprawling. His head made a crack like a bowling ball as it hit the floor.

He lay motionless as the rest of us stood over him. Ash had a shallow cut over one eye. The room smelled of beer sweat and kerosene and cigarette smoke, and the only sounds were of Denny sobbing and Ash's labored breathing.

Will let out a moan as Ash prodded him in the side with the toe of his work boot.

"Get up."

Will struggled to his feet, sagging against the broken table as he tried to find his balance. A strand of bloody saliva swung from his bottom lip as he shook a shock of black hair from his face. There was a depraved gleam in his eyes in the lamplight as he shifted his gaze from one of us to the other, his mouth crooked up at one corner, like the party was just getting started.

"You listen to me, you little shit," Ash said. "I've never trusted you as far as I could throw you. But as long as I thought you were what Denny wanted, I swore to myself I'd keep out of it.

"But I want you to know that, as of right now, all bets are off. You ever show your face here again, I'll nail your ass to the wall six ways from Sunday. You understand me?"

Will was still grinning that crazy grin when Ash gave him a shove down the cinder-block steps and sent him tumbling out into the yard, and tossed his boots and his keys out after him.

DENNY'S FINGER WASN'T broken, just dislocated, in Ash's professional opinion; it had happened to him lots of times. "A little tape, a little ice, and she'll be good as new in no time."

"She needs to get this seen to," I said as I grabbed a skirt out of the laundry basket and stepped into my Keds. It was my professional opinion that there might be more that needed healing than just Denny's finger.

The road was black and empty, a fat moon dangling in the windshield, as I gripped the wheel with both hands, taking the turns like a stock-car driver. Denny was silent in the passenger seat, her face turned to the window.

"How're you feeling?" I asked as we sailed through the blinking four-way light at the Corners.

"Okay."

"Is there anything you feel like talking about?"

"No, ma'am."

"Did he ever hurt you before?"

"No! Never."

She turned on the radio, and we listened to the first two verses of Steve Earle singing "My Old Friend The Blues" before she switched it off again.

"You know," she said, "I just figured he'd be relieved when I left him, so he could fool around all he wanted. I didn't know he'd come after me. Like I was some, some guitar he'd just remembered and decided to claim from the pawnshop."

I looked over and saw her crying silently, fat tears rolling down her face and into her lap.

"Oh, honey," I said.

"This is my fault," she said.

"Don't say that. Why would you say that?"

"I used to think Will was like Daddy! You know, sort of wild and hot-tempered. But Daddy's nothing like Will turned out to be."

"Well, you know, your daddy's settled down a good bit this past year. I guess he finally figured out what he had to lose, and he made up his mind he didn't want to lose it."

"I saw Ty tonight," she said. "He came looking for me at the Round-Up."

"I told him you were there. I hope that was okay." She shrugged, wiping her eyes with the back of her wrist. "So, what happened?"

"He said I needed to make up my mind. About him, and Will . . . I guess he sort of feels like I've been stringing him along. But it's more complicated than that, you know?"

"How so?"

"I care for him. I do. But I was thinking tonight, when I was getting ready to talk to Will, that maybe I need a little time to figure things out on my own. I mean, I *wanted* Will to leave, but I wanted it to be because *I* wanted him to, not because of Ty. Does that make any sense at all?"

"Sure."

"The thing is— What if Ty won't wait?"

The lights of the hospital appeared on the horizon, a busy space station in the middle of a vacant moonscape.

"I'll tell you something your daddy said to me, when we were first together," I said. "I had terrible cold feet—the worst. I'd never felt anything like what I felt for him, but I was scared to death of it, too. I'd just lost Mitchell, and it seemed like what was happening with your daddy and me was too much, too soon. Ash was the one who told me, 'There are no guarantees.' You put your heart out there, you might get it smashed as flat as a pancake."

"No offense, but I guess I don't see what that has to do with me."

"I just think that if it's meant to be, it will be."

"Meaning?"

I glanced over at her as we pulled into the driveway under

the red-and-white sign marked EMERGENCY. "Never mind," I said. "Sometimes this mama stuff is over my head. You'll find out what I'm talking about soon enough."

I turned the key and the engine died. Denny's face in the glow of the vapor lights was pure tear-stained misery. I was supposed to say something hopeful about how everything would work out for the best, how one day tonight would be a hazy memory. But she was smarter than that—kids always were. They could smell lies on you like liquor on your breath.

"This sucks," she said.

"Yeah," I said. "It does."

I didn't have the heart to tell her, but that was pretty much the full extent of what I knew about being a mama.

CHAPTER 17

Denny

EVERYTHING I KNEW about hospitals was from TV, so I was kind of surprised that the ER was empty— nobody staggering around with gunshot wounds or knives sticking out of them, no great-looking interns making out with each other in the halls.

A nurse in pink scrubs came through the double doors. She took a quick look at my hand, then sent Lucy to the waiting area with a stack of paperwork.

"Come with me, sweetie," the nurse said, planting an arm around my shoulders, and led me back to a cubicle surrounded by a flower-patterned curtain. Inside was a counter full of shiny instruments, a folded gown at the foot of an examining table. "Have a seat," she said. "I'll go find Dr. Sunjari."

I sat at the edge of the table, cradling my right hand in my left, and tried to decide what I'd tell the doctor. I wondered if he'd be able to tell from looking at me how this had happened, or if I could lie and say it was an accident. Not that I wanted to let Will off the hook, exactly. It was more that I was embarrassed. I didn't want to be the kind of girl who'd let a guy treat her this way. I didn't want to be the kind of girl who'd get mixed up with that kind of guy in the first place. And the last thing I needed was the sheriff getting involved, my name and Will's, and maybe Daddy's, in the papers.

The curtain opened, and I looked up to see a caramel-skinned woman wearing a white coat and carrying a clipboard. "Miss Farrell?"

"Hi," I said, giving her my best stage smile.

"You hurt your hand?"

I held it out and she took it gently between both of hers. I'd been trying not to look at my little finger, the way it stuck out sideways from the rest of my hand. The pain was dull but steady, throbbing in time with my heartbeat.

"My daddy said it's no big deal," I said. "That I'd probably just need some tape and some ice."

I couldn't read her face. "How did this happen?"

I opened my mouth, then shut it again. The doctor looked up at me, her brown-velvet eyes peering into mine. Something in her face seemed to loosen a well of feeling in me; tears sprang to my eyes and I bit my lip to hold them back.

"Your father," she said. "Did he have something to do with it?" Her voice was low and musical, hypnotic.

"No! I mean, no, ma'am."

"Did someone else do this to you?"

"I'd rather not say if I don't have to."

She rolled back on her wheeled seat. "Is there anything else you'd like to tell me?"

"I'm pregnant. If that makes a difference."

"How far along?"

"I'm not sure. Eight or nine weeks?"

"You haven't seen a doctor?"

"Just one of those stick tests."

She made a note on her clipboard. "I'm going to send you upstairs for an X-ray. We'll get the films and then we'll take care of this hand. And then we'll talk about what to do next."

The nurse came back a few minutes later to take me up to X-ray. I could hear the technicians out in the hall, talking about some game that involved terms like hip check and power play. Somebody had tacked a poster of sunflowers to the ceiling, and I leaned back and stared at it, thinking about Ty in his room at the Piney View, asleep maybe, or watching TV. The motel wasn't that far from here; I thought about getting up and crossing to the window and looking out, trying to find his light.

The technician came in, a chubby guy with a face as round as a salad plate. He didn't look old enough to have any kind of job other than a paper route.

"You follow the stars?" he said, opening my chart and flipping through it.

"I'm Virgo," I said. "But I don't know anything about cusps or any of that stuff."

He cracked up laughing. "It's a hockey team."

"Oh."

He started in with every reason and then some why hockey was the greatest thing since sliced bread, and he never shut up the whole time he was taking pictures of my hand. It was a relief, in a way, just to turn myself over to these people, to let them be in charge. Maybe, if the music thing didn't work out, I could get a job in the medical profession.

The nurse finally showed up again and took me back downstairs. Something was happening in one of the examining rooms; people were rushing around with carts and equipment, their voices low and urgent. After a while it got quiet again. I was starting to wonder if they'd forgotten I was there when Dr. Sunjari came back carrying my X-rays.

"This isn't as bad as it looks," she said as she clipped the films to a light board. "We'll put it back in line and splint it, give you Tylenol if you want it. Ice will help with the swelling. You should get it looked at again in a week or so, to make sure the ligaments are healing."

"How long before I can play the guitar?" I said.

"Well, that depends," the doctor said. "Could you play it before?"

She smiled at me over her shoulder. She was making a joke.

"I want you to make an appointment with Dr. Crawford on Monday," she said, taking a roll of tape out of a drawer. "To have a healthy baby, you need vitamins, rest, proper diet. A minimum of stress. Babies are like plants. Some will survive no matter what, but most need a healthy environment in which to grow." She locked eyes with me. "Hard as it can be sometimes, we must put their needs ahead of our own."

It hurt like hell when she popped my finger back into place—a white-hot jolt of pain, like an electrical shock. I felt lightheaded afterward as she taped up my hand. The room, I realized, was freezing, but I didn't feel it. I felt like I did waiting to go on before a show, like the center of me was a pool of bright, blossoming calm as I thought about what Lucy had said earlier, about a baby belonging to the world. I'd always thought that music was all I was good at, the only gift I had to offer. But maybe all along I'd been dreaming too small.

The doctor put her hand into her pocket and held out a couple of Tylenols.

"This will take care of the pain and help you sleep," she said. "Do you want them?"

I nodded my head, yes. I wanted them.

CHAPTER 18

Lucy

I
T WAS NEARLY two by the time we got home. Denny slept the whole way. I kept glancing over at her in the passenger seat, her face smoothed out in a way I hadn't seen since before she'd first showed up a year earlier, flaunting Will Culpepper like a carnival prize.

I pulled in behind Ash's truck and cut the engine. The porch light came on, and Ash came out into the yard.

"Everything okay?"

"Just a dislocated finger, like you said. The doctor taped her up and gave her a pill. She'll probably sleep till morning."

"That son of a bitch. I wish I'd . . ." Ash's hands flexed, like he was imagining them around Will Culpepper's neck.

"I know, but it's too late now. Come on, let's get her inside."

He opened the Blazer's rear door and scooped Denny into his arms, carried her upstairs, and laid her gently on her bed.

She didn't wake when I pulled off her boots and tugged the comforter up to her chin. Ash and I stood over her for a few minutes, watching her breathing in the moonlight.

"I figured you'd be mad at me," Ash said as the ceiling fan ticked softly over our heads.

"What for?"

"Getting into it with Culpepper. Last time this happened, you had your nose out of joint for a week."

I put my arm around his waist. "Well, I was wrong. I should have let you cut him up in little pieces and bury him in the backyard."

He smiled. "What was it you used to tell me, about letting kids make their own mistakes?"

"That was before I had any of my own."

"Kids, or mistakes?"

"Kids," I said. "I've always had plenty of mistakes."

"I think I'm too old for this shit," Ash said. I lifted my head and looked at him. "Is it too much to ask, expecting your daughter to bring home a guy you don't have to punch out every time you see him?"

"Well, you may be in luck. I think Ty Briggs is next in line."

"Good," Ash said. "Now let's just hope Culpepper gets gone and stays that way."

"You don't really think he'd come back, do you?"

"I don't know, Lucy—I guess I missed class the day they gave the lecture on crazy sons-in-law."

We washed and undressed and got into bed, but I was too wired to sleep. The slide show of the evening kept flickering inside my closed eyes, and beside me Ash's body felt hot and as tense as a coiled spring. After a while he got up and put on his pants and went out, shutting the door behind him.

When daylight came, I found him sitting in the porch swing with a cup of coffee, the shotgun resting across his knee as casually as a newspaper. The day was overcast, the pond flat and green in the morning air.

I sat down beside Ash and took a sip of his coffee. There were circles under his eyes, a dusting of dark beard on his jaw.

"Maybe we ought to call the sheriff," I said.

"What for?"

"We could file a report. Or get a restraining order, something."

"Do you really think a piece of paper would be enough to stop a guy like Culpepper?"

"Well, you can't spend the rest of your life sitting sentry." I reached out and rested the backs of my fingers against his face. "You know, Denny's not the only one around here I'm worried about."

Ash set down the gun, propping it beside the front door.

"I called that doctor Punch told me about," he said. "I've got an appointment with her day after tomorrow."

"Good."

"You think?"

"I think it might help to talk to somebody who can stand back and give you a clear view of things."

He took his cup from me and set it on the porch rail, then pulled me to him and folded me into his arms, smelling of damp and coffee, his hand in my hair. I remembered something he'd asked me once, when we'd had a falling-out over something so small I couldn't recall what started it anymore. "What was it you signed on for?" he'd asked. How could I have known then that this, sitting in the circle of his arms while the rest of the world spun crazily around us, would be the answer?

DOVE WAS ON her way to take me to buy plants for the garden, the last thing I felt like doing under the circumstances, but Ash insisted that I go. I shook Denny awake at noon, just to be sure she was okay. By the time I'd heated a pan of chicken noodle soup and carried a bowl upstairs, she'd already fallen back asleep.

"Let her be," Ash said. "Jude and I'll keep an eye out, find some stuff to do around the place."

"If she wakes up, make sure she eats something," I told him. "I'll have my cell, so call me if anything happens, okay?"

"Go and have a good time. Us guys'll hold down the fort."

"And, Ash—don't try and be a hero. If Will shows up again, call the sheriff."

"I'm betting Will Culpepper's halfway to Nashville by now and counting his lucky stars."

In spite of the fact that my Blazer had more cargo space, I let Dove drive her Lincoln. It turned out to be a blessing. Once I'd brought her up to date, I didn't have to make conversation if I didn't feel like it, didn't have to do a thing but lay my head against the cool window glass and drift off to Conway Twitty on the radio.

When I opened my eyes we were three counties over, near Palestine. I was starving, so we stopped at Sonic, then started to hit the plant farms that dotted the roadside every half mile or so up and down Highway 79. We filled the trunk with flats of half-grown tomato plants, peppers, squash, herbs, and a variety of annuals Dove claimed would add not just color but therapeutic value to the vegetables. She picked up a few hanging baskets for her front porch, and we gassed up the car and headed back toward Cade County with the sun hanging low in the rearview mirror.

I offered to take the wheel, and before long, Dove was dozing in the passenger seat. The road curved smoothly through the pines, and I snuck glances at my aunt as she slept. A whole life was in that face, mapped out in spots and wrinkles. I hoped that I would learn to wear my age with the same careless pride, and not turn into one of those frantic women who spends what time she's got left chasing after some miracle from a surgeon's knife or a cream in a jar. Just the thought of Dove having a face-lift made me laugh out loud, and she jerked awake, looking wildly around.

"You cracking yourself up over there?"

"I'm going to be a grandma, Dove. Isn't that the funniest thing you ever heard?"

"Seems like just the other day you was finding out you'd be a mama your own self."

I lowered the volume on the radio, where Tanya Tucker was singing "Delta Dawn." "Did you ever wish you had a crystal ball and could look ahead and see how everything would turn out?" I asked.

"Oh, sure, all the time, back when I was your age. But lately, I've gotten to where I kinda like surprises. Even the ones that don't seem so good at first, I figger I'll get a chance to find out what I'm made of."

"Pure gold," I said. "That's what you're made of."

"Ha! More like an old pickup, you ask me. Scrap metal and balin' wire."

"The engine's good, though. That's what counts."

"You got the same engine under your hood, Lucy Bird. Don't you forget that."

"I wonder if I ought to call Ash. See if there's anything going on that I need to be worrying about."

"We'll be home in an hour. You'll find out then, regardless. Might as well enjoy the ride." She sat forward and turned the radio back up. "Whatever happened to Miss Tanya, you reckon?"

"She raises cutting horses, I heard. I think she still sings a little now and then."

"It's an ugly business. I'm not sure them that's grabbin' for the brass ring always knows that when they get into it."

"We didn't, that's for sure."

"You think Ash ever misses them days?"

"I don't know, Dove. The early part, probably, when it looked like everything was going his way. I wish there was some way to get back to that, to make him believe that just because he had a run of bad luck, it doesn't mean he can't still write and play." I swung out to pass a hay baler creeping along the shoulder in the dusk. The driver lifted a hand as we passed, and we waved back. "Punch Laughlin gave him the name of some doctor down in Marshall. Ash is seeing her in a couple days."

"Is that good news?"

"I guess so. I mean, I don't know how much I can do for him anymore."

"You do plenty, Lucy Bird. Every day he wakes up and sees your face is a blessing right there."

"I'm not sure it's enough."

"You ask me, the trouble with the world today is everbody wantin' everthing in such an all-fired hurry. Sometimes you got to sit back and let things come to you, 'stead of the other way 'round."

When we got home, we found Ash grilling chicken-and-pineapple kabobs on the deck. Denny was down at the dock with Jude, helping him with his fishing line. Jude had yet to catch a single fish out of our pond, but that didn't stop him from trying. His daddy had told him that a hundred-year-old catfish lived at the bottom among the rocks and reeds, and even though I begged Ash not to lead Jude on, I think he was just as enchanted as Jude was with the fantasy.

I gave Ash a quick kiss. "Everything okay?"

"Copacetic."

"How's Denny doing?"

He flipped a strip of pineapple with metal tongs.

"Still a little woozy. But she's already complaining about the splint on her hand. I take that for a good sign."

Dove and I unloaded the trunk, putting the flats of seedlings in the shed for the night, and went inside to wash up for supper. We ate at the picnic table under the electric lanterns with plastic tumblers full of sweet tea, citronella candles burning in galvanized buckets to keep the mosquitoes away. We had a dewberry pie Dove made for dessert, then sat peacefully in the twilight, listening to the frogs and watching flies drown in the dregs of our dessert. In spite of the bulky splint on her hand, Denny seemed more tranquil than I'd seen her since she'd first arrived.

"Remind me to call Geneva after a while," I said. "She can probably get you in to see Dr. Crawford in the morning."

"Okay."

I was trying to think how to ask her if she'd heard from Will when headlights appeared on the road, weaving their way toward us through the trees. Ash and I looked at each other across the table, and he got up wordlessly and went into the house.

"Jude," I said, "I think it's time you started getting ready for bed."

"But I'm not sleepy!"

Ty's black truck came into the yard and rolled to a stop, and I let out my breath.

"Evening, folks," he called, climbing out in a crisply pressed shirt, creased Wranglers, and spit-shined boots. "Sorry to interrupt your supper."

"The chicken's gone, but there's some pie left," Denny said. "Dove makes the best dewberry pie in East Texas."

"How can I say no?" Ty winked at Dove, who for possibly the second time in her life turned as pink as a Tyler rose.

He was digging into his pie when Ash stepped out onto the porch with the shotgun over his shoulder.

"Whoa," Ty said, his fork halfway to his mouth. "Maybe I should have called ahead, made sure I haven't worn out my welcome." I waved to Ash, who went back inside, taking the gun with him. "What's going on?" Ty said, a half smile frozen on his face as he looked from Denny to me and back again.

"Come on, champ," I said to Jude. "We need to get your bath. Tomorrow's a school day, remember?"

"Is Daddy gonna shoot something?"

"Don't be silly," I said. "Get up, now, and let's let Denny and Ty have themselves a private visit."

I sent Jude upstairs while Dove and I cleared the table. As we loaded the dishwasher, I snuck a glance out the window over the sink. Denny slowly took her hands out of her lap and stretched them across the table, and Ty set down his fork and took her right hand in his. I could only guess at what he was saying as he came up off the picnic bench, leaning forward over the sputtering candle. For Will's sake I hope what Ash had said was true and he'd gotten himself far, far away, because the list of folks who wanted to do him harm was growing longer by the minute.

Dove nudged me out of the way to rinse a plate in the sink.

"Never a dull moment 'round here, that's for sure," she said.

"When are we going to get those plants in the ground?" I said. "I've got to work tomorrow, and try to get Denny to the doctor."

"I reckon I can handle it," she said. "All the manpower you got on the premises, ought not to take more than a few hours, tops."

"We're one less man than we were yesterday," I reminded her.

"That one weren't worth much to begin with." We watched as Ty sat back down, holding on gently but firmly to Denny's hand. She shook her head at something he said, but he didn't let go. "That one there, on the other hand," Dove said, "I reckon he's got what it takes to shoulder the load."

"I hope you're right."

Dove and I stood hip to hip at the window, scraping the last bits of crust and berry out of the pie tin with one shared fork, until the candle on the picnic table guttered out and there was nothing to see but the shapes of the trees on the far side of the pond against a violet sky.

CHAPTER 19

Denny

D R. CRAWFORD WAS about a hundred years old, with a scrubbed pink face and bright little eyes. The whole time he was examining me, he told me stories about how he'd delivered not only Jude but both Lucy and Daddy, making it sound like it had happened just a day or two before and not forty-some-odd years ago. Finally he patted my leg and told me I could sit up.

"You're about nine weeks along," he said. "That puts you on track to deliver . . ." He paused to consult a clipboard. "December fifteenth. We'll do an ultrasound in a few weeks that will be more accurate. At your age, I see no reason to order one now, though. Have you been taking good care of yourself?"

I wasn't sure how to answer him. Hadn't he seen the splint on my hand?

"I drink too many Cokes," I said.

"Well, I'll give you some material to read at home," Dr. Crawford said as he scribbled something on a pad and handed it to me.

"What's this?"

"A prescription for prenatal vitamins. And I want lots of fresh food, no junk, plenty of water. Walk as much as you can, so long as you're feeling up to it. You don't smoke, do you?"

"I quit," I said. "Very recently."

"Good. No alcohol—that goes without saying—and get as much rest as possible."

"I'm a musician, like my daddy," I reminded him. "My band played two hundred dates last year."

The doctor looked at me over the tops of his glasses. "That sounds hard enough on a regular person, much less one with a baby."

"Yes, sir, I know. Daddy and Lucy are gonna help me take care of her once she's born. I'm not sure how yet, exactly, but we're gonna make it work."

"Then I'd say your job is to make sure she gets the best start you can give her. Can you take it easy for the next few weeks? You haven't got a world tour in the works or anything like that, have you?"

"No, sir," I said. "I'll take it easy, I promise."

LUCY AND I stopped off at the Sav-Mor to pick up my vitamins, got milk shakes at the Dairy Queen, then crossed the square together toward the flower shop, where my truck was parked.

We found Peggy and Audrey sitting on the showroom floor drinking Diet Cokes and sorting greeting cards, trying to figure out which ones could be sent back for credit and which ones should go into the clearance sale. Lucy excused herself and went into the restroom.

"I just think it's so awesome that you're having a baby," Audrey said. "Joe and I want about ten of 'em. I was all for going ahead and getting started right away, but my mom said she'd murder me if I turned up pregnant at my own wedding."

"When is it, again?"

"Less than two weeks now. The day after graduation. We were planning to stick around the rest of the summer and try and save up some money before we moved to Dallas, but now that Peggy's closing the shop, there's no reason to stay. We're gonna drive up there next weekend to look for an apartment."

"I grew up in Dallas," I said. "What are y'all hoping to do there?"

"Joe's already got a job lined up installing satellite dishes. I guess I might sign up at the community college, take a few courses, if I don't get pregnant right away."

"You can go to school even if you do have kids," Peggy said. "A girl needs to be able to make her way in the world, whether or not she's got a man to look out for her. Take me. Where would I have been when Duane died if I hadn't had this shop?" She looked around her with a startled expression, like she'd just then realized what she was giving up.

"I wish I could do what you do," Audrey said to me. "It must be the coolest thing in the world, standing up on a stage in front of hundreds of people, hearing them cheer for you."

"Well, it looks like I'm not gonna be doing that for a while," I said. "Doctor's orders."

"You planning on staying put for a while then?" Peggy asked.

"I guess so. If Lucy and Daddy will have me."

We stopped talking and glanced toward the back of the shop, where the water had been running for a couple of minutes.

"Maybe I better go see if she's okay," I said. It hadn't been too long since I was the one hiding in Faye's restroom, wanting to run from the latest curveball life had thrown me.

"Just a second," Lucy called out when I knocked.

The door opened and she came out, dabbing her nose with a tissue.

"Hey," I said.

"Sorry." She tried to smile, but it wasn't really working. "Just having myself a little hormonal moment."

"Isn't that supposed to be my excuse?"

"It's silly, I know. It's just a job, right? I should be able to let go, like Peggy. Like Audrey. Pick up and move on."

I took her arm and we stepped out the back door into the parking lot. Heat rose off the asphalt, the tarry smell clashing with the azaleas blooming along the curb.

"You know what my problem is?" Lucy said. "I never wanted anything but this. To live in Mooney and be married to your daddy, to work in the flower shop. Now Peggy's going to Florida to be near her grandbabies, and Audrey's moving to Dallas with Joe. I feel like the whole world's heading off and leaving me behind."

I didn't know what to say that wouldn't hurt her feelings. From the time I'd picked up my first guitar, I'd dreamed of nothing but the road, of letting music carry me to the ends of the earth and beyond. Now I was going to have to stay put for a little while. But I would leave again, eventually, and one day I'd take my baby with me. Where would Lucy be then? What could I tell her to hang on to and hope for?

She blotted her eyes with the tissue and stuffed it into her skirt pocket.

"I guess I better get back inside," she said. "Earn my pay-check while I've still got one to earn." She leaned forward and gave me a hug. "You ought to go home and put your feet up. Maybe check on Dove and see how the garden's coming along. Make sure she's not killing Ty." The night before, he'd agreed to come back out and help Dove with the planting.

I waved good-bye as I backed my pickup out of the lot and turned onto Front Street. It was late morning, not quite time yet for the lunch rush, and I drove slowly around the court-house square, then out the FM road toward home. I rolled the windows down and pushed a CD into the slot, letting the cab fill up with the voice of the great Loretta Lynn.

"Hear that?" I rested my hand on my still-flat belly. "That's your namesake."

I was a couple of miles past the city-limits sign when an ancient, moldy-green Ford appeared in my rearview. It was coming up fast, and I started to pull over to let it pass when its headlights began to flash. I slowed up and squinted into the mirror, recognizing the dreadlocks brushing against the headliner.

I steered onto the shoulder and Erasmus tucked the Ford in behind me and got out, coming around to the passenger side.

"Excellent ride," I said through the open window. "Top of the line."

"I was just heading out to see you."

I reached out and turned down the stereo. "Climb in if you want. I bet that heap you're driving doesn't have A/C."

He got in, and I put up the windows and turned on the air-conditioning. A silver-bellied propane truck lumbered by on the blacktop, and in a pasture across the road a pickup bounced along between rows of new green sorghum.

"What happened to your hand?"

"It's kind of a long story."

"For Pete's sake, Denny."

"Look, just save the sermon, okay? He's gone."

"What do you mean, gone?"

"I mean, Daddy threw him out and told him not to come back unless he wanted to get crucified."

"I'll bet that scared him."

I shrugged. I was trying not to think about it too much. "What were you coming to see me for?"

"I'm fixing to take off," he said.

"Take off? Where?"

"Back to New York. I thought I should tell you in person."

"You said you were staying till next week! Did a gig come up or something?"

"No gig. It's just that—well, it's time, that's all. It happened sooner than I expected."

I wrapped my left hand around the steering wheel. There was a pale strip of skin on the fourth finger of my left hand where my wedding ring had been; I'd taken it off that morning and stuck it between the mattress and box spring, till further notice.

"Is this because of Camille?" I asked.

"Partly."

"You miss her."

"I miss my real life. I need to get on with things, and so do you."

The A/C was blasting like a wind tunnel, and he reached forward and turned it down.

"Look, me hanging around here isn't doing either one of us any good," Erasmus said. "Especially now that I've gotten a look at Ty Briggs up close and in person. I just think we need to put a little space between us for a while."

It didn't seem to me that New York was a little space, never mind France, but I nodded, squinting at the highway through a haze of tears.

"I don't know what a guy like you has any business doing in Paris or New York," I said. "You're too . . ." I shook my head. "Simple" wasn't the word I was looking for, and "nice" wasn't right, either. "When are you leaving?" I asked instead.

"Pop's driving me to Dallas this afternoon."

Things were happening too fast. It didn't seem right that people could come and go from your life like little tornadoes, tearing up the landscape and then moving on.

Erasmus took my hand, the one with the splint, and held it in both of his.

"I better go," he said. "I've got to pack. And I need to get this fine set of wheels back to the shop."

"Aren't you gonna say good-bye to Daddy before you go?"

"You tell him for me, okay? Tell him if he and Lucy take a hankering to see Paris, the door's always open." I had to smile at the thought of Daddy strolling in a long coat and beret up the Champs Élysées. "That goes for you, too," Erasmus said. "Maybe you'll come over on your next honeymoon."

"Promise you'll call," I said. "I need to know where I can find you."

"You always know where to find me." He pressed the tip of one finger briefly, lightly, against my collarbone.

Hot air rushed into the cab as Erasmus opened the door and stepped out onto the asphalt. I watched in the mirror as he climbed behind the wheel of the Ford, executed a three-point turn, and drove off the way he'd come. I sat there for a long time after, my skin tingling where he'd touched it as the heat rose off the blacktop and the sorghum shimmered like bottle-glass in the breeze.

WHAT DO YOU mean, she *left*?"

I stared at Contessa, her bosom quivering in her rose-printed dress. "She's eighty years old! She's out of her head! How did she manage to just get up and walk out?"

"Believe me, honey, these old folks can fool you. They're a lot more spry than they let on, some of 'em. Got all kinds of tricks up their sleeves."

Evelyn lay on her back on the white iron bed, her mouth open, the quilt rising and falling as she slept. It was hard to believe that the day before she'd strolled out the front door pretty as you please and wandered off into the woods, that it had taken two deputies and a team of volunteers from the Antioch Church of Christ combing the countryside for four hours before they found her, napping on a blanket of pine needles half a mile off the paved road.

"You're sure she's okay?"

"Nothing but a few bumps and bruises. They kept her overnight in the hospital, put an IV in her, just in case."

"God." I walked in and sat down in the chair under the window. "Why didn't somebody call me?"

"Didn't know the number. Anyway, there weren't nothing much to tell. You can see for your own self, she's back now, safe and sound."

I wanted to wake my grandmother, to see her black eyes look into mine, even if they wouldn't recognize me. *Where were you going, Evelyn?* I wanted to ask. *What did you hope to find?* Was she on a mission of some kind, or did she just get a hankering to take a walk, enjoy the warm spring air? Was she having a fine old time, or had she realized she was lost and been scared to death? I hated that I'd never know, that her mind had already filed the episode away in a shadowy corner where she wouldn't be able to touch it.

I sat forward, laying my hands on the quilt. "This isn't right," I said. "She doesn't belong here."

"What do you mean?" Contessa's face was suddenly stony, her back straight as a board.

"I mean, I want to take her home."

CHAPTER 20

Lucy

PULLING INTO THE yard that evening, I was met by the sight of Jude and Lily in the garden along with Dove and Ty Briggs, all of them on their knees in the dirt. Dove took off her sun hat and waved, a gesture that I first took for a sign of greeting but quickly realized, as she clambered to her feet and kept flailing the hat back and forth, was something else.

"What's up?"

"Better get inside. Ash and Denny's goin' after it like two cats in a sack."

I grabbed my purse and hurried toward the house. Was it too much, I wondered, to expect to come home of an evening and find things sweet and peaceful, somebody to hand you a cold drink from the icebox and invite you to put your feet up while they listened to you tell about your day?

As I made my way toward the kitchen, I heard Denny say, "I can't believe you're acting this way!"

"Girl, I'm telling you, you're taking it too far! This is *my* house, and no way, no how are you telling me who I'm gonna let in it!"

I dropped my purse on a chair, and both Denny and Ash turned toward me. They stood at either end of the long oak table, looking like a pair of gunfighters squared off across the OK Corral.

"What in heaven's name is going on here?" I said. "I could hear y'all all the way out in the yard."

"You started it," Ash said to Denny. "You tell her."

"It's Evelyn," Denny said.

"What about her?"

"I drove up there this afternoon to visit her. She'd gotten out."

"You mean they released her?"

"I mean, she waltzed out the front door and into the woods! It took two deputies and a whole bunch of other folks four hours to find her."

"My Lord—is she okay?"

"They took her to the hospital, kept her overnight. But there wasn't anything wrong except a little dehydration, so they sent her back to Contessa's."

"But that's good, right?" I cast a sideways look at Ash.

"Lucy!" Denny said. "We can't just *leave* her there! What if it happens again? What if next time they don't find her in time?"

"I've heard about as much of this story as I care to." Ash spun on his heel, ready to walk out.

"Hold on a minute," I said.

He stopped and jabbed an index finger in my direction, fixing me with his dark stare.

"I'll tell you what I've been telling Denny for the past half hour, not that it's gotten me anywhere," he said. "As far as I'm concerned, this person you're boo-hooing about, Evelyn LeGrande, is dead. She has been for forty years. Are you forgetting she gave me away, like a puppy you bring home for Christmas and decide you don't want? Christa Keller was my mama, God rest her soul. Evelyn LeGrande can rot in the woods for all I care. If you ask me, it's no less than she deserves."

"Oh, Ash." This was such an old, sad song in our family, one that got brought out and played from time to time, and it always ended up giving everybody the blues. After eight years, I'd learned to live with it, if not exactly accept it. But unlike him, I'd always been able to see another side of the story, to understand in theory if not reality what Evelyn had done. I never for a moment believed, as Ash did, that she'd handed him over like a homeless stray, without an ounce of compunction. She'd known she couldn't love him the way a mama was supposed to, and so she'd turned him over to someone who could. Giving her baby boy to Christa Keller to raise had not been just an act of desperation on her part, but an act of charity. How could I, could any of us, say what we'd have done in her shoes?

But I wasn't the one she'd wounded, and forgiveness had never been Ash's strong suit. I turned to Denny. "What are you suggesting, exactly?"

"I think we need to bring her here."

"Over my dead body!"

I ignored Ash's outburst. "Now, honey," I said to Denny. "Do you really think that's sensible?"

"Why not? This house has five bedrooms!"

"It's not a matter of space. It's more a— Well, who's going to look after her? You said yourself, she's practically helpless."

"She's not helpless. She's just senile. It's not the same thing."

"She's old and sick, and she needs taking care of. It's not like we'd just be able to stick her in the guest room and pretend she wasn't there. She'd need somebody to feed her and help her get dressed, maybe take her to the bathroom . . ."

"I cannot believe I'm having this conversation," Ash said.

"You *aren't* having it, so hush up a minute," I said. "Denny, seriously. I know you mean well, but have you really thought this through? It just doesn't seem realistic."

"I'll do it," she said firmly. "I'll take care of her."

"You don't even live here!" Ash exclaimed. "You just come around whenever you get yourself in some kind of trouble, and you stay until things sort themselves out, and then you go on your merry way!"

"Ash—" I began, but he cut me off.

"Jesus Christ, Denise! Isn't it enough that we're gonna be raising your baby? Now you want to dump a crazy old lady on us, too. . . . What happens after you go back out on the road, huh? Have you thought about that? Who's gonna deal with all your leftover baggage then?"

All the color drained out of Denny's face. For a long moment she stared at Ash like she'd never seen him before.

"Fine," she said, her voice so low I had to strain to hear her. "You know what? Just go and sit out there in that studio you built, telling yourself what a raw deal you got and how misunderstood you are. You don't want to be bothered with me and my *baggage*? Well, I managed the first fourteen years of my life without you, in case you don't recall, and I can do it from here on out, too."

"Denny," I said, but she was already crossing the room, almost running, the sound of her boot heels hammering on the hardwood as she made her way up the hall. The front door opened and slammed.

Ash gripped the edge of the drain board, his knuckles white.

"Thanks for getting my back just then," he said. "I really appreciate it." Out front, Denny's pickup engine fired.

"What are you talking about?"

"Didn't I back you up when you said you wanted to help Denny raise the baby? Is it really too much for me to expect you to be in my corner on this?"

"I never said I wasn't in your corner."

"Well, you have a funny way of showing it."

"I'm just trying to see everybody's side here. Just because you don't want to hear what Denny's saying doesn't mean there might not be something to it."

He looked over his shoulder at me, scraped the hair off his forehead with one hand.

"You know, maybe I'm the one ought to leave," he said. "I don't seem to be doing much good around here."

"Ash, stop it. Stop talking crazy."

"I just don't know why I worked so hard to quit drinking. What was the goddamned point?"

I lifted the cordless phone out of its cradle and thrust it toward him. "Call Heather."

"What for? So she can give me the usual bullshit about giving it over to God?"

"She's your sponsor. Isn't that her job?"

Grudgingly, he took the phone. While he punched in the numbers, I went into the living room and turned on the TV, where a man in a white chef's coat was throwing handfuls of something—mussels, mushrooms?—into a pot of bubbling sauce.

A couple of minutes later Ash appeared in the doorway.

"She said to come over," he said. "We might just hang out for a while, or we might go to a meeting." I started to get up, but he held out his hand to stop me. "Don't. Just— I can't talk about it anymore right now, okay? I'll be home after a while."

I sank back onto the couch, listening to Ash gather his keys and wallet from the table in the front hall and let himself out the door. "And now," the TV man said in a heavy, exotic accent, "we let it simmer while we prepare the pasta. A nice linguini is just the thing, no?"

I allowed a black wave of fury to wash over me, for whatever it was—entitlement, carelessness, balls—that gave Ash the right to say "Screw it" and walk out the door, leaving me holding the bag. Times like this I couldn't help but wonder what might have happened if I'd stayed on the farm after Mitchell died, hired somebody to help me with the crops and livestock. Or suppose I'd packed my bags and moved to some city full of strangers and skyscrapers, where I could have reinvented myself as anybody at all? People did those kinds of things every day: threw caution to the wind, chose the road less traveled over the one that was safe and known.

"Hey there."

I looked up to see Dove standing at the end of the couch.

I picked up the remote to turn off the TV. "I was just thinking I better do something about supper."

"Is that what you was thinkin'?" She sat down beside me. "Don't you know by now, I can see straight through you? Anyhow, it'd've been hard to miss all the shoutin' and door slammin', folks peelin' outta the yard like the house was on fire."

"I just can't figure out how it's possible to love a person and want to strangle them at the same time."

"You talkin' about Ash, or Denny?"

"Both, I guess." I brought her up to speed on what had happened. "All I was doing was trying to point out that there might be a middle ground, but where did that get me? Now they're mad at each other and me, too."

"Well, you know how Ash feels about his mama," Dove said. "I can see how's he might feel Denny's tryin' to put him in a box he don't want to be in."

"I've been asking myself what I'd do if it was somebody on our side of the family. Mama, for instance. If she got to where she couldn't look after herself, would I bring her here to stay with us?"

"Well? Would you?"

"I guess I would. I don't think I could live with myself otherwise."

Dove reached out and patted my knee. "You're a good girl, Lucy Bird. But you got to remember, this is Ash's mama we're talking about, and it's his home, too. Just 'cause Denny's taken some notion of rescuin' Evelyn don't mean she's got the right to go over her daddy's head to do it. Those two got to wangle it out between 'em."

"And I can't do a thing but stand in the middle and watch the fur fly." I got up and walked over to the window. "How's the garden coming?"

"All done. That Tyler Briggs is a saint, I'm tellin' you. I'd marry him myself if I was forty years younger. 'Course, his hat's already set for somebody else."

"Good. Maybe he'll take her and her grandma and go back to Nashville, and things will be peaceful again."

"Ha! Things ain't been peaceful since the first time you and Ash Farrell locked eyeballs."

"Somehow this isn't quite what I bargained for."

"Very few of us gets what we bargained for," Dove said. "Keeps things lively, though, don't it?" She stood, brushing her hands on the fronts of her slacks. "How about I help you rustle up some supper 'fore I run Lily home?"

We threw a tuna-and-noodle casserole into the microwave and put together a salad, then went outside to set the picnic table for supper. I insisted Ty stay and eat with us, though he said he didn't want to impose.

"You spent the whole day busting your butt in the hot sun

on my account. How could a plate full of tuna casserole be an imposition?"

I sat down across from him at the table while Jude and Lily followed Dove inside to wash up. Clouds were gathering in the west, the tops high and white, the bottoms reflecting the red and gold of the setting sun. A fish jumped in the middle of the pond, a quick slash of silver, then gone, the water green and dimpled in its wake.

"It's nice here," Ty said. "I can see why you wanted to come back."

"From Nashville, you mean?"

"It's a whole different world, isn't it? You can hear yourself think."

"That's what Ash says. I'm not sure it's always for the best, though."

"How do you mean?"

"Just that there can be a little *too* much time to think. If you get my drift."

I looked across the table at Ty, his sweat-soaked T-shirt and his big, capable hands folded in front of him. It occurred to me that, if Dove was right, he might be part of this family someday. He might be part of it already.

"I guess Denny's talked to you some about what's going on with her daddy," I said.

"I know her side of it. I can't exactly say I feel like I've got the whole picture."

"Well, you won't exactly get an unbiased version from me, either."

"Still, I'd like to hear it."

I thought of how Ty reminded me of my brothers, the certainty that what you saw would change very little from one day to the next, that it would always be there to lean against. Funny, how I'd chosen someone so like them for a first husband, and so much the opposite for my second. I admired those qualities, was drawn to them, even; but in the end I'd cast my lot with the pirates, not the soldiers. Did that make me a pirate, too, or just a damsel in distress, waiting for the good guys to rescue me?

"At first I thought it was a good idea when he decided to build this house," I said. "Actually, that's not true. At first it seemed completely crazy. He was still drinking then, living in the trailer out behind our old house. But if there's one thing Ash knows, it's how to talk the talk. This was going to be a new beginning for him, for all of us, a way to put Nashville behind us and get a fresh start.

"And for a while, it really did seem like things were headed that way. I loved watching him with Jude, doing stuff like homework or fishing off the dock. They'd never really had that before, and— Well, neither Ash or I knew our daddies, growing up. It was a big deal for both of us.

"But somewhere along the way, he—Ash, I mean—started to drift. I didn't really notice it at first. He was busy finishing the house, and then he started working on the studio. I don't know if Denny told you, but it used to be an old hired man's shack. He spent months getting everything just right, making sure the equipment was first-rate.

"I figured it would take some time for him to get comfortable with the idea that he could go back to where he'd been before Nashville, to get in touch with that part of himself again. And at first he'd spend hours out there. But after a while I realized he wasn't doing anything except listening to CDs—other people's CDs, I mean. The handful of times I've heard him picking out some tune on the guitar, I'll ask him if it's a new song, and his face just closes up like a fist when he tells me it's something, oh, Lyle Lovett wrote, or some fellow down in Austin who's written all these big hits for George Strait and the Dixie Chicks. It's like he doesn't trust himself anymore. He acts like he got his one shot and he blew it, and the vault sealed shut. And now here Denny comes blowing in, stirring everything up . . ."

Ty smiled. "I hear you."

"Did she tell you what happened today?"

"With her grandma? She told me."

"If there's anything in Ash's life that's a sorer point than Nashville, it's his mama. She gave him up to foster care when he was a baby, and he's never forgiven her. We wouldn't even know where she was if it wasn't for Denny. She's the one who hunted Evelyn down in the first place, who's tried to keep the ties going. But I never dreamed she'd end up suggesting that Evelyn come and live here. I don't know why she'd even bring up such a thing, knowing how her daddy feels." I got up to switch on the electric lanterns. "There doesn't seem to be a middle ground, and neither Ash nor Denny is likely to give an inch."

The front door opened and Jude and Lily came out, carefully balancing a big wooden salad bowl between them.

"It's too bad we don't get to choose the people we love," I said. "We might save ourselves a lot of grief if we could."

"Yeah, but think what we'd miss. I don't know about you, but I'll take the hard stuff any day, if it means that I get a crack at the good parts."

Ty stood and stretched, working the cricks out of his back. "You mind if I run inside and wash up before we eat? I must smell like a pigsty."

"I'm sorry. Of course. You know where the half bath is, off the kitchen?"

"I'll find it."

"I could get you one of Ash's clean shirts, if you'd like."

"I've got one in the truck, but thanks."

"Denny didn't happen to tell you where she was going?" I asked as Ty turned toward his pickup.

"No, ma'am. It seemed like she was in a pretty big hurry."

"You know, I used to be the one who always took off at the first sign of trouble," I said. "Now I'm the one holding down the fort. How funny is that?"

AFTER SUPPER TY walked with Jude and Lily down to the dock while Dove and I cleared the table. He'd entertained us over our tuna casserole with stories of life on the road, and I was grateful for his company, the sense it gave me that, even though someone else might be steering the boat, there was at least one other kindred soul in it with me.

"I like that boy," Dove said as she squirted detergent into the casserole dish. "Too bad Denny couldn't of run inta him before she got tangled up with that Culpepper fella."

"She did," I reminded her. "Ty's been her manager for

three years. She only met Will last spring. But I guess this is one of those things she just had to learn the hard way."

"We all got our share a those," Dove said.

"Everybody but you," I said, reaching past her to rinse a stack of plates.

"Oh, I got a few."

"You do? Like what?"

Sliding the plates into their rack in the dishwasher, I looked up to see Dove staring out the window over the sink, her eyes filmy and distant, her hands floating in the soapy water. It put a chill in me, because I couldn't remember ever seeing that look before. Dove was a great one for making philosophical pronouncements and shelling out advice, solicited or not. But if she had regrets about the course she'd taken, she'd always kept them to herself. That wasn't, I realized shamefaced, the same thing as not having them.

"What?" I said. "What are you thinking?"

She slowly unhooked her gaze from the window. To my surprise, her eyes shone with tears. She laughed, lifting her hands out of the sink and wiping them on a dish towel.

"Nothin'," she said. "Just bein' a silly old fool."

"Sit down, and I'll make us some coffee."

"Naw, I got to be gettin' on home. Rowena and me is headin' down to Marshall in the morning, to the pottery."

"Are you sure? You don't want to stay and talk awhile?"

"You got better things to do than listen to an old lady yammer."

"Name one." I pulled out a chair, but she shook her head.

"Maybe another time, Lucy Bird." She handed me the dish

towel. Her eyes were dry, her face the same brown, time-worn one I'd always known. "You mind that garden, now. You got to keep it weeded and watered. Might want to get Ash to run you some hosing out there so you don't have to tote no buckets."

Good luck with that, I thought, as I walked my aunt to the door and called Lily up from the pond.

"I guess I'll be getting back to the Piney View," Ty said as Dove and Lily drove away.

"You're welcome to wait on Denny," I said. "I could put on some coffee if you want to stay awhile."

"Thanks, but I've been waiting a good long time already," he said. "Anyway, she knows where to find me."

Our company gone, Jude and I walked down to the garden, where he ran between the rows, proudly pointing out to me the different types of tomato plants, the furry green cilantro and dark, shiny-leafed basil.

Dove was on to something, I thought. Maybe it was seeing ourselves in new and unexpected ways that led us to find out things about ourselves we never knew.

I knelt and gathered a handful of rich pine mulch, made a ball of it in my fist. "Doggone it, I'm a gardener," I said out loud. Jude started to laugh, and I did, too. I felt like Scarlett O'Hara at Tara. That scene in the movie got me every time.

CHAPTER 21

Denny

ONE ADVANTAGE OF having an emotional crisis in Cade County as opposed to Nashville was that you could drive aimlessly for hours and not have to think about a thing. Nashville was all noise and hustle, having to be on top of your game every single minute of the day, whereas in rural northeast Texas you could just set the cruise control and the radio and let your mind roam where it wanted. The worst that could happen, you might hit a possum, instead of a guy with a guitar and a demo tape in his pocket. Come to think of it, I'd probably have felt worse about hitting the possum.

I drove without watching the odometer or the highway markers, crossing into neighboring counties and looping back again, passing familiar markers—the Miracle Mart, and Willie B.'s barbecue shed, closed for the night—and some I'd never seen before, like McLean's Hair Salon and Gun Shop, where a lighted sign out front read:

SHAMPOO & SET $7
SMITH & WESSON SALE!!!

The sky did its slow fade from pale lilac to dark, bruised purple, and I switched on the headlights and rolled down the windows to let the wind catch my hair and the cab fill up with night smells and John Hiatt singing, *Love comes out of nowhere, baby, just like a hurricane.*

I stopped at a little filling station at the Marion County line to top off my tank. Going inside to pay, I had to walk past an icy tub of soft drinks, racks of Little Debbie snack cakes and Fritos calling my name. If I headed home now, I might still make it in time for supper. I tried to picture my-self walking in through the front door, telling Daddy I was sorry.

But I wasn't; I couldn't let it go. Anyway, when you got right down to it, this was partly his fault. Stubbornness was a Farrell thing, passed down through the genes. His mama had it—at least before her mind started to unravel—and Loretta Lynn would probably have it, too.

Daddy had cut himself off from the world too much lately, and it was starting to show. His nerves were shot, not on ac-count of me, or even because he'd quit drinking, but because he was a man who wasn't meant to be bored. He needed something to bring him back to life, keep the juices stirred.

Climbing back behind the wheel of the truck, I thought

about that priest Daddy was always talking about, the one who ran the AA meetings. I'd never met the man, couldn't even remember his name, except that it was something weird. Still, there couldn't be that many priests in Jefferson, and maybe he could help me figure out a way to smooth things over with Daddy. It wasn't the greatest idea I'd ever had, not by a long shot, but it seemed like as good a place as any to start.

JEFFERSON WAS A pretty place, especially compared to Mooney. The streets were wide and manicured, a lot of the old houses converted into shops or restaurants, and the main street was full of tourists in shorts and sneakers toting shopping bags. Live music poured from the doors of one establishment. I slowed down long enough to make out someone mangling an Eagles song. The drummer had supposedly grown up around here, and the town was milking it for all it was worth.

"Oh, sure, you mean Punch Laughlin," said the checker at Brookshire's grocery. She was about my age, her face pitted with acne scars and the backs of the knuckles on her left hand tattooed with the name RIKKI. "St. Jude's. Just take a right at the corner. It's four or five blocks the other side of downtown. Redbrick building. White steeple. It's, you know, a church." I wasn't sure if she was yanking my chain or not, but I got out of there in a hurry, saying a little prayer of thanks that I hadn't ended up clerking in a small-town grocery store, at least not yet.

The parking lot at St. Jude's was full of cars. I was standing beside my truck wondering what the hell I was doing there when a maroon van pulled into the empty slot next to mine and a heavyset man in a Texas Rangers shirt got out.

"Howdy," he said. "You here for the meeting?"

"I'm not sure," I said truthfully.

"Hey, I was scared to death my first time, too," he said. "But you'll never meet a better bunch a folks. Swear to God, they saved my life."

"Oh, I'm not— I mean, I don't have a drinking problem."

The man laughed. "No offense, but that's what we all used to say, every single one of us. Come on, let me introduce you to Punch."

I fell in beside him and followed him toward the building. "You don't have to do anything but sit and listen if you want," he said. "Takes some folks a long time to get the nerve to speak up. I'm Stan, by the way." He put out his hand.

"Denise." I don't know why I decided to use my given name, I guess because it let me feel like I was masquerading as somebody else.

We walked through a courtyard full of roses and into a small meeting room, gray metal folding chairs arranged in rows before a podium, a table at the back holding a coffee urn and plastic trays of store-bought cookies. Fluorescent lights buzzed overhead, and a dozen or so people stood in twos and threes, sipping coffee in Styrofoam cups and talking. A woman burst out laughing, and it made me jump. I looked around, taking in the crowd of noisy, friendly people, the banner hanging at the front of the room, white letters on blue that read *God grant me the serenity to accept the things I cannot change, the courage to change the things I can, and the wisdom to know the difference.*

A man in running shorts and sneakers with a fringe of dark hair around his ears came over to the table to refill his coffee, and Stan steered me over to him.

"Punch, I wantcha to meet a new recruit. This here's Denise."

"How do you do," I said. *If you're a priest, I'm Mother Teresa,* I thought.

He had to set down his coffee to shake my hand. His eyes scanned my face in a way that made me feel hot under the collar. "You look familiar," he said.

I was trying to figure out how to answer that when Daddy walked in. There was a skinny black-haired girl with him, not that much older than me, wearing stovepipe jeans and a hot pink scoop-necked sweater. This must be the famous Heather Starbird, who cleaned houses for a living and was allegedly engaged to an imprisoned pot smuggler, and who just happened to be Daddy's AA sponsor. I remembered how, when Daddy first came back to Mooney the year before and started hanging out with Heather, Lucy had suspected some kind of hanky-panky going on between them, but I didn't see how Daddy, even back in his drinking days, would have stooped this low. She looked like a truck-stop groupie, the kind of girl who hangs around the tour bus and offers to do the sound guy while the band goes inside for cheeseburgers. On the other hand, she was at least partially responsible for Daddy being sober now. I guessed I shouldn't judge her on looks alone.

He was listening to something Heather was saying when he happened to see me standing between Punch and Stan. For a second his expression was like Punch's, like he was going to walk over and ask if we knew each other from some-place.

Just then, a woman in a baggy blue dress stepped up to the podium. "Ladies and gentlemen, could you take your seats, please?" she said. "We've got a lot to cover this evening."

Daddy gave a quick, angry jerk of his chin, and I excused myself and made my way against the tide of people filing into the rows of chairs.

"What are you doing here, Denise?" His eyes were stormy, the way they'd been when I told him about Evelyn that after-noon.

"I didn't mean to crash the meeting," I said.

"You need to leave."

"I've got to talk to you. Please."

I wish I could say that his face changed, that it softened or flooded with tenderness, but that was just wishful thinking on my part. It was a bad habit of mine, one I couldn't seem to break no matter how much real life taught me otherwise. He did reach out and touch me, but it was to wrap his hand around my arm and maneuver me to the door.

"You can't be here," he said to me once we were outside in the courtyard. "Do you understand?"

"No, sir. I guess I don't."

"What happens here is private. You can't just come waltzing in off the street like this is some party you decided to crash."

"I said I was sorry! I didn't know there was a meeting. I came to talk to Father Laughlin."

Through the open door, we could hear the priest calling the meeting to order.

"You were looking for Punch?" Daddy said. "What for?"

"I don't know. I remembered you talking about him. He sounded like a cool guy. I thought maybe he could tell me how to— Well, to fix what happened this afternoon." I shook his hand off my arm. "Never mind. Bad idea. I seem to have a lot of those lately."

I turned around and started to walk back across the courtyard to the parking lot. I was unlocking the truck when Daddy caught up with me.

"Hang on," he said. I turned and looked at him. He was still mad, but his face had gotten lighter somehow, around the eyes. "Come with me."

I followed him around the side of the building, up a set of concrete steps, and through a set of double doors into the church sanctuary. It was dark as a cave in there, with a scary-looking Jesus hanging by bloody nails on a wooden cross over the altar and rows of wooden pews gleaming in the light of dozens of tiny white candles. I remembered hearing somewhere that every candle represented a prayer, that as long as the flame burned the prayer was still alive.

"You can wait here," Daddy said. "The meeting'll be over in about an hour. Then you can talk to Punch, or whatever it is you came here to do."

After he left me there, I stood for a while at the back of the room, letting my eyes adjust to the darkness. I could count on one hand the number of churches I'd been in in my life. Ma wasn't real big on God when I was growing up, except sometimes at Christmas or Easter, when she'd get a surge of old Christian guilt from childhood and drag me off to places like this, with its smells of mildew and incense, plaster saints whose names I'd never learned gazing down from little cubbies in the walls. It would be nice to be a saint, I thought, to have people set flowers and candles at your feet in return for whatever it was they needed, hope or redemption or forgiveness. On second thought, I guessed it wasn't all that different from what I did for a living, minus the part about eternal life.

Daddy'd been raised Catholic before Ma wore it out of him, so maybe that's why I felt like I'd been here before as I made my way down the center aisle, the dark-red carpet spongy under my feet, and slid into a pew. I stared at Jesus on the cross, his face twisted in agony, and wondered if I should pray, but I didn't really know how. What were the rules? Could you just talk to him, or did you have to have some kind of holy permission first? I decided to give it a shot anyway. *Hi*, I said silently. *Maybe you remember me—St. Alban's in Dallas, about fifteen years ago, Christmas Eve? I was in a green corduroy jumper that rode up under my arms and black patent-leather shoes, and I wanted to go up and take communion but Ma wouldn't let me, because I wasn't baptized. I wanted to see if it was true, like they said, that the wine and bread turned into your blood and flesh. I wanted to see for myself how it tasted. But now that I think about it, it was your*

birthday and there were a lot of people that night, so you prob-
ably don't remember.

I waited, giving Jesus a chance to say something back, but the only sound was of the air conditioner ruffling the pages of a bible on the pulpit. I closed my eyes, breathing in the musty air, feeling the kinks go out of my neck. It was nice there in the cool, dark church. Maybe Jesus wouldn't mind if I just sat for a while and let my mind drift. Maybe, even though my soul was impure, he'd still enjoy the company.

It seemed like only a few minutes later that Daddy was reaching into the pew, shaking my shoulder. I was sorry to have to get up and go with him out into the muggy spring night, the voices of the AA members loud and lively as they walked to their cars in the parking lot. I felt fuzzy-headed and couldn't quite remember why I came. The events of that afternoon seemed like they'd happened to somebody else, and Daddy, too, seemed different, less angry, more like his old self.

"I can take you to Punch's office if you want," he said. "He'll be finished up here in a few minutes."

"That's okay. It's you I really wanted to talk to."

He stood looking at me like he didn't know how to take this.

"Give me a minute," he said, and went back inside the meeting room. In a few minutes he came out again with Heather, and they walked together across the parking lot to an old brown station wagon. After a short conversation, she got behind the wheel and drove away, and he came back to where I stood waiting at the foot of the steps.

"Have you had your supper?" he asked.

"No, sir."

We drove past a place called Dee's on Austin Street that he swore had the best potpie he'd ever tasted, but the lights were out and the sign on the door said CLOSED, COME AGAIN. So we went instead to one of those big, bustling twenty-four-hour places out on the highway, lit up like high noon and jammed with patrons and waitresses in polyester uniforms toting trays of food and carafes of coffee. Everything on the menu looked like stuff that would go straight to your hips or your arteries and stay there for the next thirty years. I ordered the Sunnyside Up platter—scrambled eggs and French toast, bacon and hash browns, an extra-large orange juice. Daddy just asked for coffee.

We didn't talk while we waited for the food. Neither one of us seemed to know where to start, and I was beginning to think this was a mistake, that I could just show up out of the blue and make him open his heart to me. How was it, I wondered, that he was able to talk about his darkest secrets in front of total strangers when he couldn't even look his own daughter in the eye?

"Listen," I said after the waitress had brought his coffee and my juice. "About what happened at the house today. I guess maybe it is crazy to think you could just let Evelyn into your life after however many years. I can see that. But I got left behind, too, don't forget, when I was a baby. So don't think I don't know how it feels, because I do." Daddy stared at me over the lip of his coffee cup. I thought about the eyes of the statues in St. Jude's, and pressed on. "But what else I know is that you can carry it around and let it eat you up, or you can try to set it aside and open up a place in your heart. I did the second thing, and I've never been sorry. Well, hardly ever."

For a long time Daddy just sat, turning his cup slowly around and around in its saucer.

"It's funny," he said finally.

"What is?"

"The lesson at tonight's meeting was about Step Four. 'Knowing yourself.' False pride, humility, selfishness. Admitting mistakes. Forgiveness and understanding." He smiled, a little. "Make a plan, Punch said, and then go out and live it! He made it sound as simple as making out a grocery list."

The waitress arrived, set down my platter, and topped off Daddy's coffee. I took a bite of the runny, watery eggs. They tasted like heaven.

"How come you were looking for Punch, anyway?" he asked.

"I was driving around and I remembered you talking about this priest in Jefferson. I guess maybe I was hoping he might be able to tell me how I could find a way for you and me to talk."

"Is that what you want?"

"Yes, sir. I do."

"All right, then," he said. "Let's talk."

I stopped eating, my fork in midair. "Seriously?"

"Whatever you want to know."

"Tell me about Evelyn," I said.

"Oh, for Christ's sake, Denise!"

"I mean it. Tell me. Everything you remember about her."

He sighed and sat back in the booth.

"Not much, to tell you the truth. I was only three when she left. Most of what I know is stuff Christa told me."

"Like what?"

"Like how she got up in front of the whole town at the Dogwood Days festival and sang 'I Fall to Pieces,' knocked everybody on their ass. Better than Patsy Cline, they said." I didn't tell him I already knew that story; I wanted to hear it from his lips. "My daddy was a dickhead to walk out on us," he said. "She never had the backbone to make it on her own. Not like your mama did. I'm not trying to say what I did was right, leaving you and Marlene. I'm just saying that I never worried whether or not you'd be taken care of. Marlene was a little ditzy, but she wasn't gonna forget about you and the bills and the groceries and the laundry. She wasn't gonna let you wind up in a closet eating dog biscuits."

I thought this over while I ate my French toast. "But Evelyn giving you to the Kellers to raise," I said. "Maybe that was the best thing she knew to do. I mean, maybe she knew that Christa would take care of you better than she could."

"You're not the first person to say so."

"You know, you've made Evelyn into this, this devil woman, all full of meanness and hate," I said. "But just because she went off her rocker when your daddy left, that doesn't mean she didn't want something better for you than she could give you. It seems to me you've spent your whole life judging her, but you've never really known her."

He pushed aside his empty coffee cup and slid sideways out of the booth.

"Don't," I said, setting down my fork. "Don't leave now."

"Relax," he said. "I'm going to the men's room. Finish your supper. I'll be right back."

He was gone a long time, long enough for the waitress to clear the table and leave the check. When he got back, his hair at the temples and the collar of his shirt were damp. He sat down, picked up the check and glanced at it, then turned it upside down again.

"I'm going to see a doctor tomorrow down in Marshall," he said.

"What kind of doctor?"

"The kind who can maybe help me get my head screwed on a little bit straighter."

I watched a couple of truckers standing at the register, joking loudly with the waitress while she rang up their tabs. The waitress looked tired but cheerful, loose breasted and heavy legged in her shiny brown uniform, and for a half a second I let myself imagine the easy rhythms of her life, tracing the same pattern in the worn carpet night after night, carrying trays of pancakes and pots of coffee, teasing the regulars and greeting strangers, doling out nourishment both physical and spiritual. It was another bad habit of mine, assuming that other people's lives were less complicated and more satisfying than mine. For all I knew, she had six kids to feed, was two months behind in the rent, was waiting for the doctor to call her back with the results of the biopsy. Or maybe she was happy as a fucking clam. This, here, was the hand I'd been dealt, and there was nothing I could do but change what I could and accept what I couldn't.

"I could go with you, if you want," I said. "I mean, if you want some company?"

"Thanks," Daddy said as he took out his wallet. "That'd be good."

We drove home, the night road wide and empty, a slice of orange moon hanging in the rearview mirror. There was so much more I wanted to ask him, but he'd sunk back into himself again: talked out, maybe, or just lost in his own thoughts. I was dying for a cigarette, but I made myself think about Loretta, floating inside me in the warm dark. I thought about her daddy, off who knows where doing who knows what, and about Ty back at the house, or at the Piney View, waiting on me. I thought about Erasmus on a jet plane, on his way back to New York and Camille, then on to Paris. All of us, in our own ways, just trying to find a way home.

CHAPTER 22

Lucy

ASH CAME HOME the next day with a bottle of pills and a booklet called *Clinical Depression and You.*

"How'd it go?" I asked, stepping out of my shoes and sitting down beside him on the bed.

"The doctor asked me a few questions about my history, what was going on in my life right now. Then she gave me these." He held up the bottle. "I'm supposed to check back in three or four weeks, let her know if they help."

I took the bottle from him and scanned the label. "I remember the commercials on TV for this," I said. "The ones where in the beginning the people can't get off the couch, and sixty seconds later they're telling jokes and dancing at parties."

Ash nodded. "I want to feel better, Luce. But—I don't know. Doesn't seem like I should have to swallow a pill to do it."

"Maybe we ought to call Geneva," I said. "Ask her what she thinks."

"Oh, for God's sake," she said when I reached her on her cell. "I can't believe they're still prescribing that crap! It has the worst side effects of anything on the market, and it's hell to come off of. Do you know that when the manufacturer was going for FDA approval fifteen years ago, the clinical trials lasted twelve *weeks*?"

"What does that mean?"

"It means that nobody had any idea how the drug would work after six months or a year, much less ten or fifteen years. Did Ash tell the doctor he used to drink?"

"I think so. Why?"

"Most alcoholics have liver damage. They don't metabolize chemicals like a regular person."

"Meaning what?"

"Meaning those pills could end up making him feel worse, not better."

"Well, hell. What should we do?"

"The first thing I'd do is call that doctor and rag her ass out."

"We thought she'd talk to Ash, not just stick a bottle of pills in his hand and send him on his way."

"Let me see what I can do," Geneva said. "There's a new, young guy at County, a psychotherapist who supposedly worked with addicts in an inner-city clinic up north somewhere before he came here. I don't know him, but everybody who's met him says he's great."

"Will you talk to Ash a minute? Tell him what you just told me?"

I handed him the phone and went downstairs to start supper: Salisbury steak, mashed potatoes, green beans from
Dove's garden. I went out to the laundry room to put some
towels in the dryer and was setting the kitchen table when I
heard Ash come downstairs.

"Supper's almost ready," I said. "I made you Dove's beans."

"Thanks, but I'm not hungry."

Before I could give him my speech about having to eat
sometimes even when you don't feel like it, he walked up behind me and put his hand on my hip. I spun around, startled,
and almost dropped the plate I was holding. More and more
lately Ash had a faraway look in his eyes, like he was listening
to voices nobody else could hear. But his gaze now was clear
and focused, locked hard on mine.

"I love you," he said. "You know that, right?"

"Of course I— Ash, you're scaring me."

"There's nothing to be scared about. I just need a little
time, that's all."

"Time for what? What are you talking about?"

I followed him into the hall. His duffel bag was parked on
the floor next to the front door, and he leaned over and
hoisted it, swinging the strap over his shoulder.

"Where are you going?"

"Promise me you won't worry, okay?" He leaned over and
kissed me gently along the part in my hair, a seemingly harmless gesture he'd adopted the year before that always seemed
to be the harbinger of something bad. "I'll call you," he said,
and before I could unravel the knot of fear in my throat,
he'd crossed the front yard and climbed into his truck. I

stood inside the screen door, watching his taillights head off up the road.

I was still standing there a few minutes later when Denny came downstairs, yawning and rubbing the sleep out of her eyes.

"What?" she said when she saw my face. I realized I was holding a dish towel in my fists, twisting it around and around, the same thing I'd done the morning my first husband, Mitchell, died. I unclenched my hands and the towel fluttered to the floorboards.

"Your daddy's gone," I said.

"Gone where?"

"I don't know. He said not to worry, and that he loved me, and that he'd call."

"That's weird."

"He had a bag."

"What kind of bag?"

"His duffel. Clothes, I guess. I don't know."

"Did you guys have a fight or something?"

"No. When I got home he told me about the doctor, her giving him the pills, and I called Geneva to ask her what she thought. She said he shouldn't take them, that they might make him sick, especially because he used to drink." My words tumbled over themselves, like the faster I got them out, the faster somebody could help me make sense of them. "He was still talking to her when I came downstairs to fix supper. The next thing I knew, he came in saying he wasn't hungry and that he loved me and there was nothing to be scared of, he just needed some time . . ."

"Time for what?"

"I don't know!"

"Why are you crying, Mama?" Jude stood at the door to the TV room, scratching one bare foot. I didn't think I could stand the look on his face; I remembered wearing it myself when I was his age, watching my own mama wail and tear her hair out over my daddy, Raymond Hatch.

"I'm not crying."

"But your eyes are—"

"Run in the bathroom and wash up," Denny said, giving him a pat on the behind. "Supper's almost ready." Jude went, shooting a suspicious look back over his shoulder. She bent and scooped the dish towel off the floor, then slid her arm around me and guided me toward the kitchen.

I sat down at the table, thinking how ignorant I'd been just a few minutes earlier, how perfectly fine my life had been, stirring flour into the gravy, setting the table. Why were our everyday pleasures always sweetest in retrospect? Why did we never understand how good we'd had it till it was gone?

"Now, look," Denny said as she turned off the burner under the beans. "I admit this is a little bizarre, but I don't think it's anything to freak out about."

"But he took a bag! Why would he take a bag unless he—"

A new scenario leapt sudden and fully formed into my mind, so terrible I couldn't make myself say it. Ash kept a couple of handguns in a lockbox in the closet; I hadn't seen them since he'd used one to shoot a snake in the woodpile last winter. It paralyzed me, the thought that he could be suffering that badly and I hadn't known it. Had I been so preoccupied by my own troubles that I'd let his grow and fester unchecked, until he'd come to believe that the only way out was the permanent kind?

"Let's call Geneva," Denny said, handing me the phone. "Maybe he said something to her that'll help us figure this out."

"He sounded okay when I talked to him," Geneva said. "Kinda down in the mouth, sure, about the doctor and all. But he asked me if I'd set something up for him with the psychologist at County. That doesn't sound like somebody who's about to walk out on his life, not to me."

"Well, he did," I said. "He packed a bag and everything."

"What was in the bag?"

"I don't know, Gen! I didn't get a chance to ask him."

"Honey, no offense, but you need to get a grip. There's bound to be a totally logical explanation for all this. I'm sure he'll call in an hour or two and tell you where he is and what he's up to, and everything will make perfect sense. A couple of days, max."

"A couple of *days*?" I hated waiting for test results, hated waiting for my photos to be developed and my rolls to rise. I was no good at patience, at letting things unfold in their own good time.

"You could call the sheriff," Geneva suggested.

"A lot of good that would do. There's no way they'll put out an APB on a man who left of his own free will and took a bag full of socks and T-shirts with him."

"I thought you didn't know what was in the bag."

"I don't! I'm just— Oh, God."

"What?"

While we were talking I'd carried the cordless upstairs and stood scanning our bedroom, looking for clues. The bottle of pills from the doctor in Marshall was still sitting on the night table, alongside Ash's cell phone.

"His phone is here. He said he'd call, but he left his phone!"

"Well, Lucy, maybe he knew they'd have a phone where he's going."

"They? Who is 'they'?"

"It's a figure of speech! Jesus."

I started pawing through the bureau drawers. The ones on Ash's side were half empty, but that might only mean half his stuff was downstairs in the laundry.

I lifted my head and caught a glimpse of myself in the mirror, wild-eyed, the phone jammed between my ear and my shoulder, my hair going in a million different directions. That's when I saw the piece of paper, folded in thirds and propped against the spare-change jar, my name scrawled across it in Ash's spindly hand.

"I'll call you back," I said to Geneva.

I sat down on the bed where I'd sat beside Ash only a few minutes earlier, my hands shaking as I unfolded the paper and smoothed it across my knees. I had to read it twice; Ash's handwriting had always been terrible.

> *Baby,*
> *I haven't felt like myself for a while now, I guess that's*
> *no big news. Seems like ever since I met you, it's been a*

crazy road. Sometimes we've walked it together and sometimes on our own. This is one of those times I have to go it alone. I hope you'll try and trust me on this, I know it's asking a lot.

Your love is the flame. I have my eyes on it all the time. Keep it burning so that I can come home to you whole-hearted.

Your old boy,

Ash

I got up slowly, refolding the paper and slipping it into the pocket of my skirt. As I went downstairs, I could hear Denny in the kitchen telling Jude not to play with his potatoes. I stopped to take the key to the studio out of the vase on the table in the front hall, then let myself out the screen door and walked across the yard.

I flicked on the lights in the studio and stood in the doorway, looking in. I didn't come out here often; it always felt like trespassing. Ash's guitars, bought in an early flush with Nashville money, stood at attention in their stands. The soundboard gleamed, spotless as a virgin. The air felt stale, heavy with dashed dreams. I couldn't feel Ash's presence there, except in what was absent: the pile of notebooks he'd kept scattered on the table and his old Martin guitar, its empty stand like a missing tooth in a row of shiny, perfect specimens.

My heart slowed, resuming its regular rhythm as I fingered the piece of paper in my pocket. I didn't know where Ash had gone. But I thought I knew why.

* * *

I DON'T GET it," Geneva said as I poured her a cup of coffee. She'd driven out as soon as I'd hung up earlier, expecting to find me climbing the walls, not up to my elbows in butter and flour.

"I told you, this is Granny Munroe's pound cake. You know, the one Granddaddy paid twenty dollars for at the church bazaar, just to get her to go for a ride with him?" I'd always loved the family story even though I had a hard time believing it; my granddaddy had been tight as a tick with money, and the only times he ever went to church were for weddings and funerals.

"I was talking about Ash," Geneva said.

"I've already told you what I know."

"You're saying this is some kind of a soul-searching thing? Like leaving home to find home?"

"Sort of, yeah." I finished pouring the batter into the pan and cracked open the oven door to check the temperature.

"Well, you know, maybe it isn't such a bad thing that that doctor blew him off," she said. "Pills don't work forever. Sooner or later, he'd still have to learn to deal with whatever he went looking for help with in the first place." Upstairs, Lily and Jude were making a racket over a video game Lily'd brought along. "You're sure you don't want me to send Bailey out looking for him?"

"Where would he look? Anyway, Ash said he'd call."

"And you believe him."

"Yes! I believe him. Is that such a crazy thing?" I balanced the cake pan on the middle shelf of the oven, then shut the door gently and set the timer. When I turned to look at Geneva, she glanced down guiltily into her coffee. "You think he's out drinking, don't you?" I said. "Or acting like a wild-ass, tearing up the countryside."

"You're putting words in my mouth."

The screen door squealed and Bailey came into the kitchen balancing Emmy on his hip. Her wispy black hair had been fastened with a pink barrette on top of her head, and she wore a diaper and a T-shirt proclaiming, for any fool who couldn't see, that she loved her daddy.

"We just saw our first june bug," he said. "I had a time convincing her it wouldn't make a tasty snack."

"Come here, june bug," Geneva said, reaching for the baby, who grinned her megawatt grin as she passed from one parent to the other. In spite of what a happy sight it was, I felt a pang at the memories it conjured up, of Ash and me when Jude was a baby, how we'd lain in bed in the mornings handing him back and forth between us like two kids with a Christmas toy, nothing from his fat little feet to the soft spot on the top of his head too trivial not to kiss and poke and exclaim over endlessly.

I excused myself and went out into the yard. The lights along the dock winked like fireflies in the dusk, and the air was heavy with the false promise of rain. The windows were open and from Jude's room I could hear his and Lily's voices, the sound of the TV that Ty and Denny were watching downstairs.

This was the house that Ash built. He'd built it for himself, to keep his hands busy and his head on straight, but he'd built it for me, too, and for our family. We never talked much about love, had never been good with the words; but who needed words when every board and nail, when the walls around you and the roof over your head, were there to testify to it? I wondered now if I'd ever really seen the gift for what it was, or if, like so many things, it was only in retrospect that I understood how much it mattered.

I tilted my chin and studied the sky, deep blue velvet overhead shading to mauve in the west. Above the pines the evening star pulsed, steady as a lighthouse beacon. Back in our Nashville days, when Ash was on the road, we had a rule, that wherever we were, we'd stop for a minute and go outside and fix our eyes on the evening star. It was how we stayed connected; and I couldn't help wondering if he was somewhere now looking at the sky and thinking about me.

The screen door opened and Bailey came out into the yard. I smiled at the sight of him. In the last year or so he'd started to thicken a little around the middle, but like the flecks of gray that had lately appeared at his temples, it only made him more attractive.

"Smells like rain," he said.

"It always does this time of night. Not gonna happen, though."

He rocked back on his heels and looked at the sky. "You know, Lucy, I could drive around a little, see if I can flush Ash out."

"Thanks. But no."

"I guess now's not the time to say I wish you'd married somebody—"

"What—normal?"

"Maybe 'ordinary' would be a better word. Like a banker, or a mechanic."

"You know, maybe this serves me right," I said. "I used to be the one who took off at the drop of a hat. Now I guess it's Ash's turn."

"Marriage is hard," he said. "Everybody needs a break sometimes."

"Come on. You and Kit are the original good guys. No way you'd ever just up and pack a bag and head out the door."

"Well, you don't always have to take off to leave. Sometimes you just get to feeling like—like the two of you aren't on the same page anymore. Gen and I've had our moments over the years, and so have Kit and Connie. The main thing is that we always found our way back home again."

"I can't hold him, Bailey."

He looked over at me. "What's that supposed to mean?"

"I always knew I'd never be able to give Ash everything he needs. Every now and then I just have to step back and let him make his own way."

"You're not worried, then."

"Sure I am. But he asked me to trust him. I guess I have to try."

My brother slipped his hand under my hair, against the back of my neck. I could feel the calluses on his palm, smell the Lava soap on his skin that had been a part of him for as long as

I could remember. I'd wondered earlier if having brothers like mine had ruined me for real life, but in fact I saw now that their sweet, solid presence had had the opposite effect on me, had given me the foundation I needed to love a man like Ash, with his whims and riddles, all his shades of gray.

We walked slowly back to the house, and Bailey headed upstairs to check on Lily and Jude. In the kitchen I found Geneva with Emmy, droopy-eyed with sleep, over her shoulder. The smell of pound cake made my mouth water.

"Let me," I said, lifting the baby out of Geneva's arms and cradling her against my chest. As I eased myself carefully into a chair at the table, she made a little pigeonlike coo of contentment and sank back into sleep.

"So," Geneva said, "what's the story on Denny and this Briggs fellow?"

"Did you meet him?"

"He came in and got a couple of Cokes from the icebox. Good-looking as all get-out, I'll say that for him."

"She hasn't told me much. All I know for sure is that there were three men hanging around a week ago, and now there's only one." I rested my chin on top of Emmy's head. "I think she's been half in love with Ty for years. Way before Will Culpepper came into the picture. The question is whether or not she'll let herself believe she deserves somebody like Ty. Somebody who won't rake her heart over the coals, like she seems to expect."

"It's funny, isn't it?" Geneva said. "How we either go looking for somebody just like our daddy, or the exact opposite? Of course, sometimes we think we're getting one thing and we end up with another." She smiled. "I remember back when Bailey was riding bulls. I thought he was just about the wildest thing on two legs. Then he got hurt and came home and started building houses with Kit, and he turned out to be a straight arrow, after all."

"Bailey always was a straight arrow," I said. "That bull-riding thing might have given him a shiny surface for a while, but inside, he hasn't changed since he was eight years old. You probably knew that from the time you first started dating him."

"When I first started dating him, all I cared about was that he was hot."

"Maybe. But you don't marry hot."

"Some do." I shot her a look, and she laughed. "I was talking about Denny, not you."

"You know, I always knew there was more to Ash than just what you get on the surface," I said. "I mean, I knew there was a real, complicated man inside. I guess I just didn't realize quite *how* complicated." I ran my finger along the ivory curve of Emmy's foot. "I wish I knew why things always seem to pile up this way. Just when it seems we're getting a chance to catch our breath, here comes Denny, pregnant and dragging a string of men behind her. And then I find out I'm losing my job, and then comes that mess with Evelyn . . ."

"What mess with Evelyn?"

"Oh, Lord. I forgot you didn't know."

I told her about Evelyn's escapade in the woods and Denny and Ash's blowup over the idea of Evelyn moving in with us.

"Ash and his mama haven't had anything to do with each

other in years," Geneva said. "Why in the world would you take her in now, a total stranger? Who'd look after her?"

"I said all those things, believe me. The thing is, I see Ash's side of it, but I can kind of see Denny's, too. We're the only kin Evelyn's got. And it's not like she's got some disease where she has to be hooked up to a bunch of tubes and monitors. Maybe she'd do better with a little homegrown TLC."

"You know what your problem is?" Geneva said, wagging a finger at me.

"No, but I'm sure you're about to tell me."

"You think that if you do the right thing, it will all turn out rosy in the end."

"Since when is that a character flaw?"

"When it means you're setting yourself up for disappointment, over and over again."

"But how do I know I'll be disappointed? How can you possibly know how things will turn out if you don't try?" Emmy made a little snuffling sound in her sleep and re-arranged herself on my shoulder.

"So is that how come Ash took off? Because of the business over his mama?"

I shook my head. "I don't think so. Oh, maybe that was part of it. But it's not the main thing."

Lily and Jude came stampeding down the stairs and into the room, Geneva doing her best to shush them about waking the baby.

"Can I sleep at Lily's tonight?" Jude asked. I started to say no, that I wanted him home with me, until I saw that the anxious look he'd worn on his face earlier was gone, erased by the prospect of a sleepover with his cousin. All Jude's life, his daddy had come and gone. Even during the worst of Ash's drinking days, when we didn't hear from him for an eight-month stretch, he'd always, eventually, showed up again, tying the circle closed. This latest vanishing act either hadn't yet registered on Jude's radar or just felt like business as usual to him. I didn't know which possibility was more disheartening.

I tried to talk them into staying until the cake was out of the oven, but they said they needed to get home and get Emmy to bed. Bailey bundled up the sleeping baby and carried her to the truck as Geneva and I followed slowly, arm in arm.

"I don't know what I'd do without you," I said. "You keep on showing up and saving my life."

"Like you haven't saved mine plenty of times."

"Remember when you first found out I was pregnant with Jude, and you left and went up to Atlanta to stay with Lynda awhile? I don't think I was ever so scared in my life. I felt like I'd lost a piece of my heart."

"Then you know how I felt when you and Ash moved to Nashville."

"Sometimes I wish we'd never left to begin with. Seems like all our troubles started when that guy from Arcadia Records showed up."

"Honey, trouble's gonna find you no matter where you are. Yours might have taken another direction if you hadn't gone to Nashville, but it always catches up with you eventually. You've just got to learn to roll with what comes your way. Duck when you need to, or stand up and face it head-on."

"You're starting to sound more like Dove every day."

"I'll take that as a compliment."

We stood next to the pickup, wrapped in each other's arms. Once, not so long before, we'd talked about seeing ourselves as gray-haired old ladies together, rocking on a porch somewhere, surrounded by pets and grandbabies. Someday, I knew, tonight would be just another story we told each other, one more "remember when."

I hugged her and Bailey one last time, gave Jude a kiss, told them all I loved them and to drive safe, then stood watching their taillights move off up the road in the dark.

After they were gone, I stood in the yard listening to the frogs down at the pond singing their hallelujah chorus. You walked along the road for a little while, following its everyday twists and turns, and then all of a sudden something you didn't see coming reared up in your path, and you had to stop and figure out a way around. Or maybe, as Punch Laughlin liked to say, you just had to step back and let God point the way. The trouble with God, in my opinion, was that he hardly ever just stuck out his arm and said, "Right this way, folks." I'd known since I first took up with Ash that he would not be an easy man to love, but it seemed to me that he'd been thrown more than his share of roadblocks.

I took the pound cake out of the oven and set it on a rack to cool, then stuck my head into the TV room where Jimmy Buffett and Alan Jackson were on the big screen, singing that it was five o'clock somewhere. Denny and Ty sat at opposite ends of the couch, but her legs were stretched in his direction and his hand rested lightly, almost casually, on her bare foot.

"There's cake in the kitchen if y'all want it," I said. "I'm going on up to bed."

I put on my nightgown and sat down to read Ash's note again, then tucked the folded paper under my pillow and switched off the lamp. Punch Laughlin's God felt very far away to me, a big shot fielding phone calls and snapping his fingers, making decisions without rhyme or reason. I crawled under the bedclothes and closed my eyes, trying without much luck to keep God on the line. *It's okay,* I told him. *I'll hold.*

THE PHONE RANG, jerking me out of a fevered half sleep as I fumbled in the dark for the receiver.

"Ash?" I said into the mouthpiece. My heart was pounding like a jackhammer. Lightning flickered outside the windows, and raindrops sheeted the panes.

"Hi, baby."

His voice moved through me, spreading slow and warm and narcotic through my veins.

"Where are you?" I asked. The clock on the night table said 1:34.

"Not too far away."

"Are you all right?"

"Right as rain. You been worried about me?"

"A little." I settled back against the pillows, cradling the phone between my shoulder and chin. "Not so much after I saw what you took with you."

His laugh was soft in my ear. "Not much gets past you, does it?"

"Not anymore."

"I'm sorry I had to do this," he said.

"It's okay."

"Is it?"

"Yeah, I think so. I mean, I think I understand."

"You're something else, Lucy Hatch, you know that?"

"I know."

We were quiet awhile. This was a thing we'd once done well, sitting in easy silence on opposite ends of a phone line from far-flung corners of the countryside.

"I'm scared, Luce," Ash said. "I'm not sure I can do this."

I shifted the phone to the other ear. "Do what?"

"I never used to have to think about writing music, you know? The songs were just kind of out there, floating around, waiting for me to grab them and write them down. But after I started making records, it started to be more like, like work. I had a product to deliver. And there were all these other people now who cared about the outcome—my managers, the record label, all those so-called fans."

"But there's no pressure now," I reminded him. "Nobody to answer to."

"You'd think that would make it easier, wouldn't you?" We sat for a while, letting silence unspool between us. "I can't help thinking that this is some kind of—I don't know—payback, I guess you'd call it," Ash said.

"Payback? For what?"

"For selling out. Trying to make a living being something I'm not."

"For heaven's sake, Ash. How much longer can you do this to yourself? You didn't sell out! You got sold out, by the guys who made you all those promises, lured you to Nashville and then left you high and dry. It was bad luck, pure and simple. But that doesn't change who you are. Not in any kind of way that counts."

"I wish I believed that."

"I wish you did, too."

"It feels like this is it," he said. "Like if I can't turn things around now, I'll never get another shot."

"Then do it. Whatever it is you need to do, however long it takes."

"You mean that?"

"It wouldn't matter to me if you never wrote another song. But it matters to you. I know that. So, yeah. I want you to do this. I don't think you'll be able to live with yourself till you do."

"I better hang up now, let you get some sleep," he said. "I miss you. It's tough, lying here listening to the rain on the roof and thinking about you and our nice, warm bed."

"It's raining there?"

He laughed. "Like I said—I'm closer than you think."

CHAPTER 23

Denny

I WOKE UP on the couch under an ugly crocheted purple-and-green afghan I'd never seen before. Across the room an old George Strait video played on the TV. I could hear somebody banging around in the kitchen. Somehow it had gotten to be morning.

I went into the half bath and emptied my bladder, then dug a tube of Crest out from under the sink and used the end of my finger as a makeshift toothbrush. When I came out, I found Ty cracking eggs into a skillet at the stove. Bacon strips were cooling on a paper towel on the drain board, and a pitcher of fresh-squeezed orange juice and a platter of home-made biscuits sat in the middle of the table.

"You want your eggs scrambled, or over easy?" he asked.

"Over easy," I said. "Please. Where in the world did you learn to make biscuits from scratch?" He'd set out butter and jam and salt and pepper, Lucy's mama's gold-rimmed china plates and cups, cloth napkins, a handful of flatware.

"My granny showed me when I was a kid," he said. "She was a strange woman, my granny. A tough broad. Not exactly the kind of person you'd run crying to if you fell off your bike or got in a fight with another kid. But she knew how to make a mean biscuit. That, and how to whistle." He began to whistle lightly, a jazzy version of some show tune I probably should have recognized but didn't.

"Aren't you full of surprises?" I said.

Ty smiled without bothering to interrupt his work. "Plenty more where those came from."

He pulled out a chair for me, and I sat.

"I'm not sure I can eat all this," I said as he set a plate of eggs and bacon in front of me.

"Now, what did you tell me that doctor said, about taking care of yourself?" He glanced back over his shoulder at me as he cracked two more eggs into the skillet. "Come on, I dare you," he said. "I dare you to resist Granny's buttermilk biscuits."

He was right; there are some things in life you don't want to miss if given the chance, and one was those biscuits, sweet and creamy, like heaven dissolving on your tongue. I ate two, along with most of the eggs, and drained a glass of juice along with my horse-size vitamin pill.

Ty had poured himself a mug of coffee and was standing with his hip against the drain board drinking it.

"Aren't you eating?" I asked.

"In a minute." He cupped the mug in his two hands and

regarded me over it, his eyes somber in the morning light. "I talked to Ziggy this morning in Nashville," he said.

Ziggy was my drummer. His real name was Paul, but we called him Ziggy because of his resemblance to the reggae singer Bob Marley's son, with his flowing dreadlocks and his island-boy personality.

"What did he have to say?"

"He said he saw Will last night at the Bluebird. Making an ass of himself, according to Zig. Standing up at the bar talking and laughing during Mike Henderson's set. They kicked him out," Ty added, unnecessarily. The Bluebird Café was the high church of songwriting in Nashville; you were expected to observe a reverent silence or else risk getting permanently excommunicated. "Marin was with him, Ziggy said."

I stared into my juice glass. "Why are you telling me this?"

"I thought you needed to know. That Will's back in Nashville, mainly. Not hanging around in the woods of northeast Texas waiting to spring himself on you when you least expect it."

I stood up, too fast. The room was spinning. I grabbed the edge of the table for balance.

"Take it easy," Ty said.

"Oh, thank you, Ty. Thanks a lot." My voice was shaking. "Will's back in Nashville, getting fucked up and fooling around with Marin Bishop, just business as usual, like nothing he and I went through ever happened. My daddy's MIA. My grandma's out of her gourd. And, oh, by the way, I'm having a baby. And your answer to all that is to take it *easy*?"

"Calm down," Ty said. "I'm only trying to—"

"You're way out of your league here."

"What are you talking about?" He set down his coffee cup.

"Do you remember the night you showed up here, with those pictures of you and Grace and Jeremy at Graceland?" I asked. "Do you remember what you said to me? That you'd finally learned your lesson. To keep clear of women with kids. You said one trip to Heartbreak Hotel was enough."

"Jesus, Denny."

"You said it! You said it, clear as day!"

"That was before," he said.

"Before what?"

"Before I knew you were pregnant, for Christ's sake."

"So, what's the difference? You're already helping raise two kids who aren't yours. Why would you even think about taking on one more?"

"I can't believe you have to ask me that."

I blinked at him across the table, taking the gray of his eyes into the blue of mine.

"You didn't think I showed up in Podunk, Texas, just for the hell of it, did you?" he said. "Rescuing your asshole husband in the middle of the night? Breaking my back out there in that garden? Cooking up my granny's scratch biscuits?"

Before I could find my breath, Lucy walked into the kitchen, dressed for work in a skirt and blouse and flats.

"I thought I smelled bacon," she said.

"Have a seat," Ty said, turning back to the stove. "Eggs'll be ready in two seconds. Coffee?"

"Please."

In the sunlight streaming through the window over the

sink, her face was pale, but the creases I'd seen around her mouth and eyes the night before had smoothed out.

"I talked to your daddy last night," she said to me as Ty put a cup of coffee in her hand.

"You did? Where is he?"

"Someplace close by, he said."

"Is he okay?"

"He sounded fine." Ty handed her a plate full of bacon and eggs. "Thanks," she said to him. "Did you do all this?"

"I'm trying to make myself indispensable," he said. He smiled like this was a joke, without looking at me.

She broke a biscuit in half, smeared it with butter and jam, and bit into it.

"My goodness," she said. "Where in the world did you learn to make biscuits like this?" She didn't seem to have any notion that she'd walked in to the middle of a serious, possibly life-changing conversation, and Ty just fixed himself a plate and sat down at the table like we were a regular family who did this kind of thing every day.

And I have to admit, it was kind of nice, listening to him and Lucy make small talk as a beam of sunshine shifted through the window and tracked slowly across the table, winking off the salt and pepper shakers and the jam jar like stones in a jeweler's case. It was nice listening to funny stories and being cooked for, instead of having to worry about hangovers or whether or not somebody might get punched out at the breakfast table.

Lucy gave me a kiss and left for work, and Ty got up and started to busy himself clearing the table, filling the dishwasher. There was an inch of coffee left in the pot. He poured it into his mug and stood looking out the window as he drank it.

"I've been thinking about what you said to me the other night," he said. "About needing some time to figure things out on your own. And I want you to know that I hear you. I do." He turned around and looked at me. "But this is how I am. I take care of things. I fix what's broken. I make things better. Can I help it if the way I feel about you makes me want to do that now, for you?"

He drained his mug and set it in the sink. "I just wanted to make sure Will was really gone. If that makes me the bad guy in your eyes, then I'm sorry. And maybe you're right. I am out of my league. But this is the only way I know."

I held out my plate, and Ty put another biscuit on it. The sun made a diamond on the kitchen floor and we stood in it, listening to the clock tick over the stove and the cheesy chorus of birds outside the window, a regular festival of springtime.

"Did Tina ever get your granny's scratch biscuits?"

"Tina was not a woman who would appreciate a scratch biscuit. Not unless there was a five-carat diamond in the middle of it."

I broke the biscuit in half and bit into it. "Her loss," I said around a mouthful of crumbs.

"I've got some demo tapes in the truck," Ty said. "I thought we could give them a listen later. You need to be thinking about the next record."

"Wow, you never let up for a minute, do you?"

"You just now figuring that out?"

"Ty?"

"Yeah?"

"I don't know how to— I guess what I'm trying to say is, I'm glad you decided to stick around."

He smiled. "Hey, no big deal. It's just breakfast."

It wasn't, but we both knew that.

CHAPTER 24

Lucy

A s soon as Peggy announced she was closing the shop, business had picked up. From the time I unlocked the front door in the morning till the close of the workday, there were almost always a couple of customers hanging around, thumbing through the greeting cards or browsing the selection of potted plants. I tried to argue that this was proof that there was still hope for Faye's in Mooney, but Peggy wasn't having any of it.

"They're rubbernecking," she said, keeping her voice low. A few of the Methodist ladies were over in the corner pawing through the vases and spools of ribbon. "Trust me, if I turned around and took the GOING OUT OF BUSINESS sign out of the window, these folks'd disappear quicker than if I hollered 'Fire.'"

A car slid by on the wet street, making a *shushing* sound.

Peggy and I both held our breath as the air conditioner kicked on with a wheeze and a shudder. The unit was probably twenty years old, and Peggy was just praying it lasted the week, when it would cease to be her problem and start being Wendell Hayes's.

The phone rang, and she walked around behind the counter to answer it. "Well, *hey*," she said, turning one syllable into three.

I walked over to the front window, where Peggy had dressed our mannequin in a blond pageboy wig and one of her old muumuus, with a lei around its neck and a frosted drink glass with a little paper umbrella in its hand under a hand-painted banner saying, KISSIMEE HERE I COME! Over the years I'd been at Faye's, that mannequin had been the centerpiece in nearly every window display, but it had taken the occasion of Peggy's retirement for her to finally create a tableau in her own image. It made me sad every time I looked at it, though she seemed to get a kick out of it and added something new nearly every day, from a striped beach chair to a scattering of seashells to a rubber shark that had once belonged to her cocker spaniel, Bones. She'd even painted the mannequin's toenails to match her own in a shade called Copacabana Coral.

"How many times do I have to tell you to stay away from the window? With that long face, you'll scare off the customers."

"What difference does it make?" I said. "We're going out of business, remember?"

Peggy put her arm around me and gave me a squeeze. "Run in back and grab the keys to the van. I need you to go out on a delivery."

"Do I have to? Audrey will be here any minute."

"This one can't wait."

In the restroom I splashed water on my face and put on some lipstick. Truth be told, I'd just as soon hide in the back at Faye's till the end of the month and not have to face the public. I hated all the questions and the knowing looks, especially now that word was getting around that Ash had moved out. I'd never really minded being gossiped about, but pity was a thing I couldn't stand.

When I came out, Peggy was standing in the middle of the showroom talking to Mrs. Cecilia Kopp about buying a lot of vases for the church at cost.

"Where is it?" I asked.

"Where's what?"

"The delivery? You know, the one that can't wait?"

She went into the cooler, grabbed a bunch of daisies in a plastic sleeve, and thrust it at me.

"Aren't you going to wrap it?"

"No time." She handed me a piece of paper. "Here's the address."

"This looks familiar," I said.

"It should."

I looked up. "Wait a minute. Is this—"

"Go," she said, steering me to the back door. "And, Lucy? Take your time. Remember, customer service is what Faye's is all about."

T WO MILES OUT of town, Highway 133 was a desolate two-lane through the woods. County Line Liquor had gone out of business years before, as had the auto-body shop nearby. A few tar-paper shacks still stood beside the road. Most were deserted, in various stages of collapse, but on one front porch an old lady in a feed-sack dress looked up from shucking corn to watch me pass.

The rain was letting up as I turned off the highway into the gravel parking lot of the Piney View Motor Court. The sign in the window of the office said VACANCY, like it always did, but I didn't stop to ask directions, just made my way toward unit number ten in back, where Ash's pickup was parked.

As I pulled in and cut the engine and the wipers, the sun broke through the clouds, transforming the cabin's dark windows to gold. There was a lawn chair set up beside the front door. I got out of the van, smoothing my hair with my palms, and reached back in for the daisies.

Ash opened the door before I could knock.

"Somebody here ordered flowers?" I said.

He stepped to one side and motioned me inside. It had been years since I'd been at the Piney View, but nothing had changed in the interim. The rooms were small and gloomy and smelled of stale cigarette smoke, the bed still draped in the same rough brown spread I remembered. There was no TV, no clock radio, nothing besides the flimsy, dark-paneled furniture but a lamp, an ashtray, and a Gideon bible.

"I see the place hasn't lost its charm." I handed Ash the flowers. "Maybe these will cheer things up a little."

He carried an empty Coke bottle over to the sink and rinsed it, then stuck the daisies into it and set it on the bedside table. They looked absurd there, like a slash of bright lipstick on a bag lady.

"I guess I was hoping for a little inspiration," he said.

"Did you get it?"

"Too soon to tell."

I laughed as he came up behind me and made a cradle for me of his arms, burrowing his face into my hair.

"Don't think I don't know what you're doing," I said.

"Is it working?"

"Too soon to tell. Have you got anything to eat? I haven't had lunch."

He didn't; he claimed to have been subsisting on twice-daily chopped beef sandwiches from Willie B.'s. I dug around in my purse till I came up with a package of peanut butter crackers that we shared, lying across the ugly brown bedspread as the window unit spewed out its tepid air.

"Remember the first time we came here?" Ash said, leaning back against the headboard. I nodded that I did. "Things were good then, don't you think?"

"You mean better than they are now?"

"Well, we know more now than we did then, that's for sure. I'm not sure that's necessarily a good thing."

I kicked off my shoes and put my feet in Ash's lap.

"Tell me," I said, closing my eyes as he ran his thumb lazily over my instep. "What it was like then. What you remember."

I ROLLED OVER, trying to get my bearings. My tongue was stuck to the roof of my mouth, my eyes swollen with sleep. Ash sat at the edge of the bed with his back to me, the curve of his spine familiar under his T-shirt, his Martin guitar across his knee. I held my breath and listened as his hands moved quietly over the frets, but what music there might have been seemed meant for his ears only.

"Lord," I said, stretching a kink out of my neck. "What time is it?"

"Almost three."

"Three!" I jumped off the bed. "Peggy's probably called out the National Guard on me."

"Relax," Ash said. "Peggy knows where you are."

"Why didn't you wake me? By the time I get the van back, it'll be almost closing time."

He stood up, setting the guitar on the bed. "What do I owe you for the flowers?"

"Five dollars."

Ash took his wallet off the bureau and opened it. "It hardly seems worth the trouble. I mean, you must have used that much gas driving out here."

"Well, you know what Peggy always says—customer service is what Faye's is all about." *Or was,* I thought gloomily as I fished my shoes out from under the bed and stepped into them.

Ash handed me a ten. "Keep the change," he said. "Better yet, bring me another bunch tomorrow."

I looked up at him from behind my hair.

"In fact, let's make it a standing order." He smiled. "You might bring us some lunch while you're at it."

"You're some piece of work, you know that?" I said, slipping the ten-dollar bill in my skirt pocket. "You came here to write music, Ash. I thought that was the whole idea."

"Like I told you—I need inspiration."

He opened the door, and I stood on my toes and kissed him, a kiss full of both promise and regret.

"Lucy Hatch, patron of the arts," he said.

I cranked the key and pumped the gas pedal, trying to get the van to start. Ash gestured that I should roll down the window. As I did, the cab flooded with the smells of damp pine and carbon monoxide.

I couldn't hear him over the engine's roar, so he stepped over and leaned in the window, raising his voice.

"I said, tomorrow I won't let you fall asleep."

CHAPTER 25

Denny

W E DROVE OUT to the Piney View so that Ty could pick up a change of clothes. The road was deserted except for an old white van that flew past, heading like a bat out of hell toward town. It had rained earlier, and the motor court parking lot was full of puddles, slick and shining with rainbows in the sun.

"Check it out," Ty said as we pulled in at the second cabin. "Isn't that your daddy's truck?"

"Shit. I wonder what he's doing here."

"Why don't you ask him yourself?" Ty said as the door of the last cabin opened and Daddy stepped out, squinting into the sun with his old Martin in his hand. There was a folding lawn chair next to the door, and he sat down in it and laid the guitar over his knee and began to fool with the tuning keys.

My boots crunched in the gravel as I approached.

"Well, hey there, baby girl," Daddy said, looking up with a grin on his face. "It's getting to be a regular family reunion here at the Piney View."

"What are you talking about?" I was ready to bless him out; him acting all happy-go-lucky threw me off my game.

"You just missed Lucy," he said.

"Lucy knows you're here?"

"No secrets, Denise. That's the key to a successful relationship."

I leaned over and looked into his face. "Are you drunk?"

"Just high on life." He lifted a hand and waved to Ty, who waved back. "How's the hand?"

"The—? Oh." I held out my right hand with its bulky splint, the tape dirty and fraying. "All right, I guess. Ty's had me practicing guitar. I'm not too great, but it's better than just sitting on my ass feeling sorry for myself."

It didn't come out the way I intended, but Daddy didn't seem to take offense.

"I hear you," he said. He struck a chord on the Martin, fiddled some more with the E string.

"I don't get it," I said. "You took off and left a note, scared everybody half to death, and now you turn up in the parking lot at the Piney View with a guitar and a lawn chair?"

He shrugged. "Sometimes a man's just gotta do what he's gotta do."

"Which is what?"

"I don't think I can say for sure."

I had to bite my lip to keep from screaming. "Are you having a midlife crisis? Is that it?"

"That'd be one way of looking at it." He twisted the tuning key, frowning in concentration. "I guess I'd rather think of it as a brand-new start. You know what those are like, right?" He looked up at me, and I nodded my head.

"So, how long are you here for?" I asked. The door to his room was open, but it was too dark inside for me to see anything. Even from here, there was an air of desperation about the place. It reminded me of his old trailer that way. But then, Daddy had always had a fondness for cast-off things.

"Depends," he said.

"On what?"

"On how far I decide to take this thing."

"What thing?"

"I don't know yet, Denise. Whatever it turns out to be."

I turned and looked over my shoulder to see what was keeping Ty, but he'd gone inside his cabin. I wondered if what was wrong with Evelyn was inborn, some dark thing passed down through the blood from her to Daddy to me. Maybe even now Loretta was stewing in it. On the other hand, Daddy seemed better than I'd seen him in a long time, more like his old self. What was crazy, anyway, other than a way of looking at the world that skewed a little bit off center from everybody else's?

"Daddy, listen," I said, all in a rush, before my better judgment could kick in. "Ty and I are headed up to Hughes Springs, to see Evelyn. Why don't you come?"

He stopped fooling with the guitar and looked up at me. "Say what?"

"You heard me." My heart was beating so hard I swear I could see it through my shirt.

"I don't think that's such a good idea."

"But you've been talking about a brand-new start. I just thought—"

He held up his hand, and I shut up. Ty came out of his room and locked the door behind him. He was wearing a fresh button-down shirt, white with thin red stripes, and sharp-creased jeans.

"Señor Farrell, *cómo estás?*" he said, coming across the parking lot.

"Not too bad," Daddy said. "Just sitting here minding my own business. Which is more than I can say for some people."

"Daddy's turning over a new leaf," I said.

"Is that so?" Ty looked from Daddy to me with a pleasant but dubious expression.

"You don't think I can do it, do you?" Daddy said to me. His mouth was still set in a smile, but his eyes were flinty. "You think I'm chickenshit."

"I didn't say—"

He jumped to his feet. "You know what? You're right, Denise. No time like the present."

I looked nervously at Ty, who shook his head. But Daddy had already set the guitar back in his room and locked the door.

All the way to Hughes Springs, I tried to tell myself that everything was going to work out fine. The sky was silvery green and spackled-looking, like fish scales. In the backseat Daddy talked a mile a minute, a running commentary on the weather and the scenery. I kept expecting him to come to his senses and holler at Ty to pull over and let him out in the bar ditch, but he didn't.

Twenty minutes later we were pulling up in front of Contessa's yellow-brick house, the lawn neatly trimmed as always, the rain barrels of petunias in full bloom. The sun was trying to break through the clouds, but the air felt heavy and still, like it does right before a gully washer.

Ty killed the engine and we sat for a few seconds as it ticked and cooled. I turned and looked over the seatback at Daddy. His bluster was gone; under the tan, his face was the same greenish gray as the sky.

"You can still change your mind, if you want," I said. "Wait here while Ty and I run in."

"Yeah—it feels like things are moving a little fast, you know what I mean?"

I started to say that forty years wasn't exactly my definition of "fast," but the look on Ty's face shut me up. "You two go on ahead," Daddy said. "Give me a minute."

"Good idea," Ty said, and we got out of the truck, leaving the doors standing open.

"You heard him," I said to Ty as we waited for someone to answer the bell. "He came along of his own free will! I didn't tie him up and kidnap him or anything."

Ty shook his head, tight-lipped. "Just remember, this is on your head."

CONTESSA DIDN'T SEEM too happy to see us. "You bring somebody from HHS to shut me down?" she said, giving Ty a head-to-toe, squint-eyed look.

"This is my friend Tyler Briggs," I said. "What's HHS?"

She ignored my question as we followed her into the living room, where as usual the big TV blared out a game show to an audience of no one.

"Evelyn's out back, in the garden," she said.

"I didn't know you had a garden."

"Joyner keeps it goin'. Them that wants to is welcome to help out. Now that the weather's warmed up good, Evelyn's taken a real shine to it."

This was how I remembered my grandmother, kneeling in the dirt, her face shaded from the sun by a big straw hat. Joyner crouched beside her, guiding her as she placed a marigold seedling into a hole he'd trowled. His voice was gentle, and Evelyn laughed as she eased the flower from its plastic cup and patted it into place with the flat of her hand.

"Look here, Evelyn," Contessa called out. "You got comp'ny."

Evelyn turned our way, peering out from under the brim of her hat.

"Hi, Evelyn," I said, reaching out a hand to help her to her feet.

"Are you from the Church of Christ? Because if you are, you can save your breath."

"No, ma'am. I'm your granddaughter, Denny Farrell."

"I once knew a man named Farrell," she said. "Broke my heart." She looked past me to Ty, sizing him up with shrewd dark eyes. "Is that what you've come for? To break my heart?"

"No, ma'am. I sincerely hope not." He leaned past me and held out his hand. "How do you do. My name's Tyler Briggs. Denny's told me so much about you."

"Well, I don't see what she could possibly know to tell. Goodness, you're a handsome thing. It's a curse for a man to be too handsome, you know." She dragged a hand across her forehead, streaking it with dirt. "Annie Childs, where is my lemonade? You know better than to leave me sweltering without something cold to drink."

"I'll run fetch you a glass of water, Evelyn," Contessa said in her long-suffering way and went back to the house.

Joyner walked toward us, wiping his bald head with a ragged bandanna. "Howdy do, Miss Denny," he said. "Miss Evelyn's bein' a big help to me today. Got to get these marigolds in, keep the cutworms off the tomato plants."

I introduced him to Ty, and Joyner excused himself to fetch a hoe from the shed.

"Lord, this heat," Evelyn said. She took off her hat and fanned herself with it.

I guided her to a lawn chair set up in the shade of a live oak tree. "I'm getting too old for this work," she said sadly as she settled into the chair and slipped off her Keds. "That hired man is some help, but I can't keep up like I used to."

"Well, you just sit here and rest awhile," I said. "Contessa's bringing you a drink of water."

She set her hat in her lap. "How's the baby doing?" she asked.

"The baby's fine," I said. I couldn't look at Ty.

"Remind me again—is it a boy or a girl?"

"A girl, I think."

"That's funny. I seem to recall a boy."

The back door opened and Contessa appeared carrying a

plastic pitcher in one hand and a stack of tumblers in the other.

All of a sudden, Evelyn gasped, her hands gripping the metal arms of the lawn chair.

I followed her gaze to where Daddy stood in the side yard, still as a statue, staring at the three of us grouped under the live oak tree.

"Frank!"

Evelyn struggled upright, then fell back again. Her voice was girlish, soft with joy and disbelief. She looked like someone who'd stepped through a secret door and found herself without warning in a world that she'd only dreamed existed, or remembered from some other, long-ago life.

She pushed herself out of her chair, tipping it over, and would have tumbled to her knees in the grass if Ty hadn't lunged forward and caught her.

"Frank! Come back!" But she was talking to a ghost in more ways than one. As suddenly as he'd appeared, Daddy was gone.

THE SKY OPENED up just after we left Contessa's, and the whole way back to Mooney the only sound was of the hiss of our tires on the blacktop and the wipers slapping time against the windshield. I kept sneaking glances at Daddy in the side mirror, but I couldn't read his face, and there was nothing I could think of to say that would make things better. I never seemed to learn my lesson, to stop sticking my nose in places it didn't belong. I just couldn't keep myself from wishing for fairy-tale endings, no matter how much real life showed me otherwise.

"I don't think this is a good idea," I said when Daddy insisted we drop him off at the Piney View.

"I believe we've all had enough of your good ideas for one afternoon," Daddy said.

Ty pulled up in front of cabin ten and let the motor idle. As Daddy climbed out, I rolled my window down.

"Why don't you come home with us? At least for supper."

He shook his head and turned to put his key in the door.

"Give Jude a kiss for me," he said over his shoulder. "Tell Lucy I'll see her tomorrow."

I opened my mouth to say something else, but he'd already gone inside and shut the door.

A T   H O M E   W E   found Lucy poking around in the freezer. Her face clouded over when I told her what had happened.

"Honey, what did I tell you, about trying to force a thing like this? You can't just expect something that goes back forty years to dissolve in one afternoon."

She went to the kitchen to start supper, and I ducked into the half bath under the stairs to wash up. I'd just dried my hands and was trying to decide whether to go up and put on a clean shirt when I heard Ty's and Lucy's voices coming through the wall. I cracked open the door to hear better.

"—know why you put up with this family's craziness," Lucy was saying. "I don't know why *I* put up with it sometimes, and I married into it."

"I've been in the music business ten years now," Ty said. "I reckon I've seen my share of craziness."

"It's a lot to take on," Lucy said. "Denny was fourteen when she came to us, and there were times I thought she'd send her daddy and me both around the bend." They both laughed. "I guess what I'm trying to say is, bringing a baby into the mix is hard enough even when it's your own."

"If you're trying to scare me off, it won't work," Ty said. "My mind was made up a long time ago."

"Good. I'm glad. It's about the only thing I have to be glad about right now, so I hope you don't mind me hanging on to it."

When I walked into the kitchen, Lucy was breading pork chops while Ty peeled a pan of new potatoes and put them on to boil. I went to the old pie safe and took out place mats and napkins and started to set the table.

"My Lord," Lucy said, "would you listen to that."

She reached over and turned up the radio. I recognized the song right away, about a fellow in a dance hall pining after a girl he'd never win, even though the only time I'd ever heard it had been on a scratchy cassette, just Hardy Knox's voice and a lone guitar. This was a full-scale studio production, with pedal steel and fiddle, the whole nine yards. Hardy's voice sounded different, too, brasher, more confident.

"So he really did it," Lucy said as the song ended, segueing into Kenny Rogers and Dolly Parton singing "Islands in the Stream." "He was always trying to convince Ash he was the real deal. I guess he had the stuff to back it up after all."

"Hardy Knox would sell a kidney if he thought it would get him where he wants to go," Ty said.

"Well, maybe that's what it takes," she said. "Maybe that's the secret, the one Ash didn't know."

"Are you kidding me?" Ty said. "Ash's got more talent than Hardy Knox in his little finger. I know half a dozen record guys who'd jump at the chance to work with him."

Lucy looked at Ty, then me.

"I think I've learned my lesson about trying to play God," she said. "You might keep that in mind, too, next time you see your daddy."

After supper I offered to help Lucy clean up the kitchen while Ty took Jude down to the dock. Side by side we worked in silence, loading the dishwasher and setting the cooking pans in the sink to soak. She poured us each another glass of tea and we carried them out to the front porch.

We sat in the swing, rocking gently. A breeze lifted off the pond, smelling of rain and algae. In the twilight we could see Jude and Ty sitting at the end of the pier with their feet hanging, hear Jude's voice over the steady hum of crickets and frogs.

But I couldn't relax. I kept waiting for Lucy to chew my ear off, but when I said so, finally, she just smiled and shook her head.

"I know you think you messed up today, with your daddy. And maybe you did. But stuff like this isn't the end of the world, even if it might feel like it at the time. You say you're sorry, and you try again."

She reached out and tucked a strand of hair behind my

ear. "The older I get, the more I think maybe that's what love is all about. Apologizing for what you did wrong, and then trying again, till you get it right."

"I thought love meant never having to say you're sorry."

She laughed. "In the movies, maybe. Not in real life."

"I'm scared," I blurted out.

"Of what?"

"That I won't be a good mother. That maybe I'm not smart enough, or nice enough . . . I mean, what if I do something wrong, make some horrible mistake? Suppose I don't love her enough? Or too much! You could ruin somebody's life!"

"Welcome to the club. Listen, nobody knows what they're doing when they start this job. I sure didn't. I was scared to death, too, and I've screwed up plenty of times. But that's sort of what I was trying to say before. I think what matters aren't so much the things we do right, but the mistakes we make. They're what gives color to things, and texture."

The lights came on down at the dock, and Lucy stood up and called out that it was time for Jude's bath.

"Heck, anybody can be there for the good parts," she said as we watched Ty and Jude meandering up past the garden toward the house. Jude said something in a high cartoon voice, and Ty laughed, low and scratchy-sounding, like gravel in a box. "It's sticking around when things get tough when you find out what somebody's worth. But I guess you already know that." She looked over at me in the dusk. "I hope you do, anyway."

"I'm starting to," I said.

"Good."

She smoothed my hair with the flat of her hand. I'd always loved having my hair touched, but nobody I cared about ever did it except Lucy.

"And Denny?" she said. "Just for the record, there's no such thing as too much love. Wait a few months if you don't believe me."

CHAPTER 26

Lucy

THE NEXT DAY I was back at the Piney View with a double begonia in a pot and a picnic basket full of cold fried chicken, Granny Munroe's pound cake, and a thermos of sweet tea.

Ash waited for me at the door, barefoot and shirtless. I shook the rain out of my hair as he took the basket from me and set it on the floor. I barely had time to drop the plant on the night table next to yesterday's daisies when he swept me, literally, off my feet and deposited me on the unmade bed.

"I have to tell you something," I said later. We were sitting naked on the brown bedspread, licking chicken grease off our fingers and finishing up our tea. "When you asked me to come to the Piney View yesterday, this is more along the lines of what I was expecting."

Ash smiled and leaned back, one arm folded behind his head against the headboard.

"In fact, I was trying to decide whether or not my feelings were hurt. I thought maybe you'd decided you cared more about flowers and food than you did about me."

"Maybe I was just biding my time."

"Well, I don't know what for. The whole town thinks I'm here so you can jump my bones. Imagine what they'd say if they found out I fell asleep yesterday. I'd never live it down."

"So now the whole town is in on this, huh?"

"Peggy says it's the number one item on the menu at the café. I think she's a little miffed that we knocked her moving to Florida out of first place."

Ash laughed, bending forward to kiss my neck. "You must be the only man in the world who gets turned on by white underwear," I said, shivering happily as his stubbled jaw grazed my skin.

"Me and Elvis," he corrected.

"You know what I think?" I said. "I think you miss how things were with us at the start—the widow and the bad boy, everybody placing bets and talking behind their hands. I think you like being the talk of the town."

"Guilty as charged. But I can't shoulder the load by myself, you know."

"Vergie Humphries called this morning," I said. "She wanted to know if it's true that you're holed up at the Piney View having a nervous breakdown."

"Vergie's just worried that I'm gonna leave her stranded with her kitchen cabinets half done."

I unwrapped the pound cake and fed him a bite with my fingers.

"Denny told me what happened yesterday, with Evelyn." Ash shrugged.

"I've been trying to write about it," he said, gesturing to the desk, where one of his notebooks lay splayed open, face-down. "About—you know—looking your fears in the face and all that shit."

I set the cake aside and slid my arms around him and rested my head against his chest, his heart galloping against my cheek.

"You know what's really weird?" he said.

"What?"

"For forty years, I've been picturing this—this monster. And after all that, she just turned out to be a little bitty, dried-up, sad old lady."

I waited for him to say how he'd discovered that he was ready to open his heart to Evelyn and forgive her all her trespasses. But he didn't, and so we lay there in a pool of yellow lamplight while rain pinged on the window unit outside and Ash's heart beat beneath my cheek and slowly, imperceptibly, the universe moved, one door opening as another one closed, throwing light into places where it's never shined before.

I FELT LIKE I was living two lives: the dreary, obligatory, everyday life, with my job and my house and my kids, fixing meals and paying bills, and the one with Ash at the Piney View, an hour or two every afternoon with the shades drawn and the sheets mussed, the window unit chuffing out its clammy air. I went about the former with dreamy impatience, suspended in a kind of walking daze, doing my time. It was only those hours at the Piney View that felt real. I could barely remember to pick up Jude from Dove's or take hamburger meat out of the freezer for supper; but alone in bed at night, I could recall in piercing detail a bead of sweat sliding down Ash's rib cage, the grit of his unshaved cheek against the silk of my thigh.

Sometimes we ate lunch first, and sometimes we went straight from the door to the bed. I quickly exhausted my repertoire of white underwear and was forced to branch out into yellow and pink, with tiny flowers and bows. I felt like Heidi, or Little Bo Peep. There was something more sweet than naughty about it. We laughed a lot, our heads under the covers while rain drummed on the roof. It wasn't a bad way to be, not for two people in their forties who'd been through hell and high water together and come out the other side.

Most afternoons, in spite of my intentions, I'd drift off with Ash's hand in my hair, listening to him talk. I'd wake with a start an hour or so later to find him sitting on the side of the bed with his guitar. He serenaded me the way he'd done so often in our early days. He sang old cowboy songs and Irish folk tunes. He sang "Rainy Night in Georgia," "Blue Eyes Cryin' in the Rain," Van Morrison's "Tupelo Honey." He sang me a gorgeous, haunting song called "Angel Eyes," and another called the "Ballad of Spider John."

"Willis Alan Ramsey," Ash said. "Know what happened to him?"

I said I had no idea.

"Me neither. He made this one great album in, like, 1972. Eleven songs, every one of them this perfect little jewel— well, ten out of the eleven, anyway, forget about 'Muskrat Love.' Then he just sort of disappeared. Every now and then he supposedly pops up in some club in Austin, but he's never put out another record."

"Oh, Ash."

I threw back the sheet and started sorting through the pile of clothes on the floor.

"I'm sorry," I said. "I'm not trying to hurt your feelings. But how long can you keep this up? So you wrote all these great songs and then, for whatever reason, because you didn't get the respect or the airplay you deserved, or because some record-company guy decided to make somebody else a star instead of you, or maybe because you're afraid you can't live up to your own hype, you got your hat handed to you and got shown the door. It just seems—I don't know—turned around, somehow. Like somewhere along the way the story got to be about you, and not the songs."

Ash had laid the guitar aside and sat with his head drooping between his shoulders.

"You've got it all wrong," he said.

I picked up my skirt and shook the wrinkles out of it. "Maybe so. Maybe all this is my fault, and things would have worked out better for you if I hadn't come along. Do you ever think about that?" I said. "I do, sometimes. Sometimes I wonder what would have happened if Geneva and Bailey had never dragged me to the Round-Up the first time. Maybe you'd have married that, that Misty Potter, or somebody like her, and gone on to Nashville and climbed to the top of the heap and stayed there. Instead of—this." I looked around the musty room, the wrinkled bed, the assortment of flowers dying on the night table.

Ash got up and took me by the shoulders.

"Listen to me. First of all, there never was a chance in hell of me marrying Misty Potter. And second of all, I don't care what you say—if it wasn't for you, I don't think I'd be here now. And I don't mean room ten at the Piney View Motor Court."

In the muted lamplight his eyes were black and bottom-less.

"You keep me in the world," he said. "Do you understand what I'm saying? Do you understand what it means?"

"I do. I just— I guess what I'm trying to say is, I think you need to write music because you love it, because you can't imagine doing anything else. Otherwise you might as well be building kitchen cabinets, or selling flowers. Something any fool can do."

I finished dressing while Ash gathered up the leftovers from our lunch and stuffed them into the picnic basket.

"Maybe tomorrow you could bring me some more of that pound cake," he said as he walked me out to the van.

I slid the basket behind the driver's seat. "I don't think so."

"Well, why the hell not?"

"Because I'm not coming back tomorrow."

His smile faded when he saw my face.

"I think I need to stay away for a while," I said. "For your own good."

"I'd like to know what's good about it."

"You told me you needed inspiration," I reminded him. "But I think it's turned into something else."

I climbed into the van and rolled down the window.

"Don't look at me like that! It's my fault as much as yours," I said. "And I've loved it, Ash. Every minute. But it's keeping you from doing what you came here to do."

I turned the key. Miraculously, the engine started on the first try.

"The best songs I ever wrote were for you," Ash said as a plume of exhaust shot out of the tailpipe and I wrangled the cranky transmission into gear.

"I know. But now you need to write one for yourself."

CHAPTER 27

Denny

I T WAS TY'S idea to take along a guitar next time we went to see Evelyn. "You said she used to be a singer," he said. "Maybe it would do her good to hear a little music."

The corn and sorghum seemed two feet higher in the fields as we drove up the farm-to-market road toward Hughes Springs. An early-morning haze had burned off, leaving the sky as clean and blue as a bedsheet hanging on a line.

"What's this, now?" Contessa said, eyeing the guitar case in my hand. She was still miffed at us for what had happened the other day with Daddy.

"We thought it might cheer her up some," Ty said.

"Huh." With her mouth puckered up like she was sucking on a lemon, Contessa let us into the house.

"Hi, Evelyn," I said. She sat staring out the window, her

gloved hands folded neatly in her lap. I lifted the guitar out of its case and sat down on the bed. "How'd you like me to sing you a song? Remember how we used to sing together, at your house out at the lake?"

I tuned the guitar and launched into a couple of the tunes we'd sung together on the pier, "I'm Sorry" and "I Still Miss Someone," making do as best I could with my bandaged hand.

When I finished, Evelyn was looking right at me, her hands twisting in her lap.

"I know you," she said. "You're Denny. Ash's girl."

"Yes, ma'am, I am."

"You have a nice voice," she said. "Not as good as mine, mind you, but nice."

"Yes, ma'am, I know. Would you like to hear some more?"

"Thank you, no. I'm expecting someone."

"You are? Who?"

"I believe Frank may be coming today. We have some unfinished business, Frank and me."

I started to open my mouth, to tell her Frank was gone, for God's sake, that their business was never going to be finished as long as she lived, but Ty interrupted me, taking the guitar and setting it back in its case, saying it was time to go.

"It's good to see you, Miss Evelyn," he said, though she hadn't said boo to him since we arrived. "We'll call again soon, okay?"

We sat in the truck in front of the house while I blew my nose into Ty's white handkerchief.

"She was *there*," I said. "For two seconds, she was the old

Evelyn, just the way I remember her. And then she just . . ." I
waved my hand in the air.

"Denny, listen. I hate to say this, but if you want to be part
of your grandma's life, you're gonna have to learn to live with
that. Sometimes she'll be the person you used to know, but
probably, mostly, she won't."

"But she said my name, all on her own, without me
prompting her or anything! That's something, isn't it?"

I couldn't stand what was in his face, the way his eyes told
me that I was creating a fiction to suit my own purposes, just
like I had with Will. "You live in a dream world, Denise,"
Daddy had said to me once when I was a teenager. I guess old
habits die hard.

Still, we kept going back, taking the guitar. One afternoon
we sat in the garden and Evelyn watched my face intently
while I sang, her fingers tapping on the arms of her chair.

"That was nice, Lynette," she said after I'd finished a Patsy
Cline song she'd once loved. "You need to work on that bit at
the end, though. Remember, you want to reach out and grab
'em by the asses, all the way to the very back row."

Another day, a handful of the residents gathered in Contessa's living room—the TV shut off for once, in honor of the
occasion—and I sang a medley of old tunes I thought the
residents might remember from happier times, but all that
happened was that one ancient man covered in liver spots
started to tremble and then sob, and Evelyn fell asleep,
slumped over on the flowered couch. "Next time," Contessa
said, her lips pursed as she escorted us to the door, "I think
it's best you leave the git-tar at home."

What was I hoping to accomplish? I asked myself as Ty and I rode back to Cade County, heat rippling in waves off the blacktop. The Evelyn I kept looking for was visible only in glimpses: the use of a certain word, a particular tilt of her head. Still, I couldn't give up. Without me there wouldn't be a single person on earth who remembered her the way she used to be, with her Luckies and her loud laugh, her finger-nails black with garden dirt, her little snub-nosed pistol, and her voice, the one I heard every time I opened my mouth.

At home we found Lucy poking around in the garden. The plants were getting taller every day, heavy with blossoms, and I walked out among them to greet her.

"What are you doing home?" I said. "It's not even three o'clock."

She knelt to yank a weed from between two pepper plants. "We've packed up most of the inventory and reconciled the books. Wendell Hayes was there this morning, walking around, figuring out where he's going to put his chairs and where to hang the barber pole. Except for Audrey's wedding, there's not much left to do."

"Well, maybe we ought to go do something fun, just the two of us," I suggested. "Run up to Texarkana and go shop-ping, or see a movie."

"That's sweet, honey," she said. "But I don't think I'd be very good company."

"Okay." I turned to go back to the house.

"Denny?" She stood and looked me full in the face, her eyes searching mine. "Have you talked to your daddy lately?"

"No, ma'am." I was still embarrassed about trying to drag

Daddy to see Evelyn, but in spite of the pep talk Lucy'd given me, telling him I was sorry was something I hadn't quite figured out how to do. "Haven't you?"

"Not in a few days. I'm trying to let him be, let him get some work done." She peeled off one cotton glove and wiped her forehead with the back of her hand. "So. How's everything with you? Are you feeling all right? How are things with Ty? Is Evelyn okay?"

I wanted to fling myself into her arms and tell her all my troubles, but mine felt so small compared to all she had to manage right then. So I pasted on a smile and told her what I knew she wanted to hear: "Everything's fine."

THAT NIGHT, AFTER Lucy and Jude were in bed, Ty sat me down on the living room couch and said he had something to say to me. I felt a shudder of dread as he took my hands in his and held them lightly on his knees.

"Look, I know I said I'd be here for you no matter what, as long as it takes," he said. "But I'm starting to wonder if I haven't been fooling myself."

"Fooling yourself how?"

"I guess I'm just starting to think— Well, maybe this isn't the best time for us."

"What are you talking about?"

"This thing going on with your daddy, for one thing. Then there's Lucy's job, and your grandma . . ."

"They're my *family*," I said.

"I know that. But what about us? What about all those

talks we've been having, about you and me and Loretta Lynn?"

I glanced toward the TV, where Tim McGraw and Faith Hill were gazing into each other's eyes like a couple of loons. Nobody could be that much in love. It must be a trick they did with cameras, or mirrors.

Ty reached for the remote and the screen went dark.

"Denny, level with me. Have you even tried calling Will?"

I looked down at my hands, the dirty tape and the wooden splint.

"Listen," Ty said. "I know you're scared. I know how hard it is, what I'm asking you to do. But sometimes you have to do what's hard. Not just for you. For your family."

He got to his feet and set the remote on the coffee table. I felt petrified with fear, the kind I'd felt as a kid when my mama left me in our condo while she went out on dates, when every shadow or sound outside the window seemed like evidence of how alone in the world I was.

Ty reached into his pocket and handed me a little white card.

"Mike Leary's the lawyer who set it up so I'd get visitation with Grace and Jeremy when Tina and I split up. He's a good guy. And trust me, he can take care of things with Will Culpepper, if you want him to."

The room was dark except for the light from the night sky coming in through the tall windows, gleaming off the hardwood floor. The card in my hand was still warm from Ty's pocket. I'd thought nothing I'd ever done in my life had been harder than leaving Will in Nashville, but that, I saw now, had been nothing but a warm-up act.

I walked down the hall and lifted the cordless out of its cradle and carried it onto the front porch. A spray of stars shone through the wispy clouds over the pond. I sat on the step for a long time with the phone in one hand and the card Ty'd given me in the other.

What the hell, I thought, and dialed the number of the condo in Nashville. I might not be ready yet to talk to a lawyer, but I could at least, in good conscience, tell Ty that I'd tried to get in touch with Will.

I listened to the phone ring twice, then three times, holding my breath, waiting to hear the familiar click of the answering machine, my own voice saying in my ear, "Hi, you've reached the Culpeppers . . ."

Instead, I heard the receiver being fumbled out of its cradle.

"Hello?"

The sound of Will's voice seemed to plunge right through me, into the soft, raw meat in my chest. It took me right back to the way it had been between us in the beginning: how he'd made me laugh, how he'd looked sitting up beside me in bed, the sheet pooling around his hips as he shook the hair out of his eyes. Never mind that that was ancient history, those sweet nights undone by mornings of shouting and tears. Never mind that I'd married Will Culpepper for all the wrong reasons, with less than my whole heart. It was harder than it should have been to let go.

"Hel-*lo*?" Will said again. "Is anybody there?"

What was the matter with me? How often had I heard that irritation in his voice and found myself scrambling to fix whatever caused it? Almost from the minute I'd met him, my life with Will had been one long dance of apology, a series of steps that, no matter how fast or in what direction I moved, always fell short.

I gazed at the dirty bandage on my hand. I hadn't realized how tired I was. I wanted to close my eyes and lay my head in a place where it was welcome. I didn't want to dance anymore.

"Who is it?" a woman's voice said in the background. It sounded like Marin, but it could have been anybody.

Light spilled from the windows into the yard. In my mind I could see Ty perfectly, sitting in front of the TV, waiting for me with his handkerchief ready, to pull my head against his shoulder and tell me everything would be all right.

"It's me," I said to Will, finding my voice at last. "I need to talk to you."

The conversation didn't take long. Afterward, I left a message on Mike Leary's voice mail asking him to call me first thing in the morning. Then I put my face between my knees and cried, for all the mistakes I'd made that I couldn't undo, and for the unearned gift of second chances.

Lucy

EGGY AND I stood in the middle of the showroom, staring at the bare, scuffed linoleum, the corners full of dust bunnies and desiccated foliage. Out on the sidewalk a boy on a stepladder scraped the gilt lettering off the window while Wendell Hayes stood smoking a cigarillo and putting in his two cents.

We were still in our good dresses, having left the VFW hall while Audrey and Joe were cutting the cake. I'd let myself savor a moment of satisfaction for how the white roses and creamy gardenias had looked against Audrey's white satin gown and fair skin, her dark hair sculpted into elegant finger waves against her scalp, her eyes lightly lined and her mouth pale pink. Brides, the saying goes, are always beautiful, but I'm not kidding when I say that the whole congregation gasped as Audrey glided slowly and gracefully across the hall on her big brother's arm and joined Joe at the makeshift altar. Even Joe looked bamboozled, like he'd gone digging inside the cereal box expecting a plastic mood ring and found a diamond the size of a walnut instead.

Now, for the first time since I'd walked into Faye's eight years before, the view was unobstructed: no potted plants or mixed bouquets, no racks of greeting cards. The cooler was empty, the ribbons and balloons, cash register and coffeemaker, gone. All that was left was the smell of flowers, a smell I knew as well and loved as much as I did the faded-cotton smell of Ash's shirtfront or the puppy-dog scent of the top of Jude's head. I wondered if it would linger for a while, a trace of narcissus or chrysanthemums teasing the nostrils of the men who lined up in Wendell's chairs for their weekly haircuts, or if in a matter of days it would be gone, replaced by the aromas of hair tonic and Clubman talc. Things hardly ever lasted like you thought they would. Nothing was irreplaceable.

"Oh my." Peggy pressed a hand to her chest.

I grabbed her arm. "Should I call 9-1-1?"

She laughed, a short, hiccuping laugh. "Not this time, honey."

I led her over to the stool behind the counter, the only stick of furniture left in the room, and got her a Diet Coke from the icebox. It could be the end of the world, hellfire and brimstone raining down, Peggy'd be all right as long as she had her Diet Coke.

"You know what scares me more than anything?" she said once she'd taken a restorative swallow. "I think I'll like

Florida just fine. But I don't know that I'll ever find friends like the ones I have here."

"It's not too late," I said. "You can still change your mind."

She gave a ladylike snort. "I'll let you be the one to tell that to Wendell," she said, and patted my hand. "I'm okay. Just sad, that's all. But I reckon I can stand it." I nodded, blinking back tears. "I'll tell you something my mama taught me, oh, some fifty-odd years ago. When something hurts, you got to learn to sit with it. Not run away, not cover it up. You got to look at it head-on, and let it come. All of it, all the way. Let it get as bad as it can get. It's the only way you'll ever manage to move past it and get on with the next thing."

"I wish you'd tell that to Ash." I hadn't talked to him since the afternoon I'd left him standing in front of the Piney View. I'd called a couple of days ago to remind him about Audrey's wedding, but he hadn't answered, and I wasn't all that surprised when he didn't show up.

"You sure you're okay?" I said to Peggy.

"I'm fine, I swear. You run on home and get out of those duds," Peggy said as she shooed me toward the door. "I'll see you tomorrow at my bon voyage party at Mary Dale's."

I drove home through a sun shower, rain falling in sheets out of a clear blue sky, thinking about what Peggy had said about facing your troubles head-on. Had I done the right thing, leaving Ash at the Piney View with a bunch of notebooks and a guitar? Come to think of it, I could have used a dose of Peggy's advice for my own. I'd been doing everything I could to ignore the fact that life as I'd known it was about to come to an end. For the first time since Mitchell died and I'd moved back to Mooney, time seemed to stretch out in front of me like a long, flat expanse of blacktop, not a single billboard or roadside attraction to break the monotony.

I turned onto Bates Road, slowing the Blazer to avoid chuckholes full of rainwater. The pastures on either side of the road shone in the dappled light. Usually I felt my heart lift as I made this trip, knowing that I was almost home, but today the thought of driving up to that big, empty house felt too much like a metaphor for my future.

The first thing I saw, passing through the canopy of pines and into the clearing, was Ash's white truck parked in front of the house.

My heart quickened as I pulled in beside it and shut off the engine. Leaving my purse on the seat, I ran up the porch steps and in through the unlocked front door.

"Ash?" My voice echoed back to me, unanswered.

I looked in the kitchen, the TV room, took the stairs double-time up to our bedroom. The closet door stood open, and Ash's black western-cut suit lay neatly on the bed, jacket over slacks, his dress boots lined up side by side at the footboard. A shiver passed through me; the clothes looked forsaken, like a ghost had shed them there and dissolved into thin air.

As I stepped back out onto the porch, breathing hard, the studio door opened. Ash stood in the doorway wearing jeans and a T-shirt, a week's worth of salt-and-pepper beard.

I walked across the yard, teetering a little in my pumps. I'm ashamed to say that my first, gut reaction was fear: he was drinking again, he was losing his mind.

"Hey," he said.

"You're home."

"Come on in."

I stepped past him into the studio. His notebooks were heaped on the table, and his Martin guitar lay on the couch.

"You missed the wedding," I said.

"I know. Have a seat," he said, and crossed the room to push a button on the soundboard. The hiss of tape came through the speakers. "I've got something I want you to hear."

AFTERWARD WE WALKED down to the dock. Sunset streaked the sky ocher and pale gray, and a light rain fell, pitting the surface of the pond.

"Sorry about the wedding," he said.

"That's okay. I was looking forward to dancing with you, though."

"You know what's funny? I was just about to give up. I'd packed my stuff and decided to chuck it all and come on home. Eleven days at the Piney View, and not a nibble. Then there I was up in our room, fixing to change for Audrey's wedding, when it hit me like a ton of bricks. I ran out here and wrote the whole thing in twenty minutes."

I smiled. "It's a good thing I'm not the kind of person who likes to say 'I told you so.' "

"Well, it's just one song. I don't even know if it's any good, much less if there'll ever be another one."

"I don't believe that for a minute, and neither do you."

A great blue heron sailed in low over the pond and came to rest on one spindly leg in the shallows on the far side.

"You never have seen those cranes, have you?" I said. "The ones Little David Bates told you about?"

"No, but that's okay. I think it's the idea of them I like more than anything. You know what I mean?"

"I can't say that I do."

"Hey." He took me gently by the shoulders and turned me to face him. "Look at me. What's going on?"

"Don't you ever wish we could just go back to where we were, before all this?" I waved my arm to indicate the house, the studio, the pond, our two trucks in the yard. "I just don't know what I'm supposed to do with myself," I said. "I mean, now that the shop's closed, and Jude's out of school . . ."

"You know what you need?"

"I hope you're not going to say another baby."

"Nah, nothing that drastic. Just something to shake you up a little. Make you remember that there's more to the world than this scraggly little piece of woods."

"Easy for you to say."

"I mean it," he said. "I had some time to, um, reflect on this while I was at the Piney View. And I think we should take a trip."

"A trip?" Since Ash had stopped performing the farthest from home we'd traveled was the Home Depot in Texarkana.

"Think about it," he said. "Think back to last spring. Wasn't there something you wanted? Something you told me you intended to do?"

He reached into his back pocket and handed me a sheaf of

papers. I unfolded them, scanning the words jumbled together at the top of the first page.

"Ash Farrell," I said slowly, "what have you done?"

"What's it look like?"

"Are you crazy? Two weeks in Italy?" Just saying the word made the hair on the back of my neck start to prickle.

"We used to talk about how we'd go after I sobered up and things settled down. You even got us passports and planned out our itinerary. You thought I forgot all about it, didn't you?"

"But things haven't settled down! I'm out of a job, and Denny's baby will be here before we know it."

"Well, Lucy, that's kind of my point. All along we've been waiting for a right time, but there's never gonna be one. So I figured, why not now? I called this travel agent I know from AA, and she set the whole thing up for me, right over the phone."

I studied his face for signs of sunstroke or chemicals, but all I could think, as he stood grinning down at me, was that I'd gotten my one true wish after all; I'd gotten my old Ash back.

"I do believe you're serious," I said.

"As a heart attack."

I pulled in a breath and held it. "I can't believe you did this without asking me."

"What can I say? Sometimes other people can see what's better for you than you can for yourself."

"Now you're channeling Aunt Dove."

"I can think of worse things."

"But what about Jude? And Denny?"

"It's all set. Dove will keep Jude. He can sleep over at Bailey and Geneva's sometimes, to give her a break. And Denny's got her own thing going on, in case you hadn't noticed."

"That's what I'm afraid of." I knew she'd been talking to a lawyer in Nashville, and it was impossible to ignore the sound of footsteps creeping up and down the hallway in the middle of the night, even though she and Ty always emerged from separate bedrooms in the morning. "You mean the rest of the family knows about this?" I said.

Ash laughed. "And you thought nobody in Mooney could keep a secret. Look, I know we never had a real honeymoon," he said. "I always used to tell you I'd make it up to you someday." Leave it to Ash to do everything bigger and better than anybody, whether he was making mistakes or making amends. "Anyway, you better get used to the idea pretty quick. We leave on Monday."

"Monday? Day-after-tomorrow Monday?" It was one thing to sit up in bed at night staring at pictures in a guidebook, but it was another thing entirely to think of winging off across the ocean to a place where you didn't know a soul or even speak the language. "Oh, Ash. I don't—"

"Now listen here, Lucy Hatch. Remember what I taught you? Put one foot in front of the other, and never stop."

Images I hadn't dared to visit lately came swimming up into my consciousness, tiny, determined fish making their way toward the surface. Hillsides of grapevines and olive trees in Tuscany. The sun sinking in gilded splendor into the

Grand Canal. A woman in a blue veil gazing down at me from an old church ceiling.

"There's one more thing I need to do before we go," Ash said, bringing me out of my reverie. "But first, I think I owe you a dance."

"But there's no music," I said.

"There's always music."

He held out his arms and I moved into them, linking my arms around his neck, and we swayed together on the wooden dock as raindrops fell in the streaming yellow light around us, with Ash leading and me following in his smooth, sure footsteps.

You're sure you want to do this?"

We sat in front of a brick ranch house, the pickup's engine idling. It seemed Ash was waiting for some kind of sign, but there was nothing to guide us, just the sight of a tidy lawn and rain barrels filled with blooming petunias.

He turned the key and the motor died. In the silence I could hear him breathing—panting, almost, like a dog. When we first met, I'd honestly believed Ash was immune to fear. But, like we'd both learned the hard way, a person can only be Superman for so long.

He fidgeted with his shirt collar as we waited for someone to answer our knock. Inside a TV blared, then the volume dropped and the door swung open. A big-bosomed woman in a flower-print dress scowled out at us, like we were here to sell her something she had no interest in buying.

"You," she said to Ash, and shook her head. "Here to get poor Evelyn all riled up, I guess. Here to make misery, like that girl of yours."

"How do you do," I said, holding out my hand. "I'm Ash's wife, Lucy. Could we just see her, please? We don't want any trouble."

"Huh," the woman said. "'Want' don't have a doggone thing to do with it." But she stepped aside, and we moved past her into a big, bright living room. A young man dressed in a windbreaker and a ball cap sat in a wheelchair, staring at *The Price Is Right* on TV.

"I'm sorry," I said as we followed the woman down a hallway, "I didn't catch your name."

"Contessa Jones," she said in a clipped voice.

"You run this place all by yourself?" I was trying to kill her with kindness, but she wasn't buying it.

"Me and my husband, Joyner. Been doing it twenty-some-odd years now. My niece comes by mornings, helps out some." She threw a glance back over her shoulder. "You want to see our license from the state?"

Before I could answer, we'd arrived at the end of the hall. The room was small but pleasant, with a pretty quilt on the bed and a handful of framed photos on the night table. A tiny, bird-boned lady in a turquoise jogging suit sat in a chair by the window. Her head hung at an odd angle, her white hair sparse and frizzed. It took me a minute to realize that she was dozing, like an old cat in a patch of sunshine.

"Naptime," Mrs. Jones said, like we couldn't see for ourselves.

Ash turned, facing her eye to eye.

"Could you leave us alone for a few minutes?" he asked.

"Well. I'll be in the kitchen, starting supper. Holler if you need help." She moved off up the hallway, trailing indignation like exhaust from a tailpipe.

We stood in the doorway for a while, looking into the room. So here was the dragon lady, the wicked Evelyn LeGrande, wrinkled and shrunken as an apple-faced doll, snoring into her lap. I felt a rogue wave of tenderness toward this woman I'd never met and who I'd heard such awful things about, the past locked inside her now like scraps of ribbon, old dance cards, snapshots in a memory box, the faces known but the names forgotten.

"Maybe we ought to let her sleep," Ash whispered. "Come back another time."

"Ash." I pressed my hand against his back, feeling his muscles flinch inside his shirt.

He moved slowly into the room and perched at the edge of the bed, folding his hands between his clenched knees. Minutes passed. Down the hall, the TV roared—"Red O'Brien, come on down!"—and pots and pans started banging in the kitchen.

A jaybird landed in the tree outside the window, and with a start Evelyn woke, her head jerking back, her eyes popping open. She gazed at the bird as it fluttered its wings and then took off again, a blur of blue, the empty branch shuddering in its wake.

Ash cleared his throat, and slowly Evelyn turned toward him, her face as blank as a baby's.

Then something began to work its way up through the crossed wires, a light burning faintly in the murk of her eyes. Her mouth had been carefully painted with a frosting of pink lipstick, so that, if you tried, you could make out a faint image, like somebody'd laid a sheet of tracing paper over her old-lady features, of the young woman she'd been, the one I guessed in her mind she'd always be.

She lowered her eyes to her lap, smiling at Ash from beneath her lashes.

"I had a dream with you inside it," she said.

"You know who I am?"

"Don't be silly. Of course I do."

"Well, it's been a long time."

"And I've been right here, all this time, waiting."

Who knew where she was at that moment, what she remembered? Did she understand that the man sitting before her was her grown son, the baby she'd given up all those years ago; or did she think he was that handsome rascal Frank Farrell, back from a few days on the road?

Evelyn lifted a hand from her lap and offered it to Ash, his for the taking. We're here now, her expression seemed to say. The sky is blue. There's meat loaf for supper. Goodness comes in many guises, and not always the ones we're looking for. But in that unexpectedness, sometimes, there's grace.

Epilogue

DENNY

BLACKNESS SO SOLID it's nearly blue, and from inside it a rustling of clothing, voices, anticipation rising like a bird spreading its wings, the flapping growing louder as it approaches. Then suddenly a burst of light hitting me full force, pinning me in its white heat. I'm startled but don't show it, instead beam right into it, the spangles on my skirt and jacket sparking like firecrackers, as a faceless voice booms out of the darkness:

Ladies and gentlemen, the return of the Stardust Cowgirl!

Behind me Ziggy counts a downbeat and I step forward, smiling, and open my throat. It's an old song, one my grandmother taught me, and for a while I forget who I am, the line between past and present blurring as I hear her voice, all its shades of dark and light, buried inside mine like a lucky charm, shaping every word and note I sing. I can feel her out there, the sturdy shape of her shoulders, the papery scent of her skin, as I wrap my voice around the final chorus, hearing it take wing like that great bird, soaring out over the crowd as they begin to chant as one . . .

"Mama! Mama!"

The dream falls away as I sit up slowly, blinking at the sight of Lola bouncing on the end of the bed in her diaper and T-shirt, her hair black as a crow's wing falling over her Culpepper-blue eyes.

"Mama, wake up!"

I rub the last crumbs of sleep from my eyes and reach for her, breathing in the milky sweetness of her, drunk on the smell of baby. Nobody warns you about this, the intoxication of motherhood, more tempting than any booze I've ever tasted. At two and a half her arms and legs are soft and white as biscuit dough, but you can already feel the tough girl in her as she wriggles in my arms and says, "Nice cream!"

"No nice cream for breakfast. Where's your daddy?" I was supposed to get to sleep in this morning, our first day home after eight weeks on the road, but as I sweep Lola into my arms and set off through the house, there's no sign of Ty except a mug with an inch of cold coffee in it sitting on the drain board.

The front door's open, and through it I can hear the sound of the mower. Lucy finally got tired of having nothing but dirt for a front yard, so last year Daddy seeded everything from the porch to the garden in Bermuda grass. He's done nothing but gripe about it ever since. "Damn nuisance," he likes to say with a scowl. "If I'd wanted a putting green, I'd of moved to the country club." You can tell he likes complaining, though, almost as much as he likes the John Deere lawn tractor he bought to keep the grass in check. Whenever Ty and I come home, he and Daddy argue over whose turn it is to mow.

"Da!" Lola shouts as Ty putters by on the mower, his face and arms brown from all the time he spends on the golf course, a habit I haven't been able to get him to break. He doesn't see us, caught up in what he calls the Zen of lawn maintenance, and I'm struck by the look of goofy carelessness he wears, a look I don't see much of anymore. Lola and I've aged him, though not in a bad way, I don't think. Like my daddy, Ty wears his character in the pleats at the corners of his mouth, the lines around his eyes. I smile, thinking of a song by Lucinda Williams. How I used to want to be her. How things turned out this way instead.

"Da!" Lola screams again as Ty executes a forty-five-degree turn and heads away from us, in the direction of the garden.

I carry her back inside and sit her, red-faced and squalling, in her high chair at the kitchen table. I stick one of Lucy's wooden spoons in her hand, and two seconds later she's banging it against the plastic tray, making throaty, happy sounds as she sees me take a bowl out of the cupboard and the Cheerios out of the pantry. IT'S GOOD TO BE QUEEN, her little T-shirt says, like any of us need reminding. "Enjoy it while it lasts, cupcake," I say, setting the cereal in front of her and watching her pluck out the little round O's with her fat fingers, but she's not paying me any mind, and why should she? She'll rule the roost here just as long as we let her. Fifty years from now I can see her still sitting at this table, being waited on hand and foot by the rest of us, her disciples, her willing slaves.

I put on a fresh pot of coffee and sit down at the table while it brews, and contentment washes over me and settles deep in my bones at the sight of my daughter stuffing cereal into her face, the way the sunlight comes in through the kitchen windows and plays across the wood and glass and chrome surfaces. For a little while it's quiet except for the sounds of the coffee perking and Lola crooning to herself, the distant drone of the mower out front. I know it won't last. A week, maybe two tops, and Ty and I both will start to get restless, start getting on each other's nerves. I try not to think about that now, the way I'm always torn between the road and home. I think instead of how lucky I am, that, for now, at least, I've managed to do what everybody said I couldn't: have my life both ways. Lucy and Daddy are responsible for that, the fact that Lola is healthy and happy, her own little person, full of piss and vinegar. If they live to be a hundred I won't find enough ways to thank them, though Lucy tells me all the time that no thanks are due, that Lola's mere being, her highly entertaining and demanding company, are their own reward. And there's no question that she's thriving like a hothouse flower in this big mess of a thing we call a family.

I pour myself a cup of coffee and lean against the counter to drink it, thinking back to last night's cookout at Geneva and Bailey's, a going-away party for Lucy and Daddy and a welcome-home for me and Ty. The whole gang was there, or almost: Lucy's brothers and their wives and all the kids except

Kit's oldest who's off studying civil engineering at Texas Tech, Aunt Dove, and Lucy's mama, Patsy, who's getting around better than she has in years thanks to her brand-new hip. Bailey cooked a brisket and we sat on blankets in the grass and ate meat and beans and coleslaw while the sky changed colors like a slide show, powder blue to pink to scarlet to indigo, and the lightning bugs came out and Clifton Chenier played his squeezebox on the swamp radio station thirty miles away, in Louisiana. The kids keep growing like weeds, but otherwise, time seems to pass by Mooney like it's some long-forgotten kingdom in a fairy tale. When I was a kid I thought that was a bad thing, but now I'm not so sure. It felt good to lie back on the grass and listen to the lazy conversation around me, the voices that run through my mind all the time like background music, to be able to go two whole hours without being asked for anything more than to pass the barbecue sauce.

Afterward, we drove home over the winding black highways of Cade County, Ty and Lola and me following Daddy and Lucy in their truck. Jude was staying the night with Lily and Emmalee; we'll drive into town this afternoon for their Little League game.

Ty slowed the pickup as we turned off the highway and we fell behind Daddy and Lucy, their taillights shrinking as we bumped up the unpaved single-lane in the dark. The old pink brick Bates house was off to our left, empty for years, though a safety light still burned on a pole in the yard.

"You really think he'll go for it?" Ty asked as we rolled past.

"I don't know," I said. "I mean, there's no good reason for him not to. But it'd be just like him to say no just to be—well, Daddy."

"He seems good, don't you think?"

"Yeah." *All the more reason not to screw things up,* I thought but didn't say.

I don't often have to tell Ty what I'm thinking, though. He reached over and squeezed my thigh.

"Don't worry about it. We'll talk to him together, after they get back."

And why shouldn't he go for it? The old house is just sitting there, the barn and the pastures going to seed. It's taken us a long time to get to this place, Ty and me, where we can start to think about putting down roots, making ourselves a home. We've looked at land all around Nashville, up near Hendersonville, down south around Bugscuffle and Wartrace: beautiful country, green and rolling, with old stone fences and the blood of Civil War soldiers in the dirt underfoot.

But I remember something Daddy used to say about the years he and Lucy lived outside Nashville, about being able to hear the wheels of the city turning even in his sleep, that he never got a minute's peace until he came back to Mooney. I want to lay my head down on the pillow at night knowing Daddy and Lucy are no more than a holler away, for Jude to teach Lola to throw a curveball and to fish in the pond, all of us running in and out of each other's kitchens, handing off babies and sacks of tomatoes, together not just for holidays and vacations but in a regular, everyday way.

Ty started rambling about the plans he's drawing up for our house, about what kind of countertops for the kitchen, whether we should dig ourselves a pond or put in a pool. A room for my trophies, he said, squeezing my leg again, and I smiled and patted his hand. He does know how to talk, that man.

"Down!" Lola commands, bringing me back to the present, and I lift her out of her chair and, carrying my coffee, lead her by the hand back out to the front porch. She toddles into the yard and sprawls in the new-cut grass like some kind of crazy caterpillar, kicking her legs in the air and singing to herself. I sit down on the top step and stretch my legs in the sun. In a couple of hours it'll be hotter than the seventh circle of hell, but right now the warmth feels good on my fish-belly-white skin. The pond is green and still in the morning light, rippling here and there as bugs skim its surface. High overhead, a jet plane tracks silently across the sky.

"Pop-Pop!" Lola points, making me laugh.

"That's right, baby girl," I say. "There goes Pop-Pop and Nonny." She's too little to understand that Daddy and Lucy are probably just now waking up in their airport hotel room in Dallas, getting ready to board the first in a series of flights that will have them, by tonight, in Rome. It's their third trip in three years. When I asked her last night why they don't go someplace else, Lucy had shrugged and smiled. "Because," she said, "I haven't seen all of what I want to see." I admit I like picturing them traipsing up and down old cobblestone streets, eating in open-air cafés as the sun sets and bells toll from church towers. Lucy, who doesn't choke up easily, still gets tears in her eyes and shakes her head, speechless, when she tries to tell about the Sistine Chapel. I'll just have to see it for myself, she says, and I guess, someday, I will.

This trip is different from the others, though, because instead of coming straight home, they're flying back by way of the British Isles, where Daddy's booked into a series of clubs and small halls, winding up at a three-day music festival in County Cork, Ireland. His record, *The Ash Farrell Comeback Special,* on a nothing little label in North Carolina, snuck up out of nowhere last year and surprised just about everybody. He's done a few shows stateside, but overseas, in Wales and Belgium and the Netherlands, they can't get enough of him. These days, wherever I go, people want to talk to me again about being Ash Farrell's daughter—not like it was a few years ago, when he left Nashville and dropped off the face of the earth, but the way they did when I was first getting started and being a chip off the old block was known as a good thing. Now and then the subject of our doing some shows together comes up, but so far it's just talk. I don't think he has the urge anymore to see the insides of big arenas or a tour bus. Maybe it reminds him too much of the old days, but I like to think, instead, that he's finally at home in his own skin and ready to own up to who he is, a damn good songwriter with a studio in the East Texas piney woods and a fan club based in Amsterdam.

And here I am, holding down the fort and thankful for what's right in front of me: my baby pulling out fistfuls of grass and making a mess of herself, Ty cutting neat swaths in the lawn, Lucy's garden, overflowing its chicken-wire enclosure. The sprinkler system comes on, sending arcs of water over the rows of tomato and bean plants, sunflowers taller than my head, and my nose fills with the smells of mown grass and pine mulch and wet greenery. These are the smells of home to me, these and chicken frying in a skillet, and pie cooling on the drain board, and sheets ironed with lavender water, and the place on the back of Lola's neck under her hair that I like to think nobody knows about but me.

I hear a car coming up the road and get to my feet, shading my eyes with my hand. It's Dove's old beige Lincoln, her head barely visible over the wheel. She pulls to a stop behind Ty's pickup and I scoop Lola into my arms and go out to meet her.

When I get up next to the car I see my grandmother's in the passenger seat, her head slowly pivoting on her neck, her eyes scanning the landscape through the windshield like a watchful bird's. It makes me happy and sad both to see her. My dream of her living here with Daddy and Lucy didn't quite work out the way I thought it would. Daddy did finally start going to see her up at Contessa's place in Hughes Springs, but no matter how often he went or what he said, she never seemed to understand who he was. It was hard for him, and it's hard for him still. Lucy and the priest, Punch Laughlin, keep trying to tell him that forgiveness is for the giver, not the receiver, but I'm not sure he's bought it yet. Evelyn lives now in the new Alzheimer's unit at Golden Years, where there are crafts and music, and they let her come out and visit anytime without a fuss. You might know that she and Dove would end up getting on like a house afire. In fact,

Dove's the only one of us Evelyn seems to recognize on a regular basis. It doesn't bother me, but that's more than I can say for some of the rest of the family.

I set Lola on her feet and open the car door for my grandmother. She looks even frailer than the last time I saw her, but her hair's washed and styled and she's all decked out in a bright-purple sweat suit and fancy new sneakers.

"Hi, Evelyn," I say, and lean down to give her a hug. "It's me, Denny." She doesn't hug back—she never was big on that kind of thing—but she does smile and pat my arm.

"Oh," she says, "look at the baby."

"This is Loretta Lynn Farrell," I tell her for the umpteenth time. "Your great-granddaughter."

"Where in the world did she get that hair?"

It's what everybody asks me, those who either don't know about or don't remember my short, not-so-sweet marriage to Will Culpepper. He's never once seen his daughter, unless you count the day our divorce was final, when I was eight and a half months pregnant. I wish I could say he acted all remorseful about what had happened between us, but my lawyer told me not to talk to him. Still, I waited for him outside the courtroom afterward, but he must have left through another door, because I never saw him again, even though I made Ty call him when Lola was born. He never returned the call, though, and after a while I just gave up and let Will go, back to wherever he came from and where, I guess, he is still, with the rest of the bottom-feeders. Ty's the only daddy Lola's ever known, but seeing's how he's so big and blond, and I'm small and redheaded, her black hair and blue eyes and high, slanted cheekbones are a constant source of comment. I like to tell people she's a direct descendant of her namesake, the great Miss Loretta herself, but that usually gets me nothing but an arched eyebrow or a cockeyed smile.

Dove comes around the front of the car carrying a big Tupperware bowl with a snap-on lid.

"Hey there, cowgirl. Surprised to see you up with the chickens."

"Not by choice." I nod at Lola, who's reaching up her arms and whimpering.

Dove bends slowly, balancing the bowl and cupping Lola's cheek with her free hand.

"How's our sweet thing this mornin'?"

"Da!"

We all look around at Ty heading back toward us across the lawn at a clip. He stops to raise the blade on the mower, then sets the brake and climbs off the tractor, grabbing Dove in a hug that nearly lifts her off her feet.

"Law!" she exclaims, laughing and brushing herself off as he sets her down again. "You got to be careful, son, these bones ain't as young as they useta be."

"Don't give me that," he says, and extends a hand to Evelyn. "Howdy do, Miss Evelyn," he says. "Tyler Briggs. Good to see you again." Her fingers disappear into his, and she blinks at him in wonder, like he's a movie star, or a god descended from some mountain to grace us mortals here on earth.

"Da!" Lola crows again, indignant at not being the center of attention for more than ten seconds, and Ty bends and scoops her into his arms and swings her high over his head.

Her cries turn to whoops as she flies through the air in his embrace, her arms spread wide, her mouth showing every one of her tiny, perfect teeth. He dips her low and aims her toward me, zooming her in for a quick kiss and then off again, skyward. I used to think happiness was a thing cooked up by poets and certain talk-show hosts, but I know better now.

"Peas in a pod," Evelyn says, and we all turn and look at her, and then laugh. Evelyn's mind is as full of holes as a fishing net, but every now and then it still fetches up something worthwhile and true. I learned from Lucy that if we're lucky we get to make our own families, not just from blood but from among the strangers who, by accident or grand design, come our way. It makes me think of Erasmus, playing the blues in Paris, about as far from home as a country boy can go. Of course he's not really a country boy, but that's how I like to remember him, standing on his uncle's front porch in a white shirt and suspenders, his ears sticking out and his fiddle on his shoulder. We talk on the phone every now and then, but it's not the same. Sometimes distance brings two people closer together, but Erasmus and I both know that the best of what was between us is in the past. That doesn't mean there isn't still an ache down in my ribs when I hear his voice across the water or when I walk, like I will tomorrow or the next day, across the road to Little Hope cemetery. There are more ghosts inside than just the bones buried there.

Dove hands me the Tupperware bowl—chicken salad, I see from a peek under the lid—and tells me to put it in the icebox, and she and Evelyn head off toward the garden, toting wicker baskets and sun hats. Dove's in charge of keeping things under control while Lucy's gone. Everybody just laughed when I claimed I could manage it. Lucy's garden, like Dove's own, has become a sort of local treasure, not to be trusted to amateurs. And I like the sight of the two old ladies moving between the rows, their heads together, the peal of laughter that Dove lets out at something Evelyn says. I want to be like Dove when I'm that age, spry and uncomplaining, still waking up thinking the world is full of surprises, more good ones than bad. It's all in how you look at it, she likes to say, and it's hard to argue with the living, breathing proof.

I go inside to put the chicken salad away and rinse out the coffeepot. The night before, after Ty carried Lola off to bed and Lucy'd gone upstairs to finish packing, I stayed behind in the kitchen, pretending to look for something to snack on, but really I was waiting to ambush Daddy. We hadn't talked, not one-on-one, since April, and that had been thirty seconds on my cell phone backstage at the Gaylord Center, with people jostling on all sides and flashbulbs going off and some lady in a shiny red dress wanting to interview me for one of those entertainment programs on TV.

He came in finally, toting a guitar case. He acted embarrassed, like I'd caught him doing something sneaky. I pulled a jar of peanut butter out of the pantry quick, like it was the exact thing I was hunting for, and set it on the counter.

"Couldn't decide which guitar to take," he said. "Can't take a chance on the Martin going missing in some airport in Dublin, or wherever."

I nodded and got a spoon out of the drawer.

"Peanut butter?" he said. "After all that food you ate at Bailey's?"

I shrugged and spooned up a mouthful.

"You're not pregnant again, are you?" he asked.

"Jesus, Daddy."

"Sorry." He was really nervous. It made me feel awful, the way I'd felt the first time I'd showed up unannounced at his house across the road and he hadn't known what to do with me. It's funny; sometimes I feel so close to him, even when we're hundreds of miles apart, and sometimes when we're in the same room, it seems like we don't even speak the same language.

"Guess I better get upstairs," he said. "We need to hit the road here pretty soon."

"Are you mad at me?" I blurted out. I wished I'd chosen something besides peanut butter. It's hard to have a serious conversation with somebody when your tongue is stuck to the roof of your mouth.

"Why would you think that?"

"You haven't spent more than two seconds in the same room with me since we got here. In fact, you haven't really talked to me since before the awards show. I thought maybe you . . . I don't know." I screwed the top back on the Jif.

"You thought maybe I've been feeling like you got the big head all of a sudden?" he said.

"Something like that."

The truth was, when I'd stood up there in front of all those people in their fancy clothes, blinded by lights and tears with the trophy gleaming in my hand, and the only name that came out of my mouth when I tried to remember who all I needed to thank was my daddy, I thought he might have gotten the wrong idea. That I was trying to say I was better than him, that what I'd done was so much bigger and more important, when all I really meant was that if Ma hadn't brought me to live with him and Lucy, I might never have known where my voice could take me. I'd probably have ended up waitressing or tending bar somewhere, thinking I was hot shit for winning first place on Karaoke Night. When I think of that summer now, I remember the air as being colored with music, so bright and thick it seemed you could scoop it up in handfuls and rub it all over you, head to toe. Daddy showed me that. He was the first person I ever knew who lived by what was in his heart and his gut instead of what somebody else tried to tell him.

All those thoughts and more went through my mind, but they were no closer to the tip of my tongue then than they'd been onstage in Nashville the night of the awards. How could I explain myself to him when I barely understood myself what I meant? If anything, I was making things worse. I'd have been better off writing a song about it.

"Nah," he'd said finally. "I reckon your head's the same size it ever was."

"You think?"

"Well, maybe a little bigger." I swatted at him with the spoon, and he laughed. "Anyway, you're allowed to be swell-headed for a while. It's a fine thing you did."

I made myself swallow the lump in my throat. The prizes we want the most seem to always be the ones we can't have;

we chase after them like babies chasing soap bubbles, trying to catch their wobbly shimmer in our hands. Still, we keep on wanting, and that's what I was doing when Lucy called from the top of the stairs, telling him to get up there and finish packing, they had to leave for Dallas in an hour. He'd hugged me quick and kissed the top of my head. "It's okay," he said, and for just a second, for no reason I could name, it was. I let him go without asking what he meant. For once, I was smart enough not to push my luck.

When I get outside again, Ty's back on the mower, one strong brown arm holding Lola tight against him as they race across the lawn. A cry wells up in the back of my throat, but I hang back and grip the porch rail until it retreats. They're not racing, not really; in fact, they can't be going more than a couple of miles an hour, and the blade's still up. The breeze lifts Lola's hair, her chubby fists gripping Ty's as she hangs on for the ride of her life. Already she has a laugh that's purely her own, loud and staccato, the kind of laugh that will turn heads one day in places like New York and L.A., maybe even Paris. There's no stopping her, this girl of mine. I think suddenly of something Daddy said last night, at the Hatch family cookout. He and Bailey were sitting in lawn chairs with glasses of sweet tea, watching Lily bossing Lola and Emmalee around. "They'll break your heart," he said, "and then hand it back twice as big as before." And he'd looked over and met my eye and winked, to let me know he knew I was listening.

Ty swings back toward the house and I run out to meet them. He rolls to a stop and I climb onto the seat, lifting Lola into my lap, and he slides his arm around us both and puts the motor in gear. And we're off, shrieking and laughing, our limbs tangled up together, peas in a pod. Heartbreak's a long way away this morning from Cade County, Texas, where the Stardust Cowgirl gets to hang up her spangles for a while and just be Ash's daughter and Ty's wife and Lola's mama, where every once in a while, instead of marching forward like the universe says it must, time stands still and lets us ride around in circles.

LUCY

The plane's cabin is swathed in darkness, nothing but the occasional pinpoint of a reading light or the screen of somebody's laptop computer. The boy across the aisle from me is playing a handheld video game, but for the most part I'm surrounded by sleepers. It's two A.M. back in Texas. I'd be asleep, too, if I were home in my own bed, instead of suspended, by laws of physics that don't invite too much scrutiny, in this metal nuts-and-bolts contraption high above the Atlantic Ocean.

It's cold up here at thirty-five thousand feet, and I tuck the scratchy airline blanket tight around my legs and scoot closer to Ash dozing in the seat beside me, his face mashed against a thin, slippery pillow. On the wall at the front of the cabin there's a little screen with a cartoon airplane on it, tracking our position. I've hardly been able to take my eyes off it since we left the runway in Atlanta six hours ago. I've followed our progress up the East Coast, out over Nova Scotia, then hours of nothingness, just periodic updates on our altitude, latitude,

and longitude, and the faith that there really is an ocean beneath us, and that, eventually, there will be land. You'd think
I'd be used to it by now, but I still get butterflies at the sight of
that little cartoon plane and the thought of all that blackness,
sky and ocean and who knows what all, outside.

A flight attendant comes up the aisle, looking right and
left to see if anybody needs anything. She's an older woman
with a neat gray pageboy and a soft layer of padding around
her hips. Somebody's grandma, probably. I feel safe at the
sight of her in her navy blue uniform and sensible shoes. It's
impossible to imagine anything bad happening on her
watch: a terrorist hijacking, or the plane plummeting end
over end into the dark sea. People like her don't die.

She sees I'm awake and smiles, and I smile back. She bends
over, close enough for me to smell her skin—Jergen's lotion,
another thing I find deeply reassuring—and whispers, "You
okay, hon? You need anything?"

"I'm good, thanks."

She glances down and sees the Michelin Green Guide to
Italy in my lap. "First trip?"

"Third, actually."

She presses a hand to her chest, next to a little gold badge
that says CYBIL. "I've been making this trip for six years now,
and I still get goose bumps every single time." Her accent,
too, is comforting, southern.

"Me, too."

"Where y'all from?" she asks, looking over at Ash with his
mouth open, snoring gently into the pillow.

"Northeast Texas," I tell her. "The middle of nowhere. You?"

"Well, I'm from outside Savannah originally. Still have family there. But I've got myself a little place in Rome now. Italy, not Georgia." She smiles. "So I guess you could say I'm on my way home."

I'm surprised, but try not to show it. Folks aren't always what they seem at first glance; you'd think I'd have learned that by now. We talk about Rome for a while: our favorite hotels, where to get the best gelato. When she says the names of things in Italian, her Georgia accent disappears and she sounds like a native. Imagine, casting off your old life like that, deciding to go and live in a place halfway across the world. I'm braver than I once thought, but not that brave.

"There's a fantastic little café in my neighborhood," Cybil says. "I could write down the name for you, if you're interested."

"Great. Thank you."

"Be right back." She pats my arm and heads back up the aisle.

I open the book in my lap and remove the bookmark, holding it up to examine it under the reading light. It's a Polaroid taken last night at Bailey and Geneva's house, the Hatch clan gathered for one of our summer cookouts. It's not the whole gang, far from it, but the main characters are all there: my brothers and their wives, Lily and Emmalee, Dove, Mama, Jude and Denny and Lola, Ash and me. It isn't a great picture by any means; half of us are looking not at the camera but at one another, our faces blurred and mouths in motion, like we couldn't stand to stop talking long enough for Ty to line up the shot. But that's exactly what I love about it.

How lucky we are, to still have so much to say to one another after all this time.

I pause and study each face, letting myself feel a pang of emotion that's particular to every one. My tall, good-looking brothers. Geneva's sassy smile. Lily with her arm around Emmalee, trying to act the big sister, in spite of the fact that Emmalee's a scowling, five-year-old Sherman tank who doesn't need protecting by Lily or anybody. Dove, in a T-shirt that says I DO ALL MY OWN STUNTS. Mama, looking fit and feisty with her new hip, her hair freshly permed, wearing a canary-yellow pantsuit.

I turn the photo facedown and close the book. I still don't know what to think about what Mama pulled last night. We were getting ready to head home; Denny and Ty had just arrived earlier that afternoon, and Ash and I had a four-hour drive ahead of us to get to the airport hotel in Dallas in time to grab a few hours' sleep before the first leg of our flight. Mama kept insisting that what she wanted wouldn't take two minutes, so I followed her into the house and waited while she searched high and low for her purse.

She found it, finally, and handed me a thick envelope the color of watery tea.

"Here," she said. "I thought you might want these."

I took it from her warily. "What is it?" Mama's notorious for foisting off her business affairs on the rest of us, presenting Bailey with her income tax records two days before the filing deadline, or handing Kit a new copy of her will to review every few months. I didn't have time for this.

"Letters," she said.

"What letters?"

"From your daddy, Raymond Hatch."

It took awhile to find my voice.

"He wrote letters? When?"

Mama waved her hand like she was shooing away a bird. "Oh, for years and years. All the time you all were growing up. I didn't want to get you all worked up then, make you believe there was any chance he was coming home. But I figured now you might be ready to see them."

"Now? *Now?* I'm forty-four years old, Mama! I'm leaving in the morning for two weeks in Europe! What made you think now was a good time for this?"

"Well, if that's how you feel." She reached for the envelope, but I snatched it back, tucking it under my arm. "I want those back when you're finished," she said, and I'd just nodded, speechless with surprise and a new, throbbing ache in my chest.

I think about that envelope now, tucked beneath a stack of nightgowns in a drawer in Ash's and my bedroom. Nobody knows it's there. I didn't tell a soul, and I haven't read anything in it yet, other than the handwriting on the first envelope on the stack inside, addressed to Kit and Bailey and me. He had terrible handwriting, my daddy, like Ash's, like chicken scratch. The postmark was Baltimore, June 22, 1968. It's all I can stand to know about him right now. Maybe by the time I get home, I'll have worked up the nerve to deal with what's in those letters, to bring myself face-to-face with the man who left us when I was six, who our mama was too stubborn and too proud to forgive. Just thinking about it, I get so mad at her my eyes cross. I have to remind myself to be here now, to breathe.

I'm lucky; Mama and I still have time, a chance to get things right. It's too late for Ash and Evelyn. By the time he was ready to put aside his old hurts and grievances and try to make some kind of peace with her, she was gone, lost inside the dim, twisted passageways in her mind. It's one of the sorrows he carries inside, like stones in his pocket, to worry with his fingers when he's tired or blue. We all have those stones, but Ash has been handed more than his share. It's part of the deal, I believe, one of the things that makes him what he is, but that's not much comfort to a boy who, even in the middle of his life, misses his mama.

The kid across the aisle tucks his video game into the seat pocket in front of him and pulls out a set of headphones. I watch his profile, bobbing in time to a song I can't hear. He's not much older than Jude, and by blurring my eyes slightly I can see Jude two or three years up the road, the same shaggy hair and downy jaw, the man's bones beginning to surface in his little-boy face. I do a double take when he walks into the room sometimes: his long arms and legs, his feet the size of footballs in his space-age sneakers. He looks more like my brother Bailey than Ash or me; he's frequently mistaken by strangers for Bailey's son, a thing that seems to suit them both just fine. I used to worry that Jude was too tender for this world. He cried when his daddy sprayed a nest of yellow jackets, when he didn't get a joke the other kids were laughing at, when he went to Good Friday services with his granny and heard the preacher talk about the way that Jesus died. But at ten his armor is starting to harden. Last year we brought him with us to Italy and he soaked up everything like a sponge, but this summer he's stayed behind, to go with Lily to baseball camp. I try not to take it personally. The tide that carries him away will carry him back again. Meanwhile, we bob, like two gulls riding a breaker, facing in opposite directions but never entirely out of each other's sight.

A woman comes up the aisle toward the lavatory carrying a sleeping child in her arms, the little girl's head nodding on her mother's shoulder. As they pass, I get a whiff of sour diaper and baby powder and something else—macaroni and cheese? Chicken noodle soup?

And without warning I'm right back home on the front porch swing with Lola in my lap. I think of her escaping naked from her bath and running through the house leaving a trail of wet footprints on the floor, and the first time Ash's old dog Booker licked her hand, her eyes going wide as dinner plates. I think of Ash dancing her around the kitchen singing that old '60s song—*La-la-la-la-Lo-la*—into her soft black hair, her little teeth white and round as pearls as she opens her mouth to laugh, and it's all I can do not to rise from my seat and run up the aisle to the cockpit, pound on the door with my fist, and yell for the captain to turn the plane around. Even now I miss her so much that the thought of her makes it hard to breathe. I must be out of my mind, flying off to Europe when I should be back home spending every minute with Loretta Lynn Farrell Briggs while I still can, drinking her in like a rare, sweet wine, tilting the bottle to my lips and gulping down every drop.

I used to think love was infinite. For thirty-three years I lived without it, and when it finally found me, I thought I'd hit upon a well that would never run dry. But our days are numbered, every one, and what we don't spend we don't get to take with us. We need to wallow in it, use it up.

I work my hand into the crook of Ash's arm, and he stirs and opens one eye.

"Hi," I say. I do this in the middle of the night sometimes, just to make sure he's still breathing.

He blinks. "Where are we?"

I look at the screen at the front of the cabin, read off our coordinates. "Oh," he says, and falls back asleep. I envy him. He sleeps on planes, in the backs of cabs; any kind of motion lulls him into unconsciousness. I, on the other hand, am the lookout, with my maps and guidebooks, plotting and planning, scouting ahead.

I open the book again and take out the picture. In it Denny's holding Lola, who's waving at the camera the way Ty, who was holding it, told her to. Jude's peeking over Denny's shoulder, making a face. All of them are children of my heart, who I love, who are, all the time, even when I'm right there in the same room, leaving me, breaking my heart, and putting it back together again every minute of every day.

Cybil reappears and crouches in the aisle next to me, slipping me a piece of paper. There's a name on it, and an address that, I'm pleased to see, I more or less recognize.

"Have the *carciofi alla giudia*," she says. "It's out of this world." I thank her, slipping the note between the pages of my guidebook. She sees the Polaroid and her eyes light up. "Your family?"

"Uh-huh. Just last night."

"What a pretty baby."

"My granddaughter. That's her mama holding her. The redhead."

"She looks like a handful." I don't know if she means Denny or Lola, but I laugh and nod anyway. In either case, it fits.

"The first few hours are the hardest," she says.

"Excuse me?"

"Traveling. Leaving the people you love. I've got to work, so I don't have to think about it too much. And then we're there, and as soon as I see the city, I forget."

"Me, too." Usually. Almost. I tuck the photo back into my guidebook and close the cover.

"Business or pleasure?" she asks.

"Oh. Well, both." I reach into my black leather tote bag under the seat and rummage around till I find the little envelope that holds my business cards and hand her one. She scans it with interest.

I smile and gesture at Ash asleep in the seat beside me. "He's the talent," I say. "I'm the brains. Such as it were."

Truth be told, I'm as proud of that business card as I am of anything I've ever done. *Lucy H. Farrell, President and Manager, Piney View Music.* Who'd have guessed it? Not me, not during that first year after the flower shop closed and Denny was pregnant with Lola. In the months after our first trip to Italy, Ash wrote one or two more songs, but mostly he was going to meetings almost every night and seeing Dr. Morales twice a week, building decks and renovating kitchens in town. I had my garden, my son, a grandbaby on the way. In spite of all we had to be grateful for, something wasn't right, but we didn't seem to be able to put it into words, much less know how to fix it.

The answer came in December, two weeks before Lola was born. I woke in the middle of the night to find Ash's side of the bed cold, unslept-in. That wasn't unusual; he doesn't sleep like a regular person, eight hours in a bed, but mostly in fits and starts in front of the TV or on the couch in the studio. Fragments of a dream danced at the edges of my consciousness, but whatever they'd been, I couldn't get them back.

I got up and put my coat on over my nightgown and went outside. The sky was clear, awash with stars, a tang of frost in the air. It was nearly Christmas, and as I walked across the yard to the studio I was ticking off a list in my head, things I needed to do and bake and buy.

When Ash opened the studio door, there was a look on his face I couldn't place, or almost could, but not quite. But before I had a chance to ask him what was going on, he pulled me inside and picked up his guitar.

"Listen," he said.

This time there wasn't just the one song. There came another and another—so many, when all was said and done, that he had to choose the best of the batch for the record, the one he made himself, there in the studio, and called, with equal parts pride and irony, *The Ash Farrell Comeback Special*.

Word got out, as word will, especially when your daughter is Denny Farrell. But Ash had had enough of those Nashville cats with their promises and their twenty-page contracts. One night he sat me down and, much as I'd done with him and the idea of our raising Denny's baby, laid out his grand plan.

I laughed at first. What he was proposing was ridiculous. Lola was four months old. I was a homemaker now, a reluctant gardener. The only job I'd had in the last twenty years was selling flowers. I didn't know squat about the music business.

"Bullshit," Ash said. He was serious.

And so, with my new son-in-law's help, slowly and painfully, I learned the ropes. My attention, so fractured and fractious, finally found something to latch upon; I hit the ground running and never looked back. It turns out I have a knack for it: the endless details, the phone calls to distributors and radio stations, producers and club owners. Like flowers, it's easy to sell something when you believe in it with your whole heart.

Ash and I are partners now, in every sense of the word. This isn't the thing either of us imagined when we first started out together, but in most ways it's better, as second comings usually are. Ash is steadier, easier on himself, more accepting of what fate has handed him. I tease him sometimes that we're like Sonny and Cher, yoked together in ways that even divorce or death can't put asunder.

A bell chimes softly from the front of the cabin, and Cybil goes off to answer the call. Ash shifts and opens his eyes.

"Are we there yet?"

"Not for a while."

"Trade seats with me. My legs are killing me."

In the window seat I sleep, a light, skimming sleep, like the bumblebees in my garden back home, zipping from flower to flower. I dream of Lola: her milk-white skin, the smell of the back of her neck under her hair that nobody knows about but me. In the dream she runs away from me and then back again, away and back, laughing her big machine-gun laugh, until I'm dizzy from trying to keep up with her. I wake up reaching for her, with that funny sense you get sometimes that what you were dreaming about is just beyond the tips of your fingers, that if you just shut your eyes again you can hang on to it. I can't say why, but something tells me that Lola will never be far away.

It's still dark, but the diagram at the front of the plane shows a finger of land just beginning to enter the right-hand side of the screen. Soon the cabin will begin to stir. Cybil and her colleagues will make their way up the aisles pushing chrome carts with coffee and juice and the tough, chewy pastries the airline calls breakfast. Folks will start queuing up for the lavatories with their toothbrushes and their makeup bags.

I raise the window shade and look out at the sky where it's begun to curve and brighten in the east. Before too long the Alps will appear, their snowy peaks glazed pink in the morning light, a thing I never expected to say I'd seen once in my life, much less time and again. Tomorrow I'll stand shoulder to shoulder with a couple of hundred other pilgrims, craning our necks to gaze at one man's vision of the beginning of the world, a testament to faith, and sacrifice, and the rest of the heavenly wonders. I'll eat *carciofi alla giudia* in a café with my husband as scooters roar by and men shout at each other on the sidewalk and then embrace and laugh, meeting as enemies, parting as friends. It's one of the things I love about the Italians, the way they wear their emotions on the surface, like a second skin. It's no wonder they've got the food they do, to say nothing of the churches. Next week, I'll stand in the wings of a stage in Ireland and listen to Ash's voice bring thirty thousand people to their feet.

I am a creature of habit. I like thinking of my spice jars lined up neatly in my kitchen pantry, the stacks of folded linens smelling of lavender in my hall closet. I like the way the sun looks going down in a fiery orb every night over the pond. I like order, and sure things. And yet, I remind myself, I'm the woman who married Ash Farrell. There's a little bit of pirate in me, after all.

Cybil's right; the first part of a trip is the hardest. But I don't think anymore about what I'm leaving behind, but all I'm moving toward. And for a little while longer the world is mine alone, the air thin and cold, the new day breaking in a fine red line at the horizon.

Also from Marsha Moyer

SMALL-TOWN LIFE,
BIG TIME SUCCESS,
AND ONCE-IN-A-
LIFETME LOVE

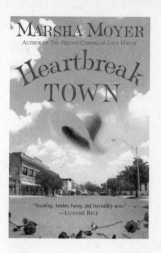

Heartbreak Town

LUCY HATCH IS NOT AT ALL SUITED for the fast life her husband was living in Nashville. Now that she's back in the small town of Mooney, life has finally stopped resembling a Hank Williams song . . . until she wakes up one morning to find a shiny white pickup parked in her yard: Her husband is back in town. He's making promises to Lucy about straightening up, but can a charmer like Ash ever change?

Heartbreak Town, A Novel
$13.95 paper (Canada: $17.95)
978-0-307-35154-8

Available from Three Rivers Press wherever books are sold